**HUSH
HUSH**

James Patterson is one of the best-known and biggest-selling writers of all time. His books have sold in excess of 385 million copies worldwide. He is the author of some of the most popular series in the past two decades – the Alex Cross, Women's Murder Club, Detective Michael Bennett, and Private novels – and he has written many other number one bestsellers including romance novels and stand-alone thrillers.

James is passionate about encouraging children to read. Inspired by his own son, who was a reluctant reader, he also writes a range of books for young readers, including the Middle School, I Funny, Treasure Hunters, Dog Diaries and Max Einstein series. James has donated millions in grants to independent bookshops and has been the most borrowed author of adult fiction in UK libraries for the past twelve years in a row. He lives in Florida with his wife and son.

Candice Fox won back-to-back Ned Kelly awards for her first two novels – *Hades* and *Eden*. She is also the author of the critically acclaimed *Fall*, *Crimson Lake*, *Redemption* and *Gone by Midnight*. Candice's first collaboration with James Patterson, *Never Never*, was a *Sunday Times* and *New York Times* no. 1 bestseller. They have co-authored three further novels featuring Harriet Blue – *Fifty Fifty*, *Liar Liar* and *Hush Hush*.

ALSO BY JAMES PATTERSON

DETECTIVE HARRIET BLUE SERIES

Never Never (*with Candice Fox*)
Fifty Fifty (*with Candice Fox*)
Liar Liar (*with Candice Fox*)

A list of more titles by James Patterson
appears at the back of this book

1 3 5 7 9 10 8 6 4 2

Arrow Books
20 Vauxhall Bridge Road
London SW1V 2SA

Arrow Books is part of the Penguin Random House group of companies
whose addresses can be found at global.penguinrandomhouse.com

Penguin
Random House
UK

First published in Great Britain by Century in 2019
This edition published in paperback by Arrow Books in 2020

A CIP catalogue record for this book is available from the British Library

ISBN 9781787462175
ISBN 9781787462182 (export edition)

Printed and bound in Great Britain by Clays Ltd, Elcograf S.p.A.

HUSH HUSH

JAMES PATTERSON

AND
CANDICE FOX

arrow books

Chapter 1

SOMEONE TRIES TO kill me at least once a day.

I usually see it coming. By definition, people in prison aren't the smartest creatures in the criminal kingdom. They tend to be violent attention-seekers, so they usually tell someone what they're planning to do.

But I'm a dirty fighter. I'll do what it takes to protect myself.

Sometimes the women are more discreet. I'd first been held at Stillwater Remand Centre, where someone caught me off guard on my third day and stuck a sharpened piece of fencing wire into the back of my neck, going for my jugular vein. I'd been tired and unfocused, worrying about my upcoming committal hearings. After the attack I'd been moved to a new remand facility, Johnsonborough Correctional Complex, to separate me from my apparent rival, but it became clear to administration not long after the transfer that *everyone* was my rival.

Today, I'd had the benefit of twenty-four hours warning before my attacker made her move. As the wake-up alarm sounded I was sitting on the floor, stretching my shoulders and strategising a solid plan of defence.

The door to my cell opened in time with a hundred others, a rolling and clunking that almost drowned out the shouts of the guards. I put on my shoes and stood to attention.

Detective Harriet Blue. Inmate 3329.

Charged with a host of crimes. The main one murder.

I'd tracked, hunted and killed a man named Regan Banks. Banks had been a serial killer who counted my brother among his victims, but that fact didn't do me any favours. The law was the law, and as a cop I shouldn't have acted like I was above it. Now I was in prison.

Any inmate who takes down a cop in prison is a hero.

But it was not going to be this cop.

Not today.

Chapter 2

DOLLY QUADDICH, MY cellmate, stepped into the count line beside me. She stretched her messily tattooed arms towards the ceiling and shook herself like a dog, but ended up looking no more revitalised. Dolly never looked entirely awake. She consumed more marijuana in prison than some junkies did on the outside.

'What's for breakfast?' she asked, yawning.

'The same unidentifiable slop they've been serving at Johnsonborough every morning for the past fifty years,' I said.

'Just making conversation, Haz.'

'Leave me alone today,' I said. 'Go sit with the other dope-heads. I'll see you in forty-eight.'

'Oh, man,' she whined. 'Again? When the hell are you gonna change your name?'

Dolly knew what seeing her in two days meant. It meant I was going to have a fight, and I'd be locked up in solitary for that time. She hated being alone in the cell because she was afraid of the dark. One hundred and seventy women living within sneezing distance of one another, eight guards touring the block every fifteen minutes and all-night security lighting that stayed bright enough for inmates to read jailhouse magazines in bed did little to abate her night-time terror. She was also convinced that if I legally changed my name, the prison population would instantly forget who I was.

I liked Dolly, but she was dumb as a brick and every time I got put in solitary she sold something of mine in exchange for drugs. I didn't have a lot of things, so my few items were precious. Usually my deodorant went first.

I sat at the table nearest the back wall of the chow hall and shoved my plate of watery eggs, soggy bread and mystery mush aside. The chow hall was a good stage for a fight. I'd seen plenty of scraps go down here – food trays flying, scalding coffee searing faces, eggs splattering on walls.

Frida, today's planned attacker, was small and wiry like me, but she had big hands for grabbing hair and gouging eyes, and a nose that looked like it had been broken more than a couple of times. I locked eyes with my challenger across the hall and her cronies looked over their shoulders at me. Everybody in the hall knew it was on. A fight is a good distraction, so it's useful to know when one is on the cards. Fights tie up guards and direct the surveillance cameras to a certain place in the room. I knew when Frida and I got together there would likely be other incidents around the chow hall. Someone shanked. Drug deals made. A smattering of robberies of weaker inmates for food, drugs or phone cards.

A woman at the head of the queue dropped her just-received tray from chest height, spraying food everywhere, drawing over the two guards in the room to assist in the clean-up. An inciting incident to kick things off. Frida stood and started moving down the aisle towards me. I was so focused on Frida as I got up and started walking to meet her that I didn't even think about her strategy.

I heard the squeak of a rubber shoe on the tiles behind me a second before an arm came around my neck.

Chapter 3

I KNEW THE second girl by her smell alone. Mel Briggs hardly ever left the smokers' corner of the yard. I reached up as she tried to drag me backwards, grabbed a fistful of her hair and twisted out of the headlock, bringing her face down on my knee. The crunch of her nose on my kneecap was like a starting gun. The women around me stood in unison, a wail of surprise, horror, excitement rising up from every mouth. I landed an uppercut to Mel's face while she was still bent double, in case she had any stupid ideas about recovering for a second run, then I dropped her limp body on the floor.

Three seconds. Frida hadn't counted on me disposing of Mel so quickly. She had used the time to take out her shank, though, a long splinter of plexiglas wrapped in electrical tape. I'd never resorted to constructing a shank of my own in prison. I'm dirty but I'm not a cheat.

Frida swung the shank at me wide and hard, going right for the face, a novice move. If you want to fight with blades you need to dance close, hug your victim to you, go for the fleshy parts – the stomach, thighs, flanks. I leaned back, gave the shank an inch clearance across the bridge of my nose, grabbed Frida's arm and shoulder as her balance shifted and used her own momentum to drive her forward into a nearby table. Women watching dove out of our path. I grabbed her hair, lifted her head and smashed her face into the table a couple of times. I could feel the impact reverberate through the steel tabletop, into the legs bolted to the floor.

The alarm above us had started wailing seven seconds into the fight. Guards shouted, trying to get through the wall of women near the counter. Red lights flashed on the ceiling. Eighty per cent of the women in the room dropped flat on the floor as they were supposed to, hands over the back of their heads, fingers interlocked.

But Frida wasn't giving up so easily, and neither were her friends.

I turned and received a palm in the face, the force of the blow snapping my head back. I grabbed a tray and batted the new challenger away with it, fell on top of her, shoved the corner of the tray into her eye socket and drove her head into the tiles.

Frida was there when I stood up again. I took a couple of jabs in the ribs and used the fury that the pain awoke, dumping adrenaline into my system, to lash out with a hard right to her cheekbone. I felt the skin split under my knuckles. I went for another blow as she fell backwards away from me. Frida was out cold before she hit the ground.

The shouting of the guards was lost in the blaring of the alarm, the screams from the inmates still standing and the ringing in my ears from the blow to the face. I stood and examined the blood on my hands, wondering how much of it was mine, as the guards swarmed me. The men swept my legs out from under me and shoved me to the ground. I realised Dolly was lying right beside me, having hit the deck when the fight started. We met eyes as I was cuffed from behind.

'See you in a couple of days, Harry.' She waved a finger clamped to her head.

'Don't sell any of my shit, Doll,' I said as they dragged me away.

Chapter 4

TOX BARNES WAS sitting at a table with his feet up on the dancers' stage at the Eruptions Club. The door opened behind him, far across the empty room. In the whisky glass near his elbow he noted the reflection of a tall man with a thick frame, broad shoulders leading to a bulging neck and a boxy head. It was a silhouette he recognised. Tox shook his head and sighed, set the newspaper he had been reading on his lap and took a packet of cigarettes out of his breast pocket. He was going to need one.

The big man who sat down beside him said nothing at first. Tox lit his cigarette and exhaled as he picked up the paper again.

'Imagine the *Telegraph* trying to come up with a headline for this,' Tox said. '*Deputy Police Commissioner visits Eruptions in uniform.*'

'Eruptions?' Woods asked. There was no sign inside or outside the club to indicate the name of the establishment.

'It used to be called the Boobie Bungalow. It's an improvement.' Tox grunted. 'What the fuck do you want?' When he exhaled smoke at the commissioner, he noticed the state of the man beside him. He was worn and tired, his name badge askew and hands clasped tightly in his lap.

'I need your help,' Woods said. 'I haven't been able to contact my daughter in eight days.'

'Well, she's not here,' Tox said.

'There has been no activity on the credit card I gave her, or on the phone number I knew her to have,' Woods continued, ignoring Tox. 'I have a pair of detectives on the case, of course. But as the days are passing I'm beginning to think I have to go harder at this. Bring in the big guns. I need you, Detective Barnes.'

'Meh.' Tox waved the older man off. 'You don't need me.'

'I –'

'If you needed me, you wouldn't have said you *haven't been able to contact* your daughter. You'd have said she was missing. You'd have played it straight. But you, me, those strippers over there at the bar and every other human being with any kind of connection to current affairs in this country knows Tonya Woods is a crackhead and a washout. Eight days? She's probably just had a good score and is on a binge. You'll find her on your doorstep wanting money for a re-up on Monday.' He went back to his newspaper. 'And don't call me detective, arsehole. Not while I'm suspended, under your orders.'

'Look.' Woods leaned in close. 'What happened with the Regan Banks case is over. I'm lifting your susp–'

'Over?' Tox sneered. 'It's not over. Not while I'm suspended, Edward Whittacker's suspended and Harriet Blue's in jail. Over? Listen to you, you self-righteous prick. I bet you thought it was over when all the magazines stopped interviewing you about your magnificent work on that case.' Tox waved at the women standing at the bar, slender, tanned beauties in fluorescent-coloured G-strings. 'Britney, dump this idiot back out on the street where you found him.'

'Barnes.' Woods stood as the woman in towering heels started walking towards him. 'My child is missing. And my grandchild is with her.'

Tox heard the strain in the old man's voice. The rumble of genuine panic thrumming through the words. He'd heard it many times before in his career. He didn't lift his eyes from the paper.

'I'll go,' Woods said as Britney took his arm. 'But I came to you precisely *because* of what happened on the Banks case. You, Whittacker and Blue – you found that man and you stopped him. I took credit for it, yes. I had you all punished for it, yes. But I'm a man with his hat in his hand here. I . . . I know it's different this time with Tonya. I know she's really gone.'

Chapter 5

WHEN DOCTOR GOLDMAN was dealing with more than one inmate at a time, one would be chained to a table in a tiny surgery while the other was seen to in an identical room next door. It was not the most secure arrangement. From the chair in which I sat, one hand cuffed to a ring on the edge of the table beside me, I could reach all kinds of things with my free hand – rubber gloves, cotton swabs, disposable rubber objects in packets. If I really went for it, I figured I could even get to the phone on the counter against the wall.

A guard whose name I had never learned was watching me silently from the corner of the room. I leaned across the table anyway, grabbed a jar of jelly snakes and extracted one. She didn't stop me, but she didn't take one for herself when I offered.

I sat quietly memorising all the extension numbers inside the prison, a game I played with myself now and then. There were posters listing the numbers on the wall of every office, classroom and work room. I closed my eyes and tested myself.

Kitchen, 312.

Infirmary, 457.

Cleaning store, 333. No, *334.*

Bernadette Goldman, a short and plump woman with wavy auburn hair, came back into the room, tearing rubber gloves from her fingers. The inmate in the other room had caught a shoe in the face during the chow-hall fight. I'd been escorted to the medical rooms behind her, following a trail of blood that dripped from a cut above her eye. Frida and Mell Briggs had been transported from the prison to a local hospital.

'You can leave us,' Goldman told the guard. 'Harry's a regular here. I'm fine.' The guard shrugged and left. There were two panic buttons in the room with us, and Goldman wore a sensor on her hip that, if tilted too far, would bring a swarm of guards down upon us. But she and I had spent hours together in this small room. She knew I was no threat.

'What's this?' I said. 'No *hello*? *How are you? How was your morning?*'

'Oh, jeez, Harry, I'm sorry.' She snorted. 'I guess you're just in here so often I forget sometimes that you actually leave.'

She gestured to my bloody clothes, hands and face.

'Who was it this time?' she said, tilting my head and feeling in my scalp for abrasions or bumps.

'I didn't see nuthin',' I said in my best criminal scumbag voice.

'Seriously, though. You need to cut this bullshit and let them put you in ad seg. You're going to run out of luck one of these days.' She started wiping my nose and cheeks of blood like a mother cleaning gunk off a kid's face. 'You take the wrong kind of blow and you could be killed. Or you could get permanent brain damage. All it takes is one good hit.'

'Who says I don't have permanent brain damage already?' I asked.

'True. You're definitely crazy, no doubt about that. Maybe I should send you for a psych assessment. That'll get you into ad seg.'

As an incarcerated cop, I should have been put into protection or 'administrative segregation', a section of the remand centre where inmates likely to be targeted by other prisoners were held for their own safety. Most of the inmates there were women who had killed children, who would be prize targets for beatings. Money and fame could also put a person in ad seg. But I hadn't been put into protection when I first arrived at Stillwater, probably because of a paperwork bungle, and that had carried over to Johnsonborough. I didn't argue. I knew that the ad seg ladies were locked up alone twenty-three hours a day in featureless glass cells. Those women were twitchy, wild-eyed creatures deprived of sensory stimuli and hungry for attention. Ad seg was a step above solitary. Solitary was in the bowels of the prison, where the shit and vomit on the walls escaped the eyes of inspectors from the Justice department and prisoner advocates. I'd always submitted to solitary, but whenever the prison had tried to stick me in ad seg I'd had a 'fainting spell' and been taken to the medical office.

Goldman took my face gently in her hands and felt my cheekbones and the bones around my eye sockets with her thumbs. I closed my eyes and let the weight of my head rest in her hands just for an instant – a second or two of trust, safety, relishing the kindness and care of another human being. For a moment she stopped feeling the bones and simply held my face. Confused, I opened my eyes and found her looking at me with an expression I couldn't read. She let me go.

'If they put me in ad seg I won't get my jelly snakes,' I said. I reached for another.

'Cute.' Goldman smiled. 'Well, I've felt your nose and it doesn't seem broken this time. I'm worried about this, though.' She poked me in the swollen flesh beside my nose. 'I wonder if we should get an X-ray.'

'Which bit are you talking about?' I felt my face. 'The zygomatic bone or the maxilla?'

'Goodness.' Goldman's red lips spread wide. 'You're a doctor now?'

'I know the names of the bones I break the most,' I said. 'If I ever have a kid I'm calling it Metacarpal. Regardless of gender.'

'Metacarpal Blue. Sounds like a rapper. I'm talking about both the maxilla and the zygomatic,' she continued. 'Any pain in your upper jaw?'

'I really think it's fine, Goldie. Gimme some ice. I'll lie down for the rest of the day.'

'If only all my patients were as medically trained as you, Harry.'

'I don't want to go to the hospital,' I said. I allowed a small whine to enter my voice. In truth, I wasn't concerned by how long the trip would take or how boring the wait in Emergency would be. I wanted the prison population to hear that Frida and her friend had been hospitalised, and I hadn't. Everything in prison is about image.

'You know . . .' Goldman said. Her voice was low. 'I'm willing to help you out here.'

'Oh?' I glanced at the window to the hall, where two guards were walking past. 'What's the plan? You stick one of the guards with a syringe full of fentanyl and I steal his gun, we blast our way out?'

'No threats to the prison staff, Harry, please.' Goldman rolled her eyes. 'I have to report those. I'm talking about diagnosing you with a mystery illness and putting you in the infirmary for a week of observation. Unexplained low platelet count. I do it all the time. They have books in the infirmary. There's a TV.'

'Thanks,' I told her. 'But no thanks. I need to walk out of here, head high and eyes bright. You know how it works.'

She nodded. The guard who had escorted me to the surgery room leaned in the doorway.

'You've got a visitor, Blue. Let's go,' she said.

Goldman and I looked at each other.

'It's not visiting hours,' the doctor said.

'Yeah,' the guard said, smirking. 'But this guy doesn't need to wait for the schedule.'

Chapter 6

I WAS BROUGHT to the door of the interview room, but when I saw who was inside I turned and tried to walk away.

'Nope!'

'Harriet.' Deputy Police Commissioner Joe Woods stood up from behind the table. 'I really need to speak to you.'

'I don't have time for this.' I struggled with the guard. 'I have more enjoyable and important things to do than waste my morning sitting here while this idiot gloats at me. I've got a ten o'clock appointment to have my eyes scratched out with a fork. Excuse me.'

I tried to get away but knew it was no use. The guard dragged me into the room by my cuffs and I let her, tired from the morning's dramatics. I noticed the red light on the camera in the corner of the room was out. My head was throbbing as the guard took my wrist and started chaining me to a purpose-built handle on the tabletop.

'I'm not here to gloat,' Woods said. 'And you don't need to lock her down, officer. She's fine as she is.'

'What's the matter with you?' I said. 'Are you having short-term memory problems? You called me a dangerous, violent criminal in the press. You're not worried I'll leap across the table and bite your face off, Hannibal Lecter style? Because I'd sure like to. I didn't eat any breakfast.'

'Inmate Blue!' the guard barked, having finally grown weary of my antics. 'I've just witnessed you threaten a visitor, the Deputy Commissioner of Police no less. I'm going to have to write you up for –'

'Please, please – just leave us.' Woods put a hand up to settle the guard. 'I don't want her cuffed. I don't want her written up. I don't want us observed. We'll be fine. I promise.'

The guard left in a huff. A coldness came over me. This wasn't the Woods I knew. The Woods I knew was snide, resentful and underhanded. He had done everything in his power to put me behind bars for taking out Regan Banks, and he had stepped on, betrayed or used the people I loved at every turn to do it. I knew immediately that something was wrong, and thought of my old boss, Chief Trevor Morris. He'd suffered a heart attack on the night that I was arrested for killing Banks.

'What's happened? Is it Pops? Is he OK?'

'Harry, I've come because I have an offer for you,' Woods said. 'I want to get you out of here.'

Chapter 7

WOODS PUT HIS arms on the table and edged closer, conspiratorial. I noticed for the first time that he had lost weight. His neck was leaner than it had been when I last saw him, and stubble trailed into the collar of his uniform shirt. I sat back in my chair, would have pushed the chair away from the table if it wasn't bolted to the floor. This man was not my friend. He was a vindictive narcissist with a badge.

'Look, you deserve to be where you are. We both know that.'

'Great start,' I said.

'You went after Regan Banks, deliberately and with calculation,' Woods reasoned. 'In your pursuit of him you committed a multitude of criminal offences, including evading police, breaking and entering, vehicular theft and assaulting multiple officers and civilians. Then you murdered Banks, just as you said you would.'

'Thanks for the trip down memory lane.'

'I have the power to quash all of the subsidiary charges against you.' He folded his hands on the table between us. 'I can have the charge of homicide knocked down to manslaughter. With my support, and testimony from Detective Whittacker, I'm confident we could get you diminished responsibility or provocation. You'd get time served, a good behaviour bond maybe. With such a defence, and considering how bad a trial would look for the police department, I believe that if I took this to the Director of Public Prosecutions, well . . . The DPP is a good friend of mine. We went to university together.'

I said nothing.

'All this would take is a couple of phone calls from me.' Woods looked at his watch. 'You could be out on bail by the end of the day, and could return to your job in six months or less.'

I stared at Woods. He had practised this speech a few times. It was convincing, tempting. He didn't need to put the icing on the cake, but he did.

'You look like you've been in an altercation.' He gestured to my face. 'You could be in a safe bed by tonight. Glass of wine, hot shower, proper meal. How does that sound?'

'It sounds as though you've lost your fucking mind,' I said. 'Or that you want something from me that I cannot possibly give.'

'You can give me what I want. You've proven yourself to be one of the only people who can.' He drew a deep breath. 'My daughter, Tonya, is missing,' he said. 'So is my grand-daughter, Rebel. I haven't seen either of them in eight days. There's been no phone contact, no activity on Tonya's bank accounts and no sightings of the two that have turned out to be credible. The last time I saw them, Tonya was taking her daughter home. They drove away from my house, and I haven't seen them again. I think that if –'

'Don't.' I held a finger up. Woods had begun taking out a photograph from the breast pocket of his shirt. 'Don't bring your baby pictures in here and try to manipulate me with them. I'm not doing a deal with the devil because of some cute-ass happy snap of your peachy little girls.'

He tucked the photograph away and instead lifted a briefcase from the floor, opened it and placed a very thick file on the table.

'You're not dealing with the devil here,' Woods said. 'I'm just a desperate father looking for his child.'

'I don't get it. What's wrong with your own detectives? Why isn't your little pet poodle Nigel Spader on this? Surely he'd have his nose crammed right up your butt crack, wanting to be your hero.'

'Everybody who is available is on this, including Detective Spader,' Woods said.

'Are Tox and Whitt working on it? Ask them to help you.'

'I approached Detective Barnes already,' Woods said. 'It was a mistake. While you're in here, I believe he and Whittacker will be unwilling to help me. I'm hoping once you're released, you could bring them on board.'

'Why do you want someone you've never liked or agreed with working a case this important to you?'

'Because you're different, Blue. You know you are. On the Banks case you proved you're willing to go outside the restrictions of law and procedure to get the job done. And if someone has hurt my family . . .'

He rubbed his face hard, biting down on the emotion. I glanced at the camera in the corner of the room.

21

'So what's the catch?' I said.

'There is no catch.' Woods cleared his throat. 'You find my family. And if someone has hurt them, you give me my time with that person before they're surrendered to custody. Your charges will be dropped.'

'Uh-huh.' I nodded. 'So if I don't achieve those things, I'll wind up right back here.' I stood. Woods looked up at me. 'Nice try. But I'm not interested.'

'Why the hell not?' Woods snapped. His face flushed interesting shades of red and purple.

'Because you said it yourself – I deserve to be here. I'm not some attack dog you can cage as it suits you. Putting me here because I wanted my own personal justice and then trying to release me so you can get yours just shows what a hypocritical, shallow piece of sh–'

Suddenly the alarm bell in the corner of the room started pealing, a shocking, ear-splitting sound.

I dropped to the floor and covered my head with my hands.

Chapter 8

'WHAT IS IT?' Woods asked, stepping around the table to the test the locked steel door. 'What do we do?'

'It's a lockdown. The bell means it's a level one. Probably another fight or something,' I said from the floor. The concrete beneath me was cold on my thighs and belly. 'I'm doing what I'm supposed to do. I don't know about you. You just sit there, I guess.'

I could hear guards running in the halls, doors and gates slamming closed. In a room nearby, guards were taking their places. There needed to be at least one guard watching every inmate while the incident, whatever it was, was taken care of. The voices of the guards reached us, muffled by thick walls.

'Get down! Get down! Get down!'

Woods hit the deck beside me, his hands under his chin.

'I'm sure you don't have to get down here, Mister Deputy Commissioner.' I frowned.

'Better safe than sorry,' he said. 'We don't know what this is. All it takes is one panicked guard with a gun.'

I watched him from beneath the table. It was bizarre to have him lying beside me on the cold, scuff-marked floor in his dazzling uniform. The thought hit me for an instant that, while he was the Grand Poobah of All Arseholes, he was also just a man. In this environment he was vulnerable, unaccustomed to the sounds and sights and activity around him. I tried to remember the first time I'd heard the lockdown alarm go off, the confusion that had swept over me as everyone around me dropped to the floor.

'What time is it?' I asked.

Woods looked at his big gold watch. 'Eleven.'

'Two lockdowns before midday,' I mused. 'Weird.'

'What was the first one?' he asked.

I pointed to my face.

'Oh.'

'Must be a full moon or something,' I said. 'Chicks in here go crazy when it's a full moon.'

I knew he was watching me. I kept my eyes on the concrete before me, examining the little sparkles and chips of rock in the mix.

'This place is awful,' he said. 'I know you hate me, but surely you want to get out of here. I'm trying to give you that chance.'

There was no time to answer. Two guards burst into the room.

'Deputy Commissioner Woods, I need to escort you out of the building, sir. Please come with me.'

'Think about it, Harry,' Woods said as he got up.

I put my hands behind my back so I could be cuffed.

'I don't know if you deserve it,' I said over my shoulder as they led the big man away.

Chapter 9

TOX BARNES PULLED his car into the parking lot of the Oceanside Motel in the south-western Sydney suburb of Punchbowl and sat looking at the area around him for some minutes, smoking and tapping his ash on the windowsill of his beaten-up Monaro. Smoking a cigarette before going into a possible crime scene was a ritual of sorts. It had saved him once from having half his face blown off by a shotgun. He'd been walking along the side of a warehouse he thought was empty, already reaching for the doorhandle, when a crew of drug runners he'd been looking for casually walked out, their guns by their sides. Tox had been in the shadows and froze as the crew appeared. They hadn't seen him. Had he forgone the cigarette in the car before he approached, he would have been dead.

The Oceanside Motel was, in fact, a fifty-minute drive to the nearest ocean – an hour and a half in peak-hour traffic – and the blue wave on its sign was cracked and faded beyond recognition. Two working girls were eyeing him from the door near reception, trying to decide if he was a customer or a pimp here to check on a girl. In the busy street, a homeless man was going from one bin to another, adding cans and bottles to a shopping trolley already half full of junk.

Woods had put his daughter up in a nice apartment in Rose Bay, an affluent suburb overlooking Sydney Harbour, near where the Deputy Commissioner himself lived. But Tox had done some digging and found out where she really lived. Tonya's history as a junkie, sometime prostitute and all-round bad girl meant that Rose Bay was too far from her friends, her sources of quick-hit cash loans and boyfriends she could sidle up to for affection or protection. When Tox had visited the Rose Bay address and talked the doorman into letting him view the apartment, he'd found it exactly as he expected it – clean, bare and unlived in. He could see right away she wasn't staying there. The milk in the refrigerator was off and there was junk mail on the floor inside the door an inch thick. Tox had called around some pimps he knew and it wasn't long before he was given the address of the Oceanside.

A few questions with the motel manager, which cost Tox fifty bucks, told him that Tonya had been renting a room sporadically, sometimes paying day by day or month by month as she was flush and then strapped for cash. Loans from Daddy, criminal pursuits or prostitution binges, Tox guessed.

He gave the working girls a nod, then walked up the stairs and along the landing to room 18. Tox had entered a thousand rooms like this one looking for girls over the years; some he had found dead, lying with their brains splattered on the walls or slumped in the shower, storm blue and still needled up. The doors of rooms like this had been kicked in by drug cops so many times that the locks were almost always faulty or crooked. All he had to do to get into Tonya Woods's room was jam his boot under the door and push upwards while giving the knob a good hard crank.

As he entered the room, Tox took in the upturned furniture, the glass on the carpet.

The scene before him was clearly the site of a violent abduction.

Chapter 10

IT WAS A sad place. The refuge of so many of society's edge-dwellers. Tox looked at the bare mattress sitting askew on an old wooden frame, pushed up against one wall. The quint-essential boxy television set, sitting on a milk crate, its black cord stretched taut near the doorway to a plug in the wall so that the set could be watched from the head of the bed. Smashed glass on the carpet, pillows and blankets on the floor. The bedside table was on its side. He pulled out his phone and took some pictures.

There were signs of furniture broken or stolen and not replaced: the outlines of two cabinets against one wall, a missing picture frame by the door. Tox stepped over the TV cord on his way out of the room and looked at the little kitchenette, where a dish rack and at least one glass had fallen and shattered on the sticky linoleum. He lit a cigarette and emptied the little plastic bin, rummaged through the contents, found a receipt and read it. Stuffed it in his pocket.

A bookshelf that had been stacked at the bottom with dozens of beauty magazines had toppled onto the end of the couch.

He stood in the bathroom and looked at the bottles scattered everywhere, the smashed mirror above the sink.

Tox crunched over broken shards to the wall where the mirror had been. There were tiny slivers of glass still clinging to the wall where something had impacted the mirror in the struggle. He would have to reach up to touch them. He thought about that for a while, opened a drawer and extracted a piece of paper stapled with a prescription. It was a hospital discharge report. On it he saw a familiar name and smiled to himself.

The smile faded when he felt the touch of a gun barrel against the back of his ear.

'Don't move, fuckhead.'

Chapter 11

TOX DREW ON the last of his cigarette and stubbed it out on the edge of the sink. The instinct flashed through him – as it always did at times like this – to react with violence. He saw himself turning and batting away the hand that held the gun, grabbing the wrist as he went, landing a punch on the guy's jaw. He'd shove the shoulder down, twist the arm back, snap it.

But instead of doing all those things, he folded the piece of paper in his hand and slipped it into the pocket of his jacket.

'I said don't fucking move!'

'Ali, what have you got?' someone shouted from the main room.

Tox turned calmly and looked at his captor, Ali. A plump Middle Eastern guy with a thin moustache clinging to the top of his lip. The guy who stepped into the small hall with them was white, also overweight. They both wore knock-off Nike hoodies and had chains running between their jeans and their wallets. The gun was small and battered.

'You know what I don't like?' Tox asked. The two bone-heads looked at each other. 'I don't like having a gun shoved in my face. I guess you could call it a pet peeve.'

'Who the fuck are you, bro?' Ali said.

'I'm Tonya's ex,' Tox said. 'Where is she?'

'Man,' Ali said. 'Your skankface girlfriend's long gone. She left us high and dry. We've been lookin' for that bitch for a week.'

'You and everyone else. She owes me, too.'

'Well, that's just too bad, so sad, bro. We ain't waiting in line. Get out of there.' Ali yanked Tox by the collar of his jacket, poked him in the back of the neck with the gun to get him to move into the hall. Tox kept his hands up, not necessarily in surrender, but to get the boneheads used to him moving his hands at about shoulder height. They backed him into the couch, tried to get him to sit down.

'Just take what you want,' Tox said. They emptied his pockets, took his wallet and phone. Then Ali held the gun on him while his accomplice started searching the apartment.

'What did she borrow money from you dopes for?' he asked.

'Baby stuff,' Ali answered. 'She was trying to buy a special kind of crib. Those things are expensive. She said her ex hocked all her baby shit. That you? You the baby daddy? What kind of deadbeat dickhead pawns all his baby's stuff?'

'This deadbeat dickhead, I guess,' Tox said.

'That's low, bro,' Ali said.

'Yeah. That's a dog act.' The second man was kicking over papers, books, magazines, looking for cash or drugs.

'Tonya ain't a bad chick, you know.' Ali turned the gun sideways, pointed the pistol teasingly at Tox's jaw. Maybe imagining himself using it on something other than Coke cans he shot off a wall for YouTube videos. 'I always thought she would make a good side bitch, but she never wanted to jump on board. She's got expensive tastes now.'

'Oh yeah?' Tox said.

'Last time I seen her, she was riding in a Beemer with some guy in a suit.'

'What guy?'

'Don't know.'

'When was this?' Tox asked.

'Like, sometime last month. Maybe if I blew her deadbeat ex's head off she might suck my dick.' He squinted, taking aim at Tox's eye socket. 'What do you think?'

'Roses are red, violets are blue, I splattered your ex's brains for you,' Tox said. He thought about it. Shrugged. 'Worth a try, probably.'

'This guy's fucking funny,' Ali grinned, showing blackened teeth. He stepped closer. The grin disappeared. 'But you're not so funny I wouldn't shoot you. I've killed before, you know.'

'Somehow I doubt that,' Tox said.

'What are you doing? You going to tell this guy your life story?' the white guy snapped. 'Bump him and let's go! There's nothing here.'

Tox knew what a bump meant. He'd known when he saw the gun that he was likely going to be clocked with it. If they'd been serious gangsters, they would have carried a serious weapon, but the little pistol with the scratches and chips all over it had spent its entire life being used as a hammer, when it wasn't starring on YouTube.

As the gun rose, Tox sprang forward.

He didn't like headbutting people. It was a risky move, to be used in close quarters only. Still, he swept the gun arm sideways and smashed his forehead into Ali's mouth. He swung Ali's hand up as he flailed and popped off two shots towards his friend. The meat-brain looking for cash grabbed his knee and hit the deck.

'Argh, shit! He shot me! Oh, God! Help!'

Tox shoved Ali down and dragged the two idiots next to one another on the floor. The two men were a bloodied mess on top of the disarray of the room.

'Don't kill us,' the white guy cried. 'Oh, God. He's gonna kill us!'

'Phones and wallets,' Tox said. 'Including mine.'

Tox tucked the goods into his pockets. 'You two morons need a mentor or something. Practical experience. You're pathetic. Stop smoking weed and watching *Training Day* and join a gang or something, for Christ's sake.'

Tox aimed and shot Ali in the calf. He put the gun in the back of his jeans while the kid screamed, spasming in pain. There was no sense in giving one of them the badge of honour of a real-life bullet wound and leaving the other out. He liked to be fair.

He left the two men writhing and sobbing on the ground, gripping their wounds, as he stepped over the debris and left the room.

Chapter 12

WITH THE ALARM still screaming in my ear, I was dragged upright and marched to the door. The unnecessarily hard grip on my bicep told me I was in the company of Officer Hugh Ridgen, but even before that I knew him from the Brut deodorant he must soak his clothes in every day.

'Oh good,' I moaned. 'It's you. My day just keeps getting better and better.'

'I heard someone gave you a kick in the face this morning, Blue,' Ridgen said. 'I'm only sorry I wasn't there.'

'I'm sorry you weren't there too,' I said. 'I remodelled a girl's face with a food tray. You could use some work on your hideous mug.'

'You're always such a flirt.' Ridgen dug into the soft flesh under my arm with his fingers. 'I understand it's frustrating in here, but if you ever want someone to warm you up on those cold nights in solitary, all you have to do is ask.'

'I spend my time in solitary fantasising about using your taser to fry your balls into tiny little bits of charcoal.'

'You do, huh?'

'It keeps me warm.'

He led me through the door and down the hall. Another officer, Tommison, who I rarely see on my wing, joined us. Tommison was Ridgen's superior, so I immediately felt safer.

'What's the trouble? Has there been an announcement?' I asked.

'Hopefully one of you bitches has gone on a killing spree over in E Wing.' Ridgen walked me along just too fast to move comfortably with my wrists secured. 'Who knows? We can only dream, huh, Harry?'

During a level-one lockdown, all inmates were to be secured wherever they could be and prison officers were directed to supervise them until further notice. One officer could supervise a maximum of twelve women. The corridors were cleared to make way for Immediate Action Teams or key officers moving between wings of the building. Ridgen, Tommison and I turned a corner and discovered another inmate, Crystal Chambers, standing looking through the windows of an empty room.

'Inmate Chambers, you're supposed to get down!' Ridgen barked. 'You must have done this drill a thousand times.'

'Sorry, sorry.' Chambers turned and put her head against a wall, her hands at the small of her back to be cuffed. 'I didn't know what to do. I wasn't thinking.'

'Probably high,' Ridgen said to Tommison as he cuffed the woman and dragged her roughly away from the wall. 'Pretty little Crystal's always high, aren't you?'

'We'll put them in workroom B,' Tommison said. 'There's a big crew of them in there, plenty of guards.'

Tommison took my arm, and the alarm bells above us stopped ringing. The silence swelled for no more than a second before a different wailing siren took over. The quickening in the guards was immediate. Tommison shoved me into Ridgen, his body hot and hard against mine.

'Jesus, level two,' Tommison said. 'You take care of these two. I'll go.'

He sprinted away, the keys at his belt jangling. In a level-two incident, all available staff were required to head to the section where the disturbance was happening. The sound made the hairs on my arms stand on end. More guards ran past us. I was so distracted by the tension and panic in the air that I almost didn't notice Ridgen was walking us past the workroom where twenty or so women were being watched over by two guards. I glanced back, saw wrought-iron chair frames on the work tables half-painted a stylish matt black, probably destined for the terrace of some corporate building in the city.

'Where are we going, Ridgen? He said to put us in the workroom,' I said.

'Yeah,' Ridgen said. 'But you two are violent inmates. I'd rather secure you by yourselves. You never know – the level two might get you all excited.'

He walked us to the end of the hall and unlocked a door. He prodded us into the small, empty education room. I realised there were no windows through which we could be seen by other guards or inmates. Ridgen took a spare set of cuffs from his belt and looped them through mine, locking me to a desk bolted to the floor beside the door. I knew we were in trouble when he went and hung his hat over the camera in the corner of the room.

Chapter 13

'IF YOU TOUCH me, I'll make it so you wish you were never born,' I told Ridgen. He laughed, leading Crystal to one of the desks in the first row of the classroom. She was taller than him but he lifted her and sat her on the desk without any trouble.

'Harry, I wouldn't touch you with a flamethrower mounted on the end of a barge pole.' Ridgen lifted Crystal's jumper and stuck his hands up beneath it. 'You just sit there quietly and watch.'

'You want me to watch?'

'Yeah.' Ridgen smiled at me. 'Get yourself some new fantasies about my balls.'

Ridgen had been right about Crystal. She was clearly high. I knew drugs were even easier to get in prison than on the outside, but most of what I saw around me was inmates spaced out on marijuana or sleeping pills. Crystal had the drooping eyes and lolling head of someone on something much harder. She came out of the haze completely for a moment and tried to wriggle away from Ridgen.

'Come on, Hughsie,' she whined. 'I don't feel like it right now.'

'Cryssie, we don't have time for you to play hard to get. We've got a couple of minutes. Start feeling like it.'

'I can't start feeling it just like that! I'm tired! I need time!'

'Ah, it's just like that scene from *The Notebook*,' I said. 'I wish I had a glass of wine and a block of chocolate to enjoy this with.'

'Shut up, Blue,' Ridgen snapped.

I sighed and sat against the wall. 'Cryssie' and 'Hughsie' had obviously arranged what a number of women in prison had over the years – an exchange of sex for perks, protection or drugs. Ridgen was notorious among the inmates for being partial to sexual favours in exchange for drugs. His favourite joke, about Johnsonborough being the perfect place to 'find somewhere for your Johnson to burrow', meant the other guards almost certainly knew about his extracurricular activities. The wailing siren, running footsteps in the hall and a second inmate watching his activities had driven Ridgen into a sweating state of passionate anticipation. I felt sick and looked around the room for something to distract myself with. On the table beside me was a stack of papers, tests marked and ready to hand back to inmates. Ridgen's groaning was halted suddenly with a grunt as Crystal kicked him in the shin.

'I said I don't feel like it!'

Ridgen pulled Crystal up from the desk and shoved her hard onto her front, so his crotch was against her backside. Crystal and I locked eyes across the classroom as he fumbled with her uniform trousers.

'Ridgen, let her go,' I said calmly. 'She's just not that into you.'

'I told you to shut up!'

'I'm giving you this one warning,' I said. 'You'd better listen.'

'*You're* warning *me*?' Ridgen ripped at Crystal's trousers. She whimpered as he shoved them down. 'I'm going to remember you said that when I'm done here.'

My cuffs, connected to the leg of the table by Ridgen's second set, gave me about two feet of chain. I stood, sliding the chain up the table leg, and knocked the stack of papers onto the floor beside me, extracting a paperclip from the top of one. I used my sense of touch alone to straighten the paperclip and tear a strip of paper from one of the pages. It was difficult with my hands behind me, but Crystal was having a harder time. She had zoned out again, her eyes half open and staring at me as Ridgen struggled to unclip his heavy utility belt. I wrapped the strip of paper around the paperclip, squeezed and scrunched it tight then curved the wire to form a U shape, and shifted over to a power point on the wall just next to the leg of the table.

'You asked for it,' I said.

Ridgen was ignoring me. I held the paper and fiddled around until the wires sank into the upper holes in the power socket. I couldn't see, but I felt the burst of heat from behind me, searing against my fingertips. There was a crack like a gunshot.

Ridgen and Crystal both jolted, and I shifted onto my knees, blindly grabbing at papers behind and beneath me. Blind to what was happening behind me, I could only hope that the paper wound around the wire had caught fire as I had planned, I began shoving test papers towards the power point, begging the universe to let the fire pass from the scrunched paper to one of the pages in my hands before it fizzled out.

'What did you do?' Ridgen grabbed at his pants. His legs were skinny and pale beneath stained white boxer shorts. 'What the hell did you do?'

The air smelled of burning paper. One of the pages had caught. I shifted away, as far as the two sets of cuffs would allow, and saw the fire spreading quickly through the papers, coiling and blue and small, but there. I shifted away, blew on the flames and watched them grow, heading for a pile of educational posters rolled and stacked under the table.

Ridgen ran for the fire beside me. As he came I kicked out, struck his ankle and sent him sprawling into the table. The fire licked and slid into the pile of posters, rising slowly like a tide through the folds, the white centres of the rolls blackening and spewing smoke as Ridgen batted uselessly at them with his hands.

I crouched beside the doorway as he ran into the hall for a fire extinguisher. The sprinklers above us sputtered and came to life. Crystal was lying still bent over the table, her pants around her ankles and her lips spread into a lazy smile.

Chapter 14

I LAY ON the concrete slab, staring at the brown swirls on the ceiling, trying to understand how the inmate who had used their own faeces to make the artworks had reached the fifteen-foot-high ceiling. The picture appeared to be some kind of angel or bird-woman emerging from a cave. The words in the angel's speech bubble were barely decipherable: *Jonsonburro gards r shit.*

'So.' The guard sitting on a fold-out chair outside my cell flipped the page of her report. 'You assaulted Inmate Jimmet, Inmate Briggs, Inmate Mallory and Inmate Scarborough. Your actions caused Jimmet and Briggs level-two injuries. You then went ahead and threatened Officer Ridgen and wilfully caused level-three damage to a facility classroom.'

'I didn't threaten Ridgen.'

She shuffled the pages. 'Did you not threaten to use his taser on his private parts?'

'I was trying to encourage him to keep them private.'

The guard said nothing. I looked over. All I could see through the hole in the cell door was a name badge that said 'Steeler'.

'What level of threat is that?' I asked.

'Level two.'

'What is it with you people and levels?' I asked. 'It fascinates me that you would spend your every available moment assigning levels to things and not scrubbing the human waste off cell walls.'

'This is a correctional facility, Inmate Blue,' Steeler said. 'Not the Crowne Plaza hotel. You don't want to stare at shit stains on the walls all night long? First, don't murder people. Second, take care of your living space. The condition of the cells is a direct result of inmate behaviour.'

'That doesn't make any sense. I'm not the one who painted the room with crap. I have no control over the –'

'You kicked Officer Ridgen in the ankle. A level-two assault.'

I yawned.

'Do you agree with the charges?' she asked.

'No, I don't.'

'Right.' Steeler stood. 'It'll go to the review board, and you can talk about it with disciplinary officers in a couple of weeks.'

'When do I get my mattress and pillow?' I asked.

'Someone will bring you your bedding shortly.' I heard the guard walk away. I sighed again. Whenever the guards say something in prison is going to happen 'shortly', it's not going to happen. My threat to Ridgen meant I was sleeping on the concrete slab, and it was more than likely that someone was going to forget my dinner, too.

I stretched and tried to settle, the base of my skull already aching against the cold surface. The constant noise of the prison – slamming doors, women shouting, guards laughing – seeming to reverberate through the slab directly into my brain.

Forty-eight hours. That was what I had been assigned for the fight with Frida. There would likely be more time stacked on for the fire in the classroom, the threat and the assault, but for now I decided to keep myself sane by counting down the first two days. Then I would decide how to handle whatever came next. You can only eat an elephant one bite at a time.

There was shuffling nearby, and I heard a familiar wheezing. I got up and went to the slot in the door, looked through the tiny airholes in the flap. Across the hall, an elderly inmate was peering through her slot at me. I knew the old woman only by her nickname, Nanna. She had been in Johnsonborough for three years, awaiting trial for poisoning another resident at her nursing home. Even the guards called her Inmate Nanna. She was a biter, and was frequently in solitary for trying to take a chunk out of other inmates or guards with her blazing-white dentures. Though I'm a cop, and should be every inmate's enemy, I had been to solitary frequently enough to befriend her.

'Did they say you assaulted Ridgen?' Nanna wheezed.

'A little kick. Nothing substantial.'

'Shame.'

'Yeah,' I said. 'I bet you'd like to get those chompers onto that son of a bitch.'

'My word,' she said. Her wrinkled face bunched as she smiled. 'Sounds like it was a big day up there. Were you there for the stabbing?'

'What stabbing?'

'The level-two lockdown,' she said. She stood and stretched, her back clicking at the effort of bending over to look through the slot. 'The doctor.'

'What are you talking about?'

The old woman bent to the slot again.

'The guards were going on about it just before they brought you down,' Nanna said. 'Someone knifed the doctor. Goldman. She's dead.'

Chapter 15

EDWARD WHITTACKER COULD feel his soul in his body. It was warm, tingling, a thing that lingered just below the surface of his skin, stretching and swirling within the limits of his limbs. He could feel the boundaries and edges of it most in the tips of his fingers. His soul flexed and expanded there, as if his hand was in a glove, the fabric bending, trying to contain the spirit.

'Counting back from ten slowly, now,' the instructor said from somewhere at the front of the room. 'Inhaling, exhaling. Ten. Inhale. Nine. Exhale.'

Whitt smelled cigarette smoke slicing through the echinacea and lavender incense. His soul recoiled. A pair of black boots clomped onto the yoga mat, either side of his face, and he opened his eyes.

'Wakey-wakey, flower child,' Tox Barnes said.

'Sir!' the instructor gasped. Around Whitt, there were dozens of sharp inhalations completely out of time with the group rhythm. Someone coughed. Tox Barnes ashed his cigarette onto the mat by Whitt's face. 'Sir, you can't smoke in here.'

'Pipe down, Bhagwan,' Tox said. 'We're outta here.' He grabbed Whitt by his T-shirt. Whitt struggled as he was hauled to his feet, the Bikram yoga room pulsing around him as he came out of his meditative state.

'Jesus Christ.' He tried to gather his mat, towel and water bottle. 'What are you doing here?'

'Leave that shit.' Tox dragged Whitt along. 'You won't need it. We're going back to the real world.'

'Sir, this is a private session!' The instructor was standing on a small platform with her hands on her hips, a tiny microphone clipped to the side of her sweaty face. 'You can't just . . . Sir? Excuse me, sir?'

Two dozen people watched them leave. Tox heaved a sigh as the door to the room shut behind them.

'Thank fuck. It's hot as hell in there. Why do you have it so hot?'

'It helps you centre your mind.' Whitt brushed back his wet hair. 'It's good for your flexibility and helps you sweat out the toxins.'

'Being toxic is a big part of my charm,' Tox said, watching the arses of a group of women in yoga outfits as they walked by. When he turned back to Whitt he stumbled a little in shock. 'Jesus. I couldn't tell when you were lying down, but you're huge!'

He poked Whitt in a pectoral muscle. It was hard as tyre rubber.

'I've been working out,' Whitt said.

'Working out? You look like you've had a head transplant. This is not your body.' Tox put his cigarette in his mouth, squeezed both of Whitt's biceps at once. 'Mother of Mary,

46

you could tour with the Thunder Down Under. Where's your locker, Arnie? We've gotta go.'

'What is this all about?'

'I need you. Consider this your spiritual calling. Deputy Commissioner Woods's daughter and grandkid are missing.' He'd started walking, following a sign that read 'Lockers'.

Whitt grabbed the older man's shoulder.

'Wait a minute,' Whitt said. 'Slow down. I'm suspended. *You're* suspended. And how the hell did Woods get you on board? You told me you wouldn't piss on that guy if he was on fire.'

'I wouldn't.' Tox took Whitt's locker key from his hand and opened his locker, grabbed a pile of stuff and threw it at Whitt's chest. 'But my curiosity got piqued. I went and looked at the girl's apartment and what I saw was marginally more interesting than the tits and arses I've been staring at for the past four months down at Eruptions. It's a hell of a lot more interesting than the ferocious wankery you were doing in that sauna.'

'That *ferocious wankery* is part of my treatment.' Whitt wiped his face with a towel. 'I'm still a resident at the rehab facility. I'm only on day release.'

'I'm your rehab now,' Tox said. 'You so much as glance sideways at any illicit substances and I'll smack you in the face with a brick. That work for you?'

Whitt had a lot of problems with what was happening, but he followed Tox down the stairs anyway, past the water cooler to the front doors of the yoga studio.

'What happened to the girl?' he asked, his heartbeat rising as he caught up with his partner's feverish pace. There was an electricity coming off Tox that he had not felt in what seemed like forever. The thrill of a mission. 'You got any leads? Was she abducted?'

'She wasn't abducted,' Tox said as he took his car keys from his pocket. 'But someone rigged her motel room to make it look that way.'

Chapter 16

DARKNESS GREW QUICKLY. I curled on my side and thought about Doctor Goldman. Hunger pangs came and went, as did the sounds of prisoners being transferred in and out of solitary, sometimes swearing and shouting, sometimes not. The impulse to cry or mourn did not come. I had shut down my emotional responses when I first entered prison, the way I had entering each and every foster home of my childhood. The best way to protect the heart and mind while in a danger- ous situation was to become like a robot. Anger was about the only acceptable reaction, and even that was quickly smothered like a flame with no oxygen. I stared at graffiti on the back wall of the cell and considered who might have killed the good doctor, weighing the possibilities against what I knew of the woman.

Doctor Goldman had been well liked in the prison. She provided a refuge, an oasis of calm in the otherwise chaotic mess of buildings that made up the facility. Her offices were safe, and she was safe – she did not have a reputation for physically or emotionally abusing patients. Inmates called her Goldie, and one wall of her private office, which I had seen only once, was plastered with letters from former inmates thanking her for her kindness while they were locked up. She had not only offered me no-questions-asked respite periods in the infirmary, but she had always tried to keep an eye on my mental state whenever I came in battered and bruised. She wanted to know if I had visitors, if I took phone calls, who my supporters on the outside were. She weighed me and insisted that I eat, asked if I had had thoughts of suicide, wanted to know what I was reading and watching when I had access to books or television.

There were things I didn't know about her. I didn't know if Goldie's warm, caring reputation also held true among the prison staff. I knew she had access to painkillers and drugs that would be appealing both to prison staff, who might sell them to inmates, and the inmates themselves. Had an inmate or a staff member killed her? Nanna didn't know when I asked. All the old woman had heard was that the doctor was dead and had been 'knifed'. A stabbing suggested an inmate had committed the crime.

When the slot in my door slid open I went over to it, hoping for dinner. Instead a manila folder slid through the hole and slapped onto the floor of my cell, spilling its contents.

'What's this?'

'From Woods,' the guard said.

'Ugh.' I slid the folder away. 'I said no to that guy.'

The guard didn't answer, just flipped the slot shut. I pushed it open again before she could lock it, peering out into the dim light of the hall at the guard's belt, inches away from the slot. She was the same guard who had interviewed me earlier, Steeler. From this angle I could see short-cropped, almost-white blonde hair. A tattoo of barbed wire running around her wrist was just visible below the cuff of her shirt.

'Hey,' I said. 'Is there any word on who killed the doctor?'

'You'll be questioned about it tomorrow morning.'

'Me?' I said. 'Why me? I wasn't there. I was with Ridgen.'

The guard tried to close the slot again.

'If it wasn't me, why do they want to talk to me?' I held the flap open with my palm. 'It doesn't make sense. Unless . . . Unless it was someone I know. Was it someone I know?'

Steeler smiled.

A chill ran through me. There was only one inmate in Johnsonborough I knew well enough to be questioned about them.

I was so shocked I forgot about my hand on the flap. The guard's baton rapped hard on my knuckles. I hadn't even seen her extract her baton from the back of her belt. I snarled a dirty word and cradled my throbbing fingers as the flap slammed closed in my face.

Steeler crouched, and I saw the blueness of her eye through the tiny airholes. 'That junkie bitch had better sleep with one eye open over in ad seg,' she sneered. 'The doctor was a lovely lady, and she didn't deserve to go like that.'

'It wasn't Dolly.' I eased the words through my teeth. 'It couldn't have been.'

'We'll see.' Steeler stood and walked away.

I knelt on the concrete, sucking my knuckles, thinking about Dolly. She would be over in administrative segregation on suicide watch, preparing to be forensically processed and interviewed about the murder. The investigation team at the prison would want to ask me if Dolly had been planning it, if she had mentioned a grudge against the doctor. I knew that gentle, naive, plainly stupid Dolly couldn't have murdered Doctor Goldman. My very bones ached with the knowledge that what was happening upstairs was a grave mistake, that the killer, whoever he or she was, was still walking the halls of the prison somewhere.

I sat against the door of my cell and picked up Woods's manila folder. My mind wanted to retreat from Dolly, from Doctor Goldman, from the emotion trying to break through the barrier that had held in place for so long. But when I opened the folder, there on the front page of the Missing Persons file was a photograph of Woods's daughter and her two-year-old child. I slammed the folder shut.

'You know . . .' a voice said. I knelt and looked out the holes in the slot. Nanna was crouched by her door again. 'I think I got some information that could help.'

Chapter 17

'WHAT IS IT?' I asked.

Nanna was silent for a long time, pausing to stretch her back, which popped and clicked like logs in a fire.

'If this Dolly person killed the doctor, and you don't think she would have done it for her own reasons, she might have been hired,' Nanna said. 'I think I heard the doctor and The Spanner had a thing.'

Anna 'The Spanner' Regent was another frequent visitor to solitary. I knew little about her, other than that she was the only child-killer in the prison who didn't spend her whole life in ad seg. She was so big and intimidating that no one messed with her, even though her crime should have made her everyone's favourite punching bag. Anna had beaten her four-year-old nephew to death with a large steel spanner, the kind used to take the bolts off truck tyres. Though she was carefully avoided by most of the prison population, now and then a downright crazy inmate, or someone wanting to make a name for themselves, challenged her and was immediately splattered on the concrete like a bug on a windscreen, and Anna ended up in solitary. I'd never spoken to Anna, but I'd seen her being walked past my own cell in solitary a number of times. She was always locked in the cell at the end of the hall, the darkest and dirtiest of them all.

'What do you mean, they had a *thing*?' I asked Nanna.

'A romantic thing.'

'What? The doctor was gay?'

'So I heard. With The Spanner.'

I sat on my haunches and thought about Doctor Goldman holding my face in her hands, looking at my eyes. The strange tenderness of it, those few seconds, when I let her take the weight of my head and rested with her warm palms against my cheeks. Why had she let me do that? How long had the moment lasted? Almost all prison gossip is bullshit. Rumours and lies circulated and embellished for entertainment purposes. The idea that a violent, child-murdering inmate and the prison doctor could conduct a romantic relationship was far-fetched. But it wasn't impossible. Guards were targeted with violence all the time, and sometimes that was because they had secret relationships with inmates that went sour.

I looked through the holes in the slot again.

'Is Anna down here?' I asked.

'I think so.' Nanna looked right, like she'd be able to see through the eight cells between hers and the end cell.

'Will you take a kite?' I asked Nanna.

'Sure. I like mysteries.'

I opened the manila folder Woods had given me, ignoring the photograph on the front page, and tore a strip of paper from the file. I worked the shoelace loose from my right shoe and found a solid patch of dried muck on the wall beside the door, probably human waste of some kind. I spat in my palm, wet the hard plastic tip of the shoelace and scratched at the muck until I had a kind of faint brown ink on the end of the plastic. The primitive writing tools wouldn't allow me to say much. In the light from the slot holes, I wrote on the strip of paper.

Dr dead, I wrote. *U know?*

I'd never spoken to Anna The Spanner before. I didn't know what level of intelligence I was dealing with, or what kind of mental illness a person capable of bludgeoning a small child to death was likely to be harbouring. I hoped Anna would be able to interpret my message, not only 'Do you know this has occurred?' but also 'Do you know anything about it?'

It was a long shot. But I felt desperate for Dolly, confused and in need of answers. I picked open the clean end of the shoelace with my teeth and divided the woven fibres until I had thin strings, which I tied end to end. I folded the note so it was tiny and flat, bound it at the end of the string and lay down on the floor.

Nanna was already lying near her cell door, having taken as long to get down there as it had taken me to make the kite. I could see one eye in the gap beneath the door. I listened for guards, and when I heard none, I set the note on the floor at the crack and flicked it out into the hall. The note came up short, a foot or so in front of Nanna's door. I pulled it back, tried again. Nine attempts, and finally the tiny note slid through the crack in Nanna's door. She pulled the note from me, and I let the string go.

I sat against the door in the dark and listened to Nanna as she tried to flick the kite to the cell diagonally across the hall from her, the cell adjacent to mine. Heard her whispered directions to the accepter of the note. It would take hours, perhaps, for the note to zigzag all the way down to Anna The Spanner's usual cell. Somewhere down the hall, a woman screamed and banged against the door. Nanna paused her mission to pass my kite as guards approached, doing rounds. The guards tramped past in their leather boots, making the line of light from under the door blink on the folder in my fingers.

I didn't know what message would return, or if Anna would answer me at all. But I had to do something. Somewhere, in another lonely, dirty cell in the prison, I knew an innocent woman was relying on me.

Chapter 18

'A BAR?' WHITT stopped between the tables on the way to the dance floor. He had been so swept up by Tox and the case, being practically abducted from his yoga session and thrown into Tox's filthy, reeking Monaro, that he hadn't taken much notice of his surroundings. 'You're interrupting my rehab to take me to a *bar*?'

'Get this guy a Shirley Temple,' Tox said to a woman who approached them. He fell into a seat near the dance floor with all the familiarity of a man who hardly left it. The woman, wearing only transparent plastic heels and a fluorescent pink G-string, didn't ask what Tox wanted.

'I can't be here,' Whitt breathed, trying not to look at the bottles behind the bar in the far corner. 'I can smell the beer in the carpet.'

'Well, this is my office.' Tox gestured to the chair across from him. 'Deal with it.'

On the painted black catwalk, a very tanned woman in a bright yellow G-string was twirling lazily around a chrome pole. Two men were talking at a table on the other side of the catwalk, and against the far wall three men were waiting in chairs to go into private rooms. Whitt sat and put his hands on the table between him and Tox, then immediately regretted it. The surface was covered with rings from the bottoms of glasses, as sticky as honey. 'What the hell do you *do* here?'

'This,' Tox said, gesturing to his seat. 'I'm the doorman.'

'The door's all the way over there.' Whitt pointed with his thumb across the huge, empty space. 'Shouldn't you stand by it and stop the riffraff coming in?'

'It's all riffraff here,' Tox said. 'They come in. After a while I put 'em back out.'

A waitress brought Whitt's pink drink and a glass of whisky for Tox. Whitt could taste the whisky from the other side of the table. Particles of it in the air mixed in with the sweat-beer-vomit-sex perfume that covered everything. He suddenly noticed that his shirt was sticking to his chest with sweat.

'Tell me what you know so we can get out of here,' Whitt said.

'Tonya Woods.' Tox put a picture of the girl on the table between them, probably adhering it to the surface forever. 'Twenty-two. Baby bad-girl. She started getting naughty at thirteen when her mother died of ovarian cancer. Climbing out the windows of the house. Riding in cars with boys. Yelling at teachers, throwing stuff. Woods yanks her out of her posh private school before she can embarrass him in front of all his lawyer and judge friends and stuffs her in a specialist program where she can cool her heels until she's seventeen. It's one of those places where the kids choose what they want to learn and light candles and tend to baby chickens. So there's no violence, but she comes out of it knowing how to make macaroni necklaces and not much else. Drops out early, sixteen.'

Whitt looked at the picture. The girl didn't resemble big, broad, square-jawed Woods at all. She was lean and pretty, with a heart-shaped face and long dark hair. The picture was a police mugshot, but it must have been early in the girl's downward slide. She was smiling a little. They always smile in the beginning, when they don't know the system – don't know that they're about to be taken out of the photography session and dumped into a cold, featureless holding cell that smells of urine while bail is arranged.

'Right after school Woods helps get her a job making coffee and being the mail girl in an office full of ambulance chasers, but she gets bored. Starts turning up late, taking long lunches, coming in hungover and scrappy,' Tox said. 'The legal firm puts up with her until she takes a company credit card and goes on a shopping spree with it. Five-thousand-dollar weekend at the Four Seasons with all her scumbag friends. Fine champagne and hotel-room damages were the major expenses. One of the guests put an armchair through the window of the sixteenth-floor suite.'

'Wow,' Whitt said. He reflected on how this all would have looked to the New South Wales Police Force. Having come from Perth, he knew nothing of the Woods family's troubles.

'Off the back of that performance, she does her first disappearing act,' Tox said. 'Six days off the radar. She turns up in jail, being questioned about a drive-by shooting. She was in the back seat when some thugs sprayed a house and killed a guy, injured a kid. She's seventeen, and the papers aren't supposed to name her but it leaks online. First big media appearance. Very embarrassing for Woods.'

Whitt leaned over and examined Tonya's face. Now that he was studying it more closely he could see her eyes were tired. Not merely physically exhausted, but the kind of weariness that comes with a long, constant trampling of the soul. Whitt felt like he was looking at a snapshot of his past. He could see a thousand days begun in hope and ended in failure. Small dreams born and crushed. *This will be the morning I get up and go to work, do my job properly. This will be the day I don't drink. This will be the person I can trust. This will be the time I make my father proud.* Whitt knew exactly what was wrong with Tonya Woods. She'd tried and failed at life too many times to wake up believing anymore.

'And here's the daughter.' Tox put another photograph on the tabletop, crumpled a little at the edges from being in his pocket. 'Two years old. Not only is the baby gone, but Tonya's not supposed to have her in the first place.'

Chapter 19

WHITT PICKED UP the photo of the infant, which made a *shluck*ing sound as it came unstuck from the tabletop. The picture had been taken at one of those child photography places. The chubby girl smiled at something just above the camera. Four teeth in her bottom jaw, lights in her eyes, her mother's dark, rich hair. *Too much hair for a baby*, Whitt thought. Funny spikes of it sticking out from behind a little pink hair band.

'The kid looks healthy,' Whitt said. 'So Tonya hasn't had custody?'

'Not so far,' Tox said, tapping a cigarette out of a box. 'Woods raised the kid.'

'Jesus.' Whitt put the pictures side by side. 'Woods and a little baby all alone? He storms around being the police department's biggest arsehole by day and goes home and warms up bottles of milk for his baby at night?'

Tox shrugged. 'I guess some people have softer sides. Not me.'

'Why did Tonya lose custody?'

'She never really had it to begin with. She was high when she had the baby. Social workers took it right off her in the delivery room because she tested positive for narcotics. They'd had their eye on her for a while. Woods sat by the humidi-crib for two weeks while the baby went through withdrawals. Tonya did another disappearing act. Three weeks this time.'

'Who's the daddy?'

'Anyone's guess. No name on the birth certificate. And she'd been hopping in and out of cars to feed her drug habit.'

'So Tonya has been having visits with the kid recently?'

'She was having supervised visits, and then unsupervised as she got clean,' Tox said. 'Woods would have her over to the house to play with the child, stay over. Sometimes, when she was sober for decent stretches, Woods would let her take the kid back to her place just for the night. That's what happened this time. He said she's been trying to get straight, be a good parent. Some bozos I ran into at the Oceanside Motel con-firmed that – they said she had borrowed money from them to buy baby things.'

'Why not borrow the money from Woods?'

'Pride, maybe.'

'So what's your theory? She tried to get clean but she slipped, and she's on a binge somewhere with the kid?' Whitt asked.

'I don't think so.'

'But why not? If Tonya's an addict and she disappears all the time, what's different about this occasion? We're only on day eight, right? She might have taken the kid overnight, fallen off the wagon and got high, and she and the baby are in a crack house somewhere waiting to be found.'

'Woods thinks it's different this time,' Tox said. 'And I think so, too.' He lay his phone on the table and opened the photo app, flipped through some pictures of a trashed motel room. 'Someone fixed the place to make it look like there was a struggle. Did all the obvious things. Knocked over a bookcase. Smashed a mirror. Threw some glasses and shit on the floor. But see here? The cord running from the television to the wall was two feet off the ground, stretched tight so the woman could watch TV in bed without having to get up to change the channels. The TV remote would have disappeared ages ago. So the cord runs right across the space between the side of the bed and the doorway.'

Whitt looked.

'OK. So?'

'Parts of the room suggest the struggle went on there, or started there.' Tox pointed. 'Glass knocked off the bedside table. Table knocked over, bed all messed up. But if there really was a struggle in that room, how did they manage not to pull the TV plug from the wall? Even if the abductor came around the other side of the bed to grab Tonya, she's supposed to have resisted capture, or at least we're meant to think so from the state of the room. But the cord is just sitting there like a giant trip-wire. Surely someone would have accidentally pulled it from the wall. And then there's the bathroom mirror.'

'What about it?'

'The point of impact on the mirror was high.' He put a hand up. 'Maybe eight feet off the ground. The bathroom's real small and the mirror's real big. I can see the mirror being smashed at shoulder height by someone falling into it. But someone had to stand inside the bathroom and raise their arm up and break it with something extended from their arm. A hammer or a piece of brick or whatever. Why would you do that when you're struggling with a petite woman in a tiny bathroom? Your hands would be down here.' He put his hands right out from his chest. 'But if you went into the bathroom *with the intention* of smashing the mirror, you'd smash it up high, right? No point smashing it in the centre and having the top half collapse over on top of you.'

'If you're right, and the struggle was staged, why has someone gone to all that effort?' Whitt asked. 'You're thinking Tonya wanted to run off with the kid, so she's trying to make it look like someone took her? That doesn't make any sense. Woods would be plenty worried if you run off with his grandchild, a child you don't have custody of. But he'll be even more worried if it looks like someone took you both. Something like that will make him bring in all the police he can spare.'

'Even suspended ones.' Tox raised his whisky glass.

Chapter 20

HE WAS BACK. Her very worst patient.

When the nurse who informed Chloe Bozer of the man's imminent arrival walked away, the trauma surgeon put her head in her hands, her elbows on the desk. Her tiny fifth-floor office at St Vincent's Hospital had been dead silent, but now it was filled with a heavy, throbbing dread. She had thought she would never see him again. In the darkness behind her palms, there was no hiding from the images that swirled of the man whose life she had saved six months earlier.

He had come into the hospital in a rush of redness, the way they all did, ambulance lights blazing in the parking bay, blood on the spotless tiles and all over the gloved hands of the paramedics. It had been a rare quiet night in the emergency room, a couple of bumps and scrapes and the usual smattering of overdoses from Kings Cross. So when the alert came, she and her staff had rushed to the doors to greet the patient. She knew it was bad from the faces of the men accompanying him. Male, early forties, multiple severe puncture wounds.

A stabbing. The paramedics informed her that he had flatlined twice in the ambulance on the way there, and he was crashing again as they wheeled him into surgery.

She knew who he was as soon as she saw him stretched out before her in the operating theatre. The name the paramedics had been yelling, trying to bring him back, hadn't reached her ears at first. His face had been a bloody mask, but a nurse wiped his cheeks and brow clean as she prepared him for anaesthesia. His eyes fluttered open and rolled towards her, wet and confused, examining the people frantically working on him. He seemed to know she was in charge of all the people there who would, or wouldn't, save him. His eyes questioned her silently, asking about his chances, perhaps, trying to read the fear on her face before unconsciousness took him again.

She knew those eyes. Then she heard the name.

Detective Tate Barnes, the man who had destroyed her life.

Chapter 21

HE CAME IN without knocking, just walked around the corner of her open door and pulled out the guest chair like he owned the place. Another man came in with him, more muscular and neater, less confident about just marching into her office.

'Chloe,' Tox said by way of greeting, sinking into the chair beside her.

'It's Doctor Bozer,' Chloe said, resisting the urge to hide her face in her hands again. 'It's always been Doctor Bozer to you. Detective Barnes, what the hell are you doing here?'

'Let me introduce my friend, Edward Whittacker.' Tox gestured to the man leaning awkwardly against the wall by the door. 'Whitt, this is Chloe. She was the head surgeon who worked on me. She saved my life. Whitt is –'

'Your partner.' Chloe nodded coldly. 'Detective Whittacker, we've met before. You charged into the emergency room on the night Detective Barnes was injured, demanding my staff stop trying to save his life to scrape some DNA evidence from under his fingernails so you could have it tested. That's if I recall correctly?'

'Oh.' Whitt scratched the back of his neck. 'Uh, yes. That was me.'

'Detective Barnes, I asked you a question.' Chloe turned back to Tox, her jaw clicking and eyes blazing. 'What are you doing here?'

'I'm on a case and I need your help.'

'You should have made an appointment.'

'I don't make appointments.'

'What the hell do you need me for?'

Tox put a photograph of a young, dark-haired woman on the table between them like a poker player setting down a trump card. Chloe stared impassively at it.

'Girl's missing.'

Chloe glanced at the picture, then took up a pen, hoping that if she went back to work Tox and his partner would just go away. Tox set down another picture, a small child. 'This one, too.'

'I've never seen them before.'

'The mother's picture's old. You have seen her,' Tox said. 'She comes in for ODs fairly regularly.'

'This is the nearest hospital to Kings Cross.' Chloe made some meaningless notes on her desk calendar. 'We get about three ODs a day. I don't usually take in faces.'

'I want to look at her medical records, and those of the child, if the child's ever been treated here. Any reports hospital staff made to the Department of Family Services. Any people mentioned who accompanied the girl here.'

'You got a warrant?'

'No.'

Chloe said nothing.

'Paging Doctor Bozer,' Tox said. 'Did you hear me?'

'I heard you. You said a bunch of things that you wanted and gave me no legal incentive to give them to you. So I'm saying no.'

'Honey.' Tox shifted closer in his chair, put an elbow on her desk, right by the corner of her calendar. She could hear the smile in his voice, though she refused to look up. 'I could get those papers from the nurses. You know I could. But I don't want to get those ladies in any more trouble.'

'If you don't take your elbow off my desk in the next ten seconds . . .' Chloe eased the words through her teeth. There was no threat that came to mind. She was not accustomed to threatening people, to the anger that was burning around her throat like a steel ring. She could smell him. Cigarettes, leather, a metallic smell that was probably gunshot residue or something. The others that had come as he lay clinging to the edge of life in the days after his surgery had smelled of it, too. Big, bruising men with gold chains. Eerie, strangely cold men in suits. There had been women, but they were all the same: a smattering of doe-eyed things in skimpy outfits, smoking and chewing their fake nails. Three of the men on different occasions had taken her aside, tried to press envelopes of cash into her hand, making vague but dangerous-sounding promises.

Just keep him alive. Do whatever you have to.

Tox took his elbow off the desk, but he didn't leave. She knew there was only one way to get rid of him.

Chloe sent a request for the documents through to the reception desk of the emergency room.

Chapter 22

THE TWO DETECTIVES walked to Tox's car, the wind warm, pressing their clothes to their bodies. Tox hugged the folder of printed records to his chest to stop the pages fluttering.

'I'm not going back there with you,' Tox said. 'Not while you're looking like that. I saw those nurses checking out your new Terminator bod. You're shaming me on my own turf.'

'Seems to me like you're shooting yourself in the foot,' Whitt said. 'That surgeon lady hates your guts.'

'I wasn't the best patient,' Tox said. 'While I was in the coma, a few unsavoury types I've come to know over the years came and hassled her about taking care of me. I'm popular among the bottom-dwellers, I guess. Doctor Bozer didn't like all the low-lifes stinking up the hospital halls and following her to her car. But I don't know how that's my fault; I was unconscious.'

'That's all it was, then?'

Tox thought. 'Well, when I woke up, I smuggled in cigarettes and booze and outside food. She didn't like that, either.'

Whitt waited.

Tox sighed. 'And then, yeah, OK – some of the nurses thought I was worth bending the physical contact rules for, and I didn't discourage them. Doctor Bozer walked in on me and a couple of them having a party between the sheets one time.'

'A *couple* of them? At once?'

'They were good friends, I think.'

'How the hell were you sleeping with the nurses when you'd been stabbed twice in the guts?'

'They're nurses,' Tox said. 'They've got a gentle touch. Plus, any stitches I popped, they'd just put them right back in.'

'I see,' Whitt said.

'So I'm not Doctor Bozer's favourite person in the whole world, but we've got the papers on Tonya.' He got into the car and slapped the file on the dashboard.

'I thought it seemed like it was more than all that stuff, though,' Whitt said, climbing in beside his partner. 'More than you just being an arsehole patient. It seemed to me like it was personal.'

'It wasn't personal,' Tox said, barely getting the words out before a sharp rap on his window startled him. Chloe Bozer was standing outside the car, her hands on her hips. Tox left Whitt in the car and slid out. He shut the door and turned, only to receive the painful poke of Chloe's finger in his chest.

'Here's how it works, dickhead,' she snapped. 'You don't ever, *ever* turn up at my office again. If you want an appointment with someone in the hospital's records department, you call ahead first and bring a fucking warrant with you.'

'Whoa.' Tox put his hands up. 'Easy, tiger.'

'It's not "tiger",' Chloe said, poking him again. 'It's not "Chloe". It's not "honey". It's *Doctor. Bozer.*'

'Doctor Bozer,' Tox said carefully. 'I was only –'

'– doing your job?' she asked. 'Right. That's what I was doing when I saved your life. If I'd known you were such an annoying, disrespectful, arrogant *twat* I might have reconsidered. So don't go waving the fact that I saved you around like it's evidence that I'll do you favours.'

'Shame,' Tox said. 'I've had some good favours done for me by the staff here. I was hoping one day you'd join in.'

Chloe shook her head. The warm evening breeze and her fury had made rose-pink clouds creep up her pale neck into her cheeks. Tox was smiling. He couldn't help himself.

'Look, I'm sorry,' he said. 'I don't mean to be a smart-arse. I've been a lot of trouble. Let me make it up to you. There's a great bar around the corner called Jangling Jack's.' He pointed. 'Get in the car and we –'

She was gone, storming off across the car park the way she had come. He shrugged to himself and slid back into the car.

'Nothing personal, huh?' Whitt said.

Chapter 23

THE DOOR TO my cell opened. I struggled awake, having drifted off into a pain-filled haze, twisted dreams about Dolly and Doctor Goldman rolling through my skull as it rested on the cold concrete. There was no telling what time it was. The hall outside was a blazing red: night lights, to save the guards' vision as they moved between the cell blocks. Two black masses shuffled into the tiny room. I heard handcuffs being removed, and then there was one form standing there, still and silent.

Anna The Spanner took a step into a shard of red light. She stayed there, only her wide face illuminated. She was broad-shouldered and boxy-headed, a spray of freckles on her nose and cheeks cast black in the red light.

A twisting, splintering feeling took hold in my chest. This woman was twice my size, and looked like she was all muscle. A guard had let her into my cell, which meant that she had sway with the prison staff. If she could get them to let her in to see me in the middle of the night, she could get them to look the other way while she strangled me. I couldn't think of a reason Anna would want to kill me. But neither could I come up with one that might have justified her beating a kid to death with a spanner.

'Well, this is a perk, the guards letting you take a tour of other cells,' I said, trying to sound non-threatening. 'You think you could talk them in to ordering us some pizza?'

'You didn't get dinner,' she said. It wasn't a question.

'No.'

Anna fumbled in the pocket of her prison tracksuit pants. I heard the crackle of a chocolate wrapper. Cherry Ripe, bent like a banana and warmed by her body. I wasn't in a position to be picky, so I took the chocolate and ripped it open.

'I didn't kill Doctor Goldman,' Anna said. She was standing strangely in profile to me, one eye watching me in the red light, like a beaten dog trying to assess a threat. 'I liked her.'

'I liked her too,' I said. 'Some people around here wonder if you two liked each other a bit more than usual.'

'She was good to me,' Anna said. 'Not a lot of people are.'

'I know the feeling.'

'It's because of what I did.' Anna looked me up and down out of the corner of her eye. 'Most people just ignore me. Or they tell me I'm a monster.'

I waited, munching the Cherry Ripe.

'My nephew,' she said. 'He was only small. I crushed his skull.'

I swallowed hard. It was clear to me that I was not dealing with a lot of intelligence here, but I wondered how attached Anna was to reality. Whether coming to talk to me had any significance in her mind other than amusement. I'd wondered, when she walked in, if she was here to convince me of her innocence. But now it seemed like she just wanted to shoot the breeze, and if that meant chatting about taking the life of a small child, I had other ways I wanted to spend my night – like shivering on the concrete and worrying myself sick.

'Doctor Goldman said I wasn't a monster,' Anna said. 'So I guess people thought she must have been in love with me.'

'But she wasn't?'

'No.' She laughed a little sheepishly. 'I don't think so.'

I fell into thought, watching Anna, waiting for her to move. She was unnaturally still, watching me.

'I was here when she was killed,' Anna said. 'In my cell.'

'I guess the records will show that,' I said.

It didn't seem safe to mention that the suggestion Nanna had made wasn't that Anna had killed Goldman herself, but that she might have hired someone to do it after their relationship went sour. I couldn't rely on Anna's word, but it was something just to have it. I felt my muscles relaxing. I'd had little to do with child-killers in my career in Sex Crimes. That was usually the territory of the Homicide division. I wondered what Anna's life was like down here in the dungeon, a freak who was now without a single friend in the world. Or maybe I was wrong about that.

'If everyone hates you so much,' I ventured, thinking as I spoke, 'how did you get the guards to let you come and see me just now? Where'd you get the Cherry Ripe?'

Anna seemed distracted. Her hearing was obviously better than mine, because within seconds the guard banged on the door. A warning that time was almost up.

'Doctor Goldman,' Anna said, circling back dreamily to the point of her visit. 'She had a lot of people who might have been angry with her. She was beautiful, and kind and nice to everyone – even people like me. My dad always said being nice can get you into trouble.'

'What kind of trouble?'

Anna shrugged.

'Did she speak to you about anyone pursuing her? Romantically or otherwise?'

'We talked about a lot of things.' Anna nodded to herself. 'Mostly she said I didn't belong here. That I belonged at the Bay. It's been a long while, and lots of paperwork, but Doctor Goldman got me a transfer there. I'm going in a few days. I'm excited. I've heard they do swim therapy there. I like to swim.'

Long Bay Correctional Complex was a sprawling prison south of Sydney that generally housed male inmates, but which had a psychiatric facility that held female inmates in maximum security. The psych facility was still a prison, but it went the extra mile in trying to rehabilitate its inmates rather than simply warehousing them. The conditions were better, and the outlook was brighter.

I wasn't surprised Goldman had won Anna a transfer to a psych ward. She seemed the type who probably believed Anna could be treated for whatever mental illness she was suffering from, that she had hope of her one day walking free and beginning again, not a danger to herself or society. Goldman had been a believer. Anna was, unlike so many people at Johnsonborough, heading somewhere good, and it was due to Goldman's efforts. I assumed Goldman's care and consideration for the child-killer was what sparked the romance rumours.

The guard banged again, and Anna left me alone in the dark, the Cherry Ripe clanging around my empty belly and my thoughts clouded with images of psych wards and dead children. In the empty room I held Dolly and Doctor Goldman in my mind, and the file Woods had given me in my hands.

Then I made a decision.

Chapter 24

THE LAST TIME I had seen Chief Trevor 'Pops' Morris, he had been in a hospital bed recovering from a heart attack.

Now the squat old man was sitting sideways in the driver's seat of his car, his legs out of the door in the morning sunshine, reading a newspaper. He was clean-shaven, his shirt ironed. I'd been allowed to leave the remand centre through the loading dock as the front car park was crowded with press covering Doctor Goldman's murder.

In the movies, the grudge between prisoners and guards seems to dissolve on release day. Hands are shaken and promises never to return are made. That morning, a guard I didn't recognise had wordlessly handed me back my street clothes and some forms to sign, and I was then led to a room to change. No one watched me undress. I sat in the room alone for a minute, just enjoying the sensation of not being surveilled by a camera or a human.

'You look terrible.' Pops smiled as I went to him.

'You look good. Retirement suits you.'

I received my first hug in four months. I'm not a hugger, and there was no swell of emotion. No urge to burst into tears of relief. But his arms were warm and strong and he smelled the way that old men smell, of carefully laundered clothes and aftershave. He thumped my back and laughed to himself, like a guy who sees a battered and bruised pet cat wander in the back door of his home after a few weeks in the wild. I had to pull away only because my jeans were slipping off my hips from the weight I'd lost on the inside.

I got in the car and we drove out of the prison complex. He glanced frequently at me, familiarising himself with my new form.

'What's all that?' he asked, eyeing a clear plastic bag I'd brought with me.

'Just some stuff I can't get anywhere else.' I brought the bag to my lap and opened it, showed him the items as I spoke. 'This strawberry jam from the commissary is the best. The toothbrushes are hard as wire, which I like. This deodorant?' I showed him the small aerosol can.

'Yeah?'

'You could spray this on a yak and have it smelling like roses.' I shook the can. 'One of the worst things about prison is the smell of hundreds of bodies living all together. I bet you can't get this stuff on the outside.'

'It probably gives you cancer.'

'Almost certainly.'

'I wish you'd taken visitors,' Pops said. 'I feel like I haven't seen you in a million years.'

'You know it would have been harder that way,' I said.

'Not for me.'

'Yes for you,' I said.

'You could have taken phone calls at least.'

'What would I have said?' I asked. '*Good morning. There's been another breakout of body lice in the prison. My arms are like Swiss cheese today. I'm really worried about hepatitis. But how are you?*'

'I get it,' he said. 'I just missed you.'

'I missed you too, Pops.' I put a hand on his leg. He took it and squeezed it.

'So where to?' he asked. 'A bar? A steakhouse? Want to drive out and see the ocean?'

'Take me home,' I said.

Chapter 25

HIS LITTLE HOUSE in Drummoyne was very much a man's house. The front yard was neatly mown but featureless. There was a pair of slippers on the porch next to a mismatched table and a single chair, placed for enjoying morning coffee and watching the street. I'd been here before, but infrequently. The double garage at the back of Pops's house had been converted into a boxing gym for local youths, and I'd turned up there a couple of times in the early days of our friendship to train.

As we approached the front door, I heard a clicking and jingling sound. I widened my eyes at him as he unlocked the house.

Three small, fluffy dogs burst across the threshold and swarmed us, barking and panting happily, snuffling, wagging tufted tails. Tags clinked on their collars.

'What . . . is . . .'

'I know, I know.' Pops rolled his eyes and walked in ahead of me. 'I've been fostering dogs. You don't get to pick them – you just turn up at the rescue place and they give you whatever they need to get rid of at that moment. I've been hoping something big and manly would come along. Pit bull or a Doberman maybe. But they keep giving me these little fluffers.'

The trio of raggedy, mop-like dogs followed us into the neat, cosy house. I stood in the midst of them as they circled and sniffed me, hairy mittens for paws scraping hopefully at my legs, black eyes shining. Pops leaned against the kitchen counter and watched me.

I burst out laughing.

He shrugged. 'What do you want me to say?'

'Why don't you just go get a Doberman, if you want a Doberman?'

'Because it's nice to foster.' He gestured at the dogs. 'They'd be put down, otherwise. The last one they gave me was a white Pomeranian someone had dyed pink. It was like a ball of fairy floss.'

I laughed hard. It felt good.

'Yeah. The women at the shelter thought it was pretty funny, too.'

He led me to his bedroom. Perfectly made bed, grey and white chequered bedspread. Lee Child books on the dresser in a stack, reading glasses.

'Your room,' he said.

'No,' I said. '*Your* room. Thanks, but I'll take the fold-out couch in the gym.'

'No you won't. You've been on a prison cot for four months. That shit is bad for your spine. You take the bed.'

'Nope.'

'You take the bed, Harry.'

'No thanks.'

'You've been released into my custody.' Pops pointed at me. 'That means you have to do what I say. While you're here, you eat. Look at you, you're muscle and bone. You look sick. I'll have you sleeping in a proper bed, and that's that.'

'I'll take the food but I'm sleeping in the gym, Pops,' I said. 'I'll feel more comfortable there.'

We both folded our arms. The trio of dogs watched us, tongues flapping from panting mouths.

'If you were my daughter . . .' he said. He made a flat hand, like he was threatening to smack me. He walked beside me towards the gym at the back of the house. I followed. The fold-out couch was already made up. It looked strange on the rubber-matted floors, under a chalkboard listing sparring partnerships between teenagers. In the middle of the big space was a boxing gym. The air was thick with the smell of sweat and leather. This was my place. I lay on the bed and the three dogs all climbed up with me.

'Hey! No, no, no. Get down. Get –'

'Yeah, they're cuddly.' He hefted a bag onto the bed beside me. 'I got you some clothes. Ladies' things. Shampoo and stuff. Figured you would need that. I wash my hair with axle grease and my body I just scrub down with steel wool.'

I put my head on the pillow and watched the old man arranging the things. Thought about what it might have been like if I was his daughter, like he'd said. The small dogs positioned themselves along the sides of my body, one curled behind my knees, another collapsing against my back, warm and shuddering as it breathed. I relented and let the littlest one crawl up under my arm. The clock on the wall said it was nine in the morning.

'When are the guys getting here?' I asked.

'Soon,' he said. 'Have a nap. I'll wake you when they arrive so we can talk about the case.'

'*Both* cases.' I yawned.

'Huh?'

'I'll tell you later,' I said.

Chapter 26

I DIDN'T SO much nap as fall into blackness, thick and smothering like ink. When I woke it was to the sound of familiar voices muffled by the brick walls of the garage. I extracted myself from the hot, hairy groove the dogs had made around me and went to the shower. My body was bruised and aching all over. The dogs watched me from behind the glass, sitting in a row, waiting for something. They tried to lick my calves and feet as I stood on the mat and pulled on new jeans and a shirt that were both a size too big.

I led the dogs out into the kitchen, where Whitt and Tox were sitting with Pops at the small round table under the windows. It was dark outside. Whitt grabbed me before he was really out of his chair, knocked the thing over, squeezed me too hard.

'Oh, Harry,' he said. He laughed and rubbed my back, smoothed my hair. Swung us in a funny rocking motion. 'You're back. You're back. You're back.'

'Leave her alone, would you?' Tox picked up Whitt's chair. 'You'll break her.'

Whitt didn't let me go. I looked at Tox over his shoulder, put a hand out. Tox put his palm to mine, a soft high five. His hand was hard and dry and smooth, like a sun-warmed brick.

'Look at you!' I held Whitt at arm's length. 'You're a man mountain!'

'I've started lifting a bit.' He pushed his glasses up on his nose, embarrassed.

I sat at the table with my crew. They had all certainly improved from when I had seen them last – Whitt had been high and drunk, and still reeling from almost being shot in the forest by a woman he'd thought he could trust. Tox had been bleeding and broken, having come out of his recovery from being stabbed far too early to assist me on the Regan Banks case. My beloved Pops had been sitting in a hospital bed, miserable, knowing I was going to jail and there was nothing he could do about it, and staring his own mortality in the face after a heart attack. We were a scarred and beaten group, war-torn and wary of further conflict, but we were hard. There were no flickers of uncertainty in the eyes of the men sitting down around me. They knew we had all survived because we belonged together, at this moment, and whatever was to come we would stare it down as one.

Beneath the table, the three dogs settled in a scruffy pile, surrounded by our shoes.

'OK,' Whitt said, laying photographs of Tonya Woods and her daughter at the centre of the table. 'Let's find this woman and her child.'

'And a killer, too.'

'Huh?' Tox frowned.

'The doctor at my correctional facility, Bernadette Goldman,'
I said. 'You would have seen her picture in the news by now.
She was stabbed to death yesterday morning in her surgery
room. A friend of mine has been accused of the murder, and
she's innocent.'

'So what?' Tox shrugged.

'So while we run this case –' I pointed to the pictures on the
table '– we also run mine.'

'Whoa, whoa, whoa,' Pops broke in. 'Hang on a minute.
Harry, you're only sitting here now because of a very flimsy
deal with Woods to find these two.' The old man also pointed
at the pictures on the table. 'If you don't put everything you
have into this case, you're looking at going back inside – for
a *long* time.'

'I don't care,' I said. 'Doctor Goldman was very well liked
among the inmates. Staff too, I'm guessing – at least the ones
who didn't want to use her for her ability to bring drugs into
the prison without raising eyebrows. My friend Dolly has
been pinned for the murder of a very popular person. She's a
target now for anyone who wants to take it upon themselves to
avenge the doctor's death.'

'Look, Harry,' Whitt said. 'We're underequipped as it is.
Our suspensions mean we won't have the resources we usually
have to handle one case, let alone two. We won't have police
databases for search capabilities. There'll be no patrol back-up
if we corner a suspect. We'll basically be civilians, without
bulletproof vests, undercover cars, radio . . .'

'Whitt, if not having a pussy vest is the only thing stopping
you from helping me on this, you'd better go buy yourself one,
because we're taking this case.'

'Perhaps I will,' he sighed. 'But listen. Your friend will be in protection, surely,' he said, googling *Bernadette Goldman murder* on his phone. 'It can wait. The guards won't let anything happen to her.'

'It can't wait. You know how this goes. The inmate winds up dead in her cell and it's ruled a suicide and no one investigates. Or she's escorted out to the exercise yard and someone throws a bucket of boiling water over her. She was my cellmate. She'd help me if the situation was reversed. I have to do something, and I've decided to do it from out here. I'll have more power that way.'

'How do you know your friend is innocent?' Whitt asked.

'That's beside the point,' Tox broke in. 'Whoever killed your doctor – they're not going anywhere. Tonya Woods and her kid? They may be in grave danger *right now*. If they turn up dead, you don't know what Woods is going to do. That guy could have you locked in solitary for the rest of your life. You need to focus on –'

'Tox, I –'

'– on what's important!'

'This *is* important to me!'

'Alright!' Pops slammed his hand on the table. Tox and I had risen out of our seats. We sank reluctantly back into them.

'We just don't want to lose you again.' Pops put a hand on top of mine. 'There are four of us. That's plenty. Harry, I'll assist you with your murder case. I've got contacts in Corrections who could help. But you'll spend the bulk of your time invest-igating with these two.' He pointed at Tox and Whitt.

Whitt put his phone on the table. On the screen was a picture of Bernadette Goldman. Beside her, Tonya Woods and her baby girl stared out. I looked at the three faces and felt a sense of dread envelop me. One of them was gone already, her last moments spent in terror, lying on the floor of her surgery while the world grew dark around her. I said a silent prayer that the other two would not share a similar fate.

Chapter 27

'THIS IS WHAT we have,' Whitt said, placing a slim stack of papers on the table before me, face down. 'Tonya Woods and her daughter were last seen by Deputy Commissioner Woods himself. He'd been letting Tonya take the baby overnight occasionally, as she seemed to be sober and doing well. He saw her drive away, supposedly to the apartment in Rose Bay that he'd been renting for her, but we know she didn't stay there.'

'How?'

'The place was not her,' Tox said. He pulled a cigarette out and glanced at Pops, who waved, resigned. 'I went in, but I didn't need to. You could tell just from looking at the building. Big secure place, nice balconies, stone and steel artwork in the gardens. Fucking posh. It's like Woods was rubbing it in his kid's face that he was successful and had money, and that he was spending it on her ungrateful arse. It was too good for her. Made her feel like a failure.'

'She's been staying at the Oceanside Motel in Punchbowl,' Whitt said. 'More her style. Closer to her connections. We believe she went there with the baby that night, and she, or someone else, rigged her room to look like a struggle had occurred there.'

I looked at the pictures on Tox's phone of Tonya's sad little motel room.

'How do you know it was done that night?'

'I found a receipt in the bin for a petrol station just up the road from the motel. The time and date put Tonya there that evening, about an hour after she left Woods's place,' Tox said. 'She bought a couple of pies, chocolate milk. Dinner. We know she didn't turn up to meet a girlfriend she was supposed to have coffee with the next morning, and there's been no activity on her social media since about six o'clock that evening. She was a voracious Facebook and Instagram user. She hasn't gone longer than twenty-four hours between checking both sites in the past couple of years, and now we've got total inactivity from that point on. No calls or texts on her phone, no bank account movement.'

'Were the pies and the chocolate milk in the motel room?' I asked.

'Not that I saw,' Tox said.

'So it's supposed to look like she got home from the petrol station, she and the kid ate dinner and then someone grabbed them,' I concluded.

We all sat silently for a while. Whitt was looking at the wine bottles sitting in a rack on Pops's counter.

'There are two reasons I can see why a person might fake an abduction,' Pops mused. 'First, you want someone to offer ransom for you. Tonya might have got together with a boyfriend and decided she wants some of the old man's money without having to ask him for it.'

'No ransom demands thus far, though,' Whitt said. 'It's been nine days.'

'Then there's the second reason. Whatever has happened to her wasn't an abduction, but it was bad,' Pops said. 'Someone wants the police all tied up in the abduction theory. They're diverting attention away from what really happened. Sending us down the wrong track.'

'Maybe it wasn't something bad that happened,' I reasoned. 'Maybe Tonya wants the police tied up so she can get away on her own.'

'Why not just run away?' Pops asked me. 'Why cause all this fuss?'

I shrugged.

'Well, the wrong track is where the police are going, either way.' Tox exhaled smoke over his shoulder. 'I spoke to the Poodle this morning about the official police investigation. Spader didn't give me anything more than the phone and internet account stuff, but he took my advice about the apartment and the fake snatch without gratitude. Their team had discovered Tonya wasn't using the Rose Bay apartment but hadn't got to where she was really living yet.'

'No wonder Woods brought us in.' Pops squeezed my shoulder. 'He knows who gets the job done around here.'

'Which brings us to this.' Whitt flipped over the pages in front of me and split them. 'Here are two hospital forms Tonya has filled out in the last twelve months. The first one is for an OD. The second is for a concussion. Spot the difference.'

The men waited while I read the reports. Tonya's handwriting was pretty; wide cursive with lots of loops, a throwback to her expensive education. On the first form, Tonya was giving her medical history after having been revived from an OD. She'd been found in her car on a lonely suburban street, unconscious in the passenger seat, a needle in her arm. It was Christmas Eve.

The second form was a report filed after Tonya had sought medical attention for a laceration above her eye. She'd needed five stitches. Tonya had told the nurses her infant daughter had thrown a toy at her face, but it was clear to the staff on duty that night that Tonya had been punched. She was given an MRI and diagnosed with concussion. The Department of Family Services had been notified of the incident, but without proof of an assault, and with Rebel having not been in Tonya's custody at the time of the incident, there wasn't much they could do.

I knew, somewhere, Tonya's Family Services file was littered with such reports. Overdoses, arrests, fights with boyfriends, assessments of her mental health by crisis teams at St Vincent's and other hospitals. My own mother had such a file, forty-five years' worth of chaos, pain and suffering housed in the cold boxes and lines of the reports. I looked at the child's name on the paperwork. Rebel. Her mother had given her a weird, alternative name, marked her for life as different from the Sarahs and Kates and Michelles who would fill the kindergarten classrooms, the teenage dances, the offices where she went for her first job. My middle name was Jupiter, something I had loathed people finding out all my life.

'Harry?'

'Yes, sorry. I was thinking.' I rubbed my eyes. Pointed to the bottom of both pages. 'I've spotted the difference. On the first form Joe Woods is listed as her next of kin. And as recently as four months ago we have a new name. Louis Mallally. Who's he? The scumbag who punched her, or her dealer?'

'Neither.' Whitt smiled. 'That would be too simple. So far, nothing about this case had been what it appears at the outset.'

'Louis Mallally,' Pops said, 'is the most expensive lawyer in Australia.'

Chapter 28

ONE OF MY tactics as a detective in the Sex Crimes unit was never to show the whole investigative team to a party being questioned. A number of times over the years I or another team member had been forced to tail a suspect or go completely undercover, which was hard if the suspect knew who everyone was. So Whitt and I set off to speak to Louis Mallally without Tox.

Whitt's phone rang as we were getting into his immaculate car. I sat in the passenger seat and thought about Dolly waking up in ad seg. If she had been brought her breakfast at all, she would be chewing it carefully, fishing through the mush for razor blades or shards of glass hidden by inmates or staff. Then she would be staring down the barrel of an unknown number of hours waiting for a lawyer to arrive, nothing but the bare walls and choking dread to occupy her mind.

Whitt winced away from the phone as soon as the caller came on and handed the device to me.

'For you,' he said.

'Why aren't you at the Oceanside Motel?' Woods barked. I could hear traffic in the background of the call. I made a mental note to get my own phone as soon as possible, to spare Whitt's ears.

'Hello, good morning,' I said. 'I'm fine, thanks. I slept OK, but –'.

'Let's get this straight, Blue,' Woods snapped. 'You've agreed to help me. You're walking free now – on bail. I can take that away at any second. So when you're talking to me, you do it on my terms. If you think I'm going to waste my time with pleasantries and chitchat, you've got another thing coming.' He drew a ragged breath. 'Nigel and his team are down here at the Oceanside, and I want to know why you're not.'

'Because we've been there,' I said. 'Tox has, anyway. I guess Nigel didn't tell you it was Tox who found the motel room in the first place. How unusual of him to take credit where it isn't due.'

'So you know Tonya and Rebel were taken,' Woods said.

'No, we don't.'

Woods gave an exasperated sigh.

'They were taken,' he insisted. 'I've looked at the scene. It's plain as day. The place is trashed. There's blood on the floor.'

'The blood is from Tox,' I said. 'Some bozos turned up when he was checking out the room and tried to shake him down, so he knocked their heads together.'

'You need to be looking into people from my past,' Woods rattled on, as though I hadn't spoken at all. 'I've arrested some big names, pissed off a lot of people. I can give you a list of men who are out, who might have organised something like this as an act of revenge. In the meantime, Nigel and his guys are going to go to the media and try to make contact with the abductors. I'll need you to handle ransom demands if they come in.'

'No,' I said. The line went quiet. I heard a distant sound, as though Woods had taken the phone from his ear and growled. Whitt looked over at me expectantly as he drove. It was Saturday, and on every corner an open-house sign flashed by, advertising a property for sale. Kids gathered in parks in sports kits, mothers waited to cross the road between cars and playing fields.

'Blue,' Woods said. I'd expected a voice full of fury, but when he said my name it was small and weak. 'I took a real gamble letting you out, bringing your team on board. I need . . . I *need* you to help me.'

'So stop blubbering and let me do my job,' I said. I disconnected the phone and handed it back to Whitt. He took it and slipped it into his pocket.

'Cold as ice, Harry,' Whitt said. I looked at him, thought for a long time, watching the suburbs roll by as we headed towards the city.

'Was it?' I asked.

Whitt seemed to have drifted off into other thoughts. 'Huh?'

'Was it cold as ice?'

'A little. The guy's just trying to find his family.'

'I'm a bit worried about that. About my coldness.' I shifted in my seat.

'What do you mean?'

'When Pops picked me up at the prison, I feel like I should have cried,' I said. 'I stood there thinking, a normal person would be feeling something at a time like this. A wave of emotion. Pops is the closest thing I've ever had to a father. He hugged me, and it was nice, but I just felt . . . blank. Same when you hugged me yesterday. It was like I was numb.'

Whitt nodded.

'Sometimes, when I was on the inside,' I said, 'I'd forget what I had done. People would ask me what it was like, killing Regan. And I'd think, oh shit. Yes. I killed a man, didn't I? I mean, I've done it before, of course. But who *forgets* about killing someone? There's got to be something wrong with me.'

Whitt thought for a while. I watched his eyes flicking between the mirror and the road ahead as he changed lanes.

'You know what happened with me,' Whitt said. 'The first time I fell off the wagon.'

I did know what had happened. He'd planted evidence in the case of a murdered child, been caught, and all but assured the release of the girl's killers back into the community. He lived every day with the knowledge that they would probably reoffend, and that whoever they harmed next, it would be his fault. His struggle with drugs and alcohol were a direct result of the case.

'I was searching for numbness when I started drinking,' he said. 'It's self-preservation. Your brain can't handle what's happening so it shuts down your emotions, becomes mechanical. When you get the emotions back, they won't necessarily be good.' He glanced at me. 'I'm not drinking. I'm not numb. And living with what I did doesn't call for very enjoyable emotions.'

I watched as the houses of the suburbs transformed into the high-rises of the inner city. Little apartments leaning over the motorway. A tiny knot of homeless people camped on a traffic island at the entrance to the Cross City tunnel, an orange umbrella their only shelter.

'So how do you cope?' I asked.

Whitt shrugged his big shoulders.

'Look at me.' He gave a sad smirk.

I nodded. 'You just exhaust yourself every day working out.'

'It's the only way I can sleep at night,' he said. 'It's this or knock myself out with a half-bottle of Jack and a couple of Xanax.'

I looked at his hard forearm extending to the steering wheel, veined and taut, leading to vice-grip hands. Whitt had made himself a living temple to his pain, a hurt being housed and protected by hard-won muscle. I knew that before the Whitt I was seeing now, the one who looked like a body builder, there had been a different kind of shield – of neatness, order, painful precision.

'You're really not OK, are you,' I said. It wasn't a question.

A rueful smile crept to his lips. 'Neither are you,' he said. 'So I'm in good company.'

I wondered what I would use as my body armour against the pain when it came. As we made our way towards the beachside Eastern suburbs, I felt vulnerable and exposed, waiting to be hit with the reality of the last few months at any moment. There were lives on the line, and that made my sanity all the more precious. I needed to get my mind together before it was too late for Dolly, Tonya Woods and her tiny child.

Chapter 29

LOUIS MALLALLY'S MANSION was perched high on the hill above Bondi Beach, with sweeping black glass balconies pointing towards the sea on one side of the building and towards the distant city on the other. There was a silver BMW convertible sitting on the street outside the double doors of the garage. The security gate beside the garage was open, so Whitt and I approached the house via a small path that led through a garden of desert plants and white stones, past a fountain made from polished concrete blocks bubbling quietly in the shade.

I reached for the doorbell, but a woman pulled the door open before I could push it.

'Oh!'

'Oh, excuse me.' I stepped back, bumped into Whitt's rigid frame. 'I was just –'

The woman squinted at me. 'Harry?' she said. 'Harriet *Blue*?'

I looked her up and down. She was wearing a black sports catsuit, the kind that's supposed to compress the muscles and make a person more aerodynamic. Long-distance runner,

I guessed. Severe ponytail and dark eyes. There was no recognition flickering through my brain, and my face must have shown it.

'I'm Shania Mallally, nee Parker.' She spread a hand with finely manicured nails on her chest. 'We went to high school together. Swan-Langley College in Randwick.'

I shrugged. 'What's your point?'

The question hit Shania like a slap. She seemed to realise through the fading novelty of my appearance at her doorstep that she hadn't even asked me or my partner why we were there. She glanced at Whitt, calculated, and decided to forge on, determined to be remembered.

'We were in the same grade. Seventh. You were there for three months, maybe more.'

'I grew up in foster care,' I said wearily. 'I must have attended seventeen different high schools. I never made a single friend at school. Not one. So if you and I went to school together, it means you were indifferent to me or you were cruel. Which was it?'

Shania recoiled again as though struck. Whitt put a hand on my shoulder, a warning. I didn't react. Shania seemed to be assessing her standing in the little battle of wills we were having on her front doorstep, so before she could come to a conclusion I cut over her again.

'Is your husband home?'

'He's by the pool,' she said. 'I was just going for a run. What . . . ah. What's this about, exactly?'

I didn't answer her question, and instead walked past her into the huge marble foyer. Before I could cross to the passageway leading to the back of the house she spoke again.

'I was cruel,' she said.

Whitt and I turned and looked at her. She was nodding, resigned. 'I was cruel. We knew you were a foster kid, my friends and I. The second-hand uniform. The ratty, worn-out backpack. We'd heard whispers between some of the parents. You'd been given a place at the school as a kindness while you were fostered by a family in the area, and we were all Swan-Langley families from generations back. We picked on you relentlessly. My friends dared me to pour my chocolate milk over your head one day and I did it.'

She looked over at Whitt again, like she was seeking an ally. He didn't offer himself.

'I only remembered it all a few months ago when I saw you on the news,' Shania said. 'The Regan Banks case. There you were. A detective. A serial-killer hunter. I could hardly believe it. I thought you were in jail now, but I guess I was wrong.'

'Are you going to stand there all day talking about yourself? Or can we get on with our job?' I said.

'When I saw you on the news I felt a tremendous sense of shame, Harry,' she said, ignoring my words. 'I'm sorry.'

I turned and walked across the hall and didn't look back.

Chapter 30

THERE WERE TWO small girls in the huge pool in the backyard, doggy paddling to the edge, climbing out, jumping back in. The water splashed all around the pool told me the cycle had been running for some time. Louis Mallally was sitting in a stylish wicker cabana with a little table and four chairs inside it, the unsettled water projecting moving patterns onto his white shirt. His black curls were scraped back over the top of his head and fell in small ringlets behind his ears. He hardly gave Whitt and I an upward glance. He was focused on the pale terracotta tiles between his shoes, a mobile phone clamped to his ear.

'Let's go back to them with five years, no parole,' he said. 'Tell them it's all we will accept. Let them sweat it over the weekend. They're firing water pistols at us, Brian. Let's not pretend they're real guns.'

I took a seat in the chair opposite Mallally, while Whitt leaned against the side of the cabana and folded his huge arms like a nightclub bouncer.

Mallally didn't get off the phone. I raised my eyebrows as he listened to the person on the other end of the line.

'No, that doesn't make sense,' Mallally responded. 'A strategy like that has been tried and tested in the courtroom and it always fails.'

I held up five fingers. Mallally frowned at me.

'The meeting's on Thursday. Susan will be there.'

I lowered my thumb, held up four fingers. Mallally looked at my eyes.

Three.

Two.

'Oh, they're posturing. Of course they are. They don't have the –'

I showed Mallally my index finger.

'Brian, will you hold on, I've just got to –'

I leaned forward and took the phone from Mallally's ear, tossed it over my shoulder into the pool. The little girls screamed with surprise or delight, I couldn't tell.

Mallally spread his empty hands like he had just disappeared a dove in a magic trick, his eyes wide.

'You – You – You can't – !' He let out a harsh breath, a well-practised huff he'd seemingly developed to expel his frustration and simultaneously regain his composure, a sound easily mutated into a laugh or sneer. Defence lawyers are used to smothering their surprise. 'That was a very important phone call.'

'Sounded like it.' I took a pair of women's sunglasses that was sitting on the tabletop, probably Shania's, and slipped them on.

'I'm going to bill you for that. For the phone and the phone call. Do you have any idea what I charge by the hour?'

'Wouldn't matter if it was a million dollars,' I said. 'I don't have it, and I don't work for anyone who does, so dry your eyes, princess.'

'I know who you are.' Mallally took in Whitt, shook a finger at me. 'Harriet Blue, right? What happened? You got bail for the serial-killer murder? Now you're looking to me for defence for the trial. Let me tell you, sister: I'm not interested. I know a dead loss when I see one. You can take your meathead body-guard and carry on to your next personal disaster.'

'Meathead?' Whitt asked mildly. He took a chair beside mine, perpendicular to Mallally. The lawyer shrank almost imperceptibly in his chair. 'I'm not sure it's time for name-calling quite yet, Mr Mallally. We're here to enquire about your relationship with this woman.'

Whitt glanced at me, a warning, telling me to get ready. Mallally's reaction to the photograph in Whitt's hand was going to be very important, and it would likely be fleeting. He was a lawyer, practised in hiding his emotions, particularly surprise or recognition. Whatever he showed, we would have to catch it before it was gone forever.

He put the picture of Tonya Woods on the table.

Mallally dropped his head into his hands.

Chapter 31

A SMALL GIRL, dripping wet, appeared at Whitt's side. She was grinning at him, her dark hair plastered to her high forehead. For a moment it seemed I was witnessing Whitt's tragedy come to life, the tiny child that haunted him materialised, teasing him from another realm. But she handed the wet and blank-screened phone to her father, giggled and ran away, splashing into the pool just behind us. Cold droplets hit the back of my neck.

'Ugh, Jesus,' Mallally sighed, rubbing his tanned cheeks. 'I knew this was going to come back to bite me.'

Mallally glanced at the kids in the pool, rubbed his palms together.

'What has she done exactly?' he asked. 'Actually, never mind. Don't tell me. I'll post her bail but I'm not representing her, and I don't know anything about any criminal activities she may have engaged in.'

Whitt and I looked at each other. I decided to bluff.

'We understand your relationship with Tonya has been complex,' I said. 'How did you meet, exactly?'

Mallally gave a rueful laugh. 'She was outside the courthouse fighting with one of her low-life friends. A dealer, by the look of him. Gold chains and big, hideous Nikes. I was leaving; I'd just finished representing a client on a fraud charge. Whatever the guy with Tonya had been involved with at the court hadn't gone his way. He smacked her. Right there on the courthouse steps. Even in a busy street. There must have been two dozen witnesses.'

Mallally rubbed his face again, tired.

'The police jumped on him. They were all standing around smoking, drinking coffee, waiting to escort people in and out of the building. Bloody idiot – I don't know where the hell he thought he was, the dealer. It boggles the mind, what these people do. Anyway, I took Tonya away, thought I'd sit her down for a cup of tea or something, but she wanted a beer, so I took her to The Crown. I wasn't trying to be the hero of the situation. It just happened.'

'When was this?' I asked.

'Eight months ago?' Mallally thought. 'I didn't, uh . . . I didn't expect it to become what it became. I gave her my phone number in case she needed anything and then before I knew it we were meeting up again.'

The little girls in the pool were calling for their daddy to watch them leap in, arms linked. He obliged, his thin lips twisted with guilt.

'My wife can't know about this,' he said.

'So how long has your affair with Tonya Woods been going on?' Whitt asked.

Mallally heaved a sigh. 'Long enough for a couple of relapses on her part. She does her best to shake off her addiction but she always falls back into the fray. Her friends drag her in. And to be honest, I don't think her father helps much.'

'The Deputy Commissioner?' I asked.

'He dumps the child on her all the time,' Mallally said. 'Long before she's ready to take responsibility for her. Tonya gets clean for fifteen bloody minutes and her father starts in with the overnight stays and weekends with the kid in her care. Tonya doesn't have any experience in how to be a parent. She doesn't know what to do with a child. The girl throws a fit and Tonya feels like a failure, heads right back down into the hole she's just climbed out of.'

Failure. I remembered Tox talking about the nice apartment Woods had been keeping for Tonya, the one she hadn't lived in. How he believed it made her feel inadequate. Had Woods finally put too much pressure on his daughter to take back her child? Had the young woman snapped and run away, or worse?

'You think Joe Woods was tired of caring for the little one?' Whitt asked.

As if on cue, one of the small girls rushed up to her father, soaking his shirt as she leaned in.

'Ella's hurting me! She's hurting me! Daddy, help!'

Whitt and I sat and watched as Mallally dealt with the squabble between the children. When he returned his shirt was sticking to his chest with damp, black chest hairs visible through the fabric.

'They can be quite tiring,' he said. 'I didn't know what the situation was with Tonya's father and the baby. We didn't talk about the Deputy Commissioner much, because it made me uncomfortable. If he were to find out we'd been seeing each other, I could have kissed my legal career goodbye.'

I nodded.

'In any case,' Mallally sighed. 'Yes, I'd been seeing Tonya. Yes, she's trouble, with a capital T. Whatever she's done this time, I certainly wasn't involved with it. I broke it off with Tonya about three weeks ago, and I would hope that as officers of the law you'll treat our liaison with the utmost discretion. I assure you it's not a factor in whatever's going on here.'

'Why did you break it off with Tonya?' I asked.

'Are you two going to tell me what this is all about?' Mallally asked. 'What's happened to her? Where is she?'

Whitt and I glanced at each other.

'We don't know,' Whitt said.

Chapter 32

THE THREE FLUFFY dogs had all crowded into Pops's lap on the couch, and though his body heat was steadily rising under the blanket of fur and warm bodies, he couldn't bring himself to move. The old man didn't know where the dogs were going next, whether they would be adopted into loving homes where snuggles on the couch would be permitted. He figured now was the time to spoil them, so as he reached for the phone on the side table he also took three liver treats and fed one into each of the scruffy mouths that rose at the sound of his hand lifting the lid from the jar.

It took ten minutes to get through the various checkpoints and barriers, even when he explained who he was. He was redirected four times, put on hold, barked at for calling outside the designated hours. Eventually a very uncertain voice came on the line, and he knew that he was through.

'Hello?'

'Dolly Quaddich?'

'Yeah, that's me.'

'My name is Trevor Morris.' Pops stroked the dogs on his lap with his free hand. 'I'm a friend of Harriet Blue. I'm calling to talk to you about what happened the day before yesterday.'

'Are you a cop? Harry's a cop,' Dolly said.

Pops could hear shouting in the background of the call, gates slamming.

'Well. Yes. Retired.'

'The lawyer said not to talk to any cops, even if they're nice to me,' Dolly said. 'And you're calling at the wrong time. We can't take calls until after midday in ad seg. It's the rules.'

'Dolly.' Pops took a deep breath. 'I know you've been asked to keep quiet about what happened, but Harry and I are going to try to help you from out here. Harry has told me she knows you're innocent. That there's no way you would have killed Doctor Goldman.'

'What do you mean "out here"?' Dolly asked. 'Is Harry out?'

'She is, yes.'

'No, she's not.'

Pops found himself pressing a fist against his forehead. 'She really is, Dolly. She made a deal with a . . . Look, you just have to believe me. You have to believe that Harry's out and I'm her friend and we're trying to help you.'

'If Harry's out, how come she isn't calling me?'

'Because she's working on another case.'

'But you just said she . . .'

Pops pulled the phone away from his ear, took another deep breath, let it out slow. One of the dogs raised its head and looked at him questioningly.

There was clatter on the line. A buzzer, some shouting. Dolly didn't speak for a long moment.

'Dolly,' Pops said, a hand clasped over his eyes. 'Do you think you could just tell me what happened? Harry says you must have gone to see Doctor Goldman right after she'd been there.'

'Yeah, well, see, I didn't think I needed to go. There was a big fight in the chow hall. I was lying under a table with my legs out, and while they were fighting someone stood on my ankle. It was just an accident. Wasn't that bad. I thought I'd just walk it off. And then after a little while that wasn't working so I thought I'd go see Doctor Goldman about it,' Dolly said. 'I was coming up the hall just as they were taking Harry away. That's why I figure she can't be out because I only saw her like the day before yesterday. When did she get out?'

'Yesterday. But try to focus on that day,' Pops said. 'What happened when you went to see Doctor Goldman? Did she fix your ankle?'

'She didn't get time, really,' Dolly said. 'She had some other girls in there from the fight. In the other room. She fixed them and sent them off. Then she came back to me. She said she thought it might be sprained. Then the alarm went off. A level-one lockdown.'

'What did Doctor Goldman do when the alarms went off?'

'Well, look, I didn't see everything,' Dolly said. 'I was on the floor. You're supposed to get down during a lockdown. She made a phone call. No, wait, she *got* a phone call. Then she went out, locked me in the room. Came back a few minutes later bleeding everywhere.'

'So she went out and locked the door. You just lay there the whole time.'

'Yes.'

'Where was she wounded?' Pops asked.

'She was stabbed in the neck, I think. And in the chest too. She was stabbed three times. She couldn't talk. I tried to ask her what happened but she didn't tell me.' Dolly was almost panting, her voice rising with tension. 'Man, it was bad. Bad bad bad.'

'So you don't know where she went after she got the phone call? You don't know who she was speaking to?'

'I told the lawyer all this stuff.'

'Well tell me, would you?'

'I don't know.' Dolly seemed to try to regulate her breathing. 'I can't remember. The blood went everywhere. All over me. All over the floor. It just spread all around. Once I saw all the blood it was like my brain just blanked out.'

Pops winced. Talk of 'blanking out', however firmly Dolly protested her innocence, would be snatched up by the prosecution in her case on what was certainly a recorded phone call. If Dolly 'blanked out' and forgot details of what had happened during the ordeal, how could she trust her memory that she had not committed the murder?

'So the alarm went off. Doctor Goldman got a phone call. She left the room, locked the door behind her, went out into the hall for a few seconds. Then she came back stabbed.'

'That's pretty much it.'

'What did she say on the phone?'

'I couldn't really hear. The alarms . . . Plus it's rude to listen in on people on the phone.'

'So what happened next?'

'The guards wanted to know where the knife went and I didn't know,' Dolly said. 'They stripsearched me for it.'

'So they never found the knife?' Pops sat up on the couch.

'Well, they were still asking me about it today. Like, an hour ago. So I guess not. It must have been a big one because there was a lot of blood. I mean *a lot*.'

'Yes, you've said.'

'The guards are really mad. They're super-duper mad. Everybody is.'

'Has anyone harmed you?' Pops asked. There was silence on the line. 'Dolly, has anyone harmed you since you've been in ad seg?'

There was a pause. 'I better go,' Dolly said. 'We're outside call time.'

With a click, she was gone.

Chapter 33

IF THERE WAS one thing in the world Tox didn't like above all others, it was a kiss-arse. He understood the psychology behind it. It had proven an effective means of gaining power and protection from the moment the first remora fish spied the underbelly of a great white shark and thought, *Hey, I have a crazy idea.* But Detective Nigel Spader was that special kind of power-clinger who not only wanted to ride the big fish to paradise waters, but didn't want anyone sharing the journey with him. Spader was a parasite, but Tox knew exchanging information in an investigation was essential, so he sat at the bar at Jangling Jack's and tapped the counter to request a second whisky before hitting the call button.

Nigel came on the line, blasting questions at him like they were already mid-conversation.

'Are you idiots going to spend this whole investigation running ahead of my team and burning witnesses before we have a chance to get anything valuable out of them?'

Tox massaged his brow. 'Depends,' he said. 'Are you going to spend this whole investigation lagging behind my team, contributing nothing, only to swoop in two seconds before we reach a conclusion to claim all the credit? Wait. Don't bother. I know the answer.'

'Blue and Whittacker got to the lawyer, Louis Mallally,' Nigel said. 'We understand he has been conducting an affair with Tonya Woods. We tried to speak to Mallally, but he's so embarrassed by having had it squeezed out of him and so worried his wife will find out that he's clammed up.'

'What do you want to know?' Tox said. 'The two were fucking. Martini-sipping douchebag has a midlife crisis, takes in a street strumpet hard on her luck, fools around with her until he gets bored and cuts her loose. Watch the Julia Roberts movie. You'll get the picture.'

'How did it end? The relationship?'

'It's still going by the end of the movie. Richard Gere climbs up a fire escape and gives her some flowers. But if you ask me, it's a doomed union.'

'Tonya and Mallally, arsehole.'

'Right,' Tox said. 'It ended as well as could be expected. She had a kid, and he didn't want that, and he was married with two of his own. Harry tells me neither of them were under the illusion that he was going to bump the purebred family out of the palace on the hill to move her skinny track-marked butt in.'

'Maybe Tonya did think that. Maybe that's *exactly* what she thought, and when it didn't come to fruition, things went south.'

'I don't think her self-esteem was that high. Girls like that have dreams but they're not stupid.'

'I guess you'd know. You've probably dated a few skels in your life, eh, Barnes?' Nigel sneered.

'Was that a thank-you?'

'No, it was a fuck you,' Nigel said. 'You check Mallally's alibi the night Tonya went missing?'

'He was sipping martinis with a bunch of other lawyers in a public bar until nine. But it's useless, because we don't know what time she disappeared.'

'What about his phone records? Did you see if he contacted her that night? I want to see those. If you've got them, send them to me.'

'I'm not your errand boy. Go get them yourself,' Tox said. 'Anything I should know about on your end? Have you found anything in our leftovers we should have paid more attention to?'

'A hot shot,' Nigel said. 'At the motel room. Little baggie of it under the kitchen sink. Looks like she decided not to get into it or didn't get the chance.'

'Interesting. What makes the shot so hot?'

'We had it tested. It's heroin, and some other chemical garbage you'd expect from cheap smack. But it was also loaded with arsenic trioxide.'

'Huh. Old school,' Tox mused.

'Why do you say that?'

Tox thought for a moment. 'Well, arsenic's not easy to get anymore,' he said. 'Back in the day, you wanted to poison someone with arsenic you could just scrape some out of ant traps or mix some rat poison pellets into your batch. But they don't use arsenic in those anymore. Too many toddlers kicking the bucket after sticking the little green candies in their mouths.

They use brodifacoum in rat poison now. You'd have to eat a barrel of it to die.'

'So where did the person who made the hot shot get the arsenic?'

'You're asking a lot more questions than you are giving answers, Spader,' Tox said, glancing around the bar. 'I'd hate for you to pull ahead in this race and find the girl and her kid before Harry gets a chance to. Our mutual friend goes back to the can if she can't prove her usefulness to Woods.'

'That's half the reason I'm out here,' Nigel said. Tox could hear the smile in the detective's voice. 'I'm going to ask if I can drive her back there myself.'

Chapter 34

CHLOE BOZER WENT to the nearest bar stool and dumped her belongings onto the seat beside her, hiding her face, pretending to search for something deep in her cluttered handbag. It had been a mistake to come here. She knew it as soon as she spied him at the bar, tapping an unlit cigarette on the surface while he scrolled through his mobile phone. Every time she saw Tox Barnes, the memories of him flooded back. She saw him as he lay clinging to life in the hospital bed, tubes and wires coming out of him, a respirator raising and lowering his chest in unnaturally jerky movements as he slept.

She'd sat beside him in the dark and looked at his body. He was heavily scarred all over, some of them from injuries that looked like they'd been stitched at home, others obvious gunshot and stab wounds. There were old, faded tattoos – pin-up girls and a big tiger on his ribs that had been disfigured by a slash wound across its face. Tox Barnes was a fighter.

Then there were the wounds she'd closed herself, obtained in a fight with a serial killer. He was obviously a violent man.

She had taken his hard hand in the dark room and looked at the fresh grazes on his knuckles. Just knowing that he was violent meant something to her, but she didn't know what. Would it all have been less painful if he'd come into her surgery a buttoned-up, law-abiding accountant hit by a car while helping an old lady across the street? She'd held the hand, stared at it, was so lost in thought that one of the cleaners had come in and apologised, thought she was sitting by a relative, holding vigil. She'd dropped his hand and walked out.

But now she was here. She grabbed her things, stood and turned to go, only to almost run into him as he headed for the door, the cigarette and lighter raised and ready.

'Well, well.' He gave a knowing smile that twisted something in her belly.

'Oh.' Chloe felt her face reddening. 'I didn't see you there.'

'I didn't see you either,' he said.

'I was just leaving.'

'No you weren't.' He sat down at the stool beside the one she'd just vacated, put his phone on the counter. Chloe went back and dumped her things again, slipped tentatively onto the stool.

'What are you drinking?' he asked. 'I can't believe you came here. I guess you don't hate me that much after all.'

'I didn't come here for *you*,' she scoffed. 'This is my local. I come here all the time.'

The bartender approached them. Chloe ordered a shiraz without looking at the wine list.

'Actually we don't serve a straight shiraz,' the bartender said. 'We have a blend, but –'

'Just, fine, anything.' She flapped a hand at him, didn't meet Tox's eye. 'Just give me something, would you?'

They sat in silence that was excruciating for her but didn't seem to bother him at all. She'd heard cops were like that, immune to awkwardness, always in possession of the upper hand. Asking the questions, not answering them. The bartender brought him a whisky without needing to be asked and Tox leaned on the bar with both arms. She focused on the cracks in the leather of his jacket, tried to breathe.

'While we're here, *by chance*.' She put her elbows on the counter, mirrored his posture. 'I suppose I did want to say I was sorry.'

'Oh, really?' He flashed a canine tooth in a delighted smirk.

'Don't torture me,' she said. 'I'm trying to be the bigger person. You might try it sometime.'

'Sounds boring.'

'I was rude,' Chloe sighed. 'You were rude, of course, and you could apologise for that. But there was no need for me to sink to your level. You were trying to do your job.'

'Doctor Bozer, you couldn't sink to my level if you tied yourself to a cinder block.'

'Chloe is fine.' She swallowed with difficulty. 'And I've heard people calling you Tox, is that right? Where on Earth does that come from? It must be a cop nickname.'

'Sort of.' His face was unreadable.

Chloe fidgeted in her chair. Perhaps this was the perfect moment to tell him. Reveal everything. But a message appeared on his phone, distracting them both. He flicked it open, read it, dismissed it. She glanced back just in time to see what he'd been reading on the screen earlier, a news article with the same photographs he'd shown her in her office. He put the unlit cigarette between his lips, thoughtful, scrolled further down the page.

'Those are your missing persons?' Chloe said.

'Yeah.' He tapped the screen. 'They're about to live stream the press conference.'

They sat, their arms almost touching, and watched as Deputy Police Commissioner Joseph Woods came onto the screen and briefed a room crowded with press about his missing daughter. Huge printed photographs of Tonya and little Rebel Woods stood on easels behind the big man in his stiff uniform.

'My daughter . . . has had a hard life,' Woods said. He put a fist to his mouth, cleared his throat. Tried to blink tears away without wiping at them. 'She's troubled and needs help. She's a strong, beautiful, *good* person. Tonya loves her baby, and I do too, and I just want to know that the two of them are safe.'

'This is so sad,' Chloe said.

'Eh.' Tox shrugged. 'Everybody's strong and beautiful and good when they're missing. He leaned on "good" too hard. Like he was defending her. I bet if I went missing, people would say I was an absolute champ. Beloved by all.'

'You're not beloved by all?' Chloe asked.

'No.' He didn't look at her. 'I've done terrible things. On the job. Off the job.'

She stiffened, trying to disguise the shudder that ran through her.

'Chances are, Tonya Woods has too,' he continued, tapping the cigarette on the bar again. 'They found a hot shot in her apartment. Could have been for her, could have *been* hers; meant for someone else. It had arsenic in it, which tells me she didn't make it herself. It was made by someone who's been doing this for a while, hasn't got with the program.'

'We had an arsenic poisoning case,' Chloe said.

Tox put the cigarette down. 'Huh?'

'A month ago, maybe.' Chloe nodded, remembering. 'We'd never seen one before. We had to bring a consultant in. The patient started with stomach cramps, moved into convulsions. I wondered if it was severe food poisoning, maybe a bit of dehydration. Then one of his kidneys failed. Definitely arsenic. The guy was a big biker type. Tattoos and silver rings.'

'You save him?' Tox asked.

'No,' Chloe said. 'He died on the table.'

Chapter 35

THERE ARE PLENTY of ways to break in to an unoccupied house. Hack the security system. Pick the locks. Climb onto the roof and go in through an upstairs window.

The best and quickest way to break in to a house, however, is to wait until someone's home and walk right in while all the doors are unlocked and the alarm is off. Riskier, but often worth it.

I had been sitting in the car watching Doctor Goldman's pretty semi-detached home in Balmain long enough to see people arriving one by one, some of them leaving again, obviously distressed. The speed with which someone opened the door after a visitor rang the bell told me it was being left unlocked between arrivals. I went to the house, entered through the front door and slipped quietly into the hall.

Someone was sobbing in the living room while others comforted her. I stood in the dark and listened to the family mourning. Goldie's death was shocking, but not entirely unexpected. Her job had been dangerous, and a man with an old, husky voice was lamenting the fact that she hadn't just stayed as a general practitioner, wondering why she'd chosen the dark path.

'She always liked people like that,' a woman said. 'Bad people. Burnouts and losers. She felt she could save them all, like stray cats. We didn't raise her like that, did we, Howard? Where did all this crying for the less fortunate come from?'

I walked down the hall, trying to decide if I was a burnout, a loser or simply bad. I'd known people like Bernadette Goldman during my time in foster care. People with sympathy for the devil, attracted to strays, the needy, the misunderstood. Lending a helping hand to bad people could be rewarding, I supposed, but it could also get you killed.

Goldie's office was at the back of the house, a small room with a single window and an orderly desk. I went to the laptop sitting on the desk and pushed it open. No password on the home computer, all the tabs available. I opened Goldie's email and scrolled through the sent items. She had emailed friends overseas, her sister, her accountant. I clicked on one sent to something called 'Safe Home Enterprises' two weeks before she was killed.

Hi there, I'd like to get a quote about upgrading my home security system. Semi-detached, two-bedroom house in Balmain with single lock-up garage.

I stared at the email. Had Goldie felt insecure in her home, or had working with criminals all day just given her a more acute sense of the possibility of a break-in? I went to the security panel on the wall by the door and examined the tiny lit screen. Goldie already had all her windows and doors alarmed. I didn't see any evidence of cameras feeding to her laptop. I went to her internet search history and found she had looked up a few different home-security suppliers. As well as the usual email and news sites, she'd also visited a website six times in the past few weeks – the guidelines and policies page of the Medical Board of Australia.

I clicked the link, which brought up a list of documents. The third in the list caught my eye.

Sexual Boundaries: Guidelines for doctors.

I heard footsteps in the hall and moved quickly away from the desk.

'I don't know,' a man shouted from the hall. 'Hang on.'

I slipped behind the door and stood rigid in the darkness, my knees bent awkwardly around a briefcase sitting there, as the man came into the room and stood just feet away from me. I watched his reflection in the window through the crack in the door beside me. He had Goldie's auburn hair. A brother, maybe. He turned on the light, paused, looked at the laptop. He was listening intently; he must have heard me hiding. I held my breath, and after a few seconds he flipped the laptop closed, turned out the light and walked away.

Chapter 36

IF THERE'S ONE thing prisons don't do well, it's meat. Meat in all forms comes minced, glued together and pressed into geometric shapes, and often without any kind of crumbed coating to hold it together. I sat at the bar at The Workers hotel in Balmain and watched the rain falling outside. A group of dock workers in their high-vis vests and big boots sat outside on the rooftop, regaling each other with apparently hilarious stories. When my burger came I was two glasses of wine in and feeling warm and tired, burning with hunger. I forgot the chips and the wine completely and took big, slow chomps of the burger, licking the meat juices from my lips and watching the majestic slide of the melted cheese down the cliffs made by my bites in the patty.

The new phone in my pocket rang and I answered it with my mouth full.

'What's it feel like, regressing to childhood?' Tox asked. 'Pops makes you dinner. Buys you clothes. Lends you money to buy a phone, lends you his car. You might stay there forever, his live-in daughter. You and Daddy and the three shaggy pups.'

'I don't know if I'd call this a regression,' I said. 'My child-hood was nothing like this. No, wait. I lie. One of the foster dads did buy me an item of clothing once. It was a string bikini. He wanted to watch me sunbaking in it.'

I finished the chips, pointed to my empty plate and caught the bartender's eye, made a 'same again' motion with my finger. The bartender obliged with his eyebrows raised.

'I've got phone records between Mallally and Tonya,' Tox said.

'Oh yeah?'

'Yeah, I'll email them to you. But don't get excited. They're brief.'

'How brief?'

'Three months' worth,' he said. I could hear him clicking a mouse, tapping keys. 'They had a little flurry of romantic exchanges early on, and then bam, they stop. Dead silence. No calls, no texts.'

'It was an eight-month relationship,' I said.

'I know.'

'So they text for three months and then what?'

'Then the wife wants to know why he's smiling at his phone all the time and they go offline,' Tox said. 'That's my guess.'

'Offline how? Letters? Hired intermediary? Carrier pigeon?'

'I don't know yet.'

'Well, get on it, Barnes.'

'Yes, boss,' he said.

I hung up. My second burger came. It was as physically and mentally pleasurable as the first one. I ate it more slowly. I realised a man was watching me as I put the last mouthful longingly between my lips.

'What are you, a reformed vegetarian?' He laughed. He was young, cute, some kind of manual labourer, judging from the big calloused hands and the paint or wood dust in his hair. A half-eaten burger lay on the plate before him.

'It's just been a while.' I munched on a chip.

'You can't deprive yourself of the good things for too long,' he said.

I wiped my hands on my napkin, nodded in agreement and raised my wineglass in his direction.

'Here's to that,' I said.

Chapter 37

THE SEX WAS GOOD. Wholesome and intimate when it needed to be, impersonal and rough at just the right moments, the fold-out in the garage taking the challenge without squeaking madly as I worried it would.

Pops's dogs scratched at the door as we lay sweating in the semi-darkness. It turned out the labourer was a fitter of kitchens. It was sawdust in his hair. That's all I knew. I lay silently, watching him try to work it out – whose house this was and why I was sleeping in the gym, why we had to be quiet and come in the back door. The bruises on my face and body. He must have wondered why I was so hungry, not just for good food and wine but for his touch. All of my possessions had been put in storage while I was in prison, unmarked boxes Whitt had shoved away for an indeterminate period. The kitchen fitter must have wondered why the only clothes I had were brand-new, still bagged beside the bed. He didn't ask.

We rolled over together. The dogs went away and I closed my eyes, our feet touching, his arm around my waist like a belt. He fell asleep first. They always do. I revelled in the feel of his breath against the back of my neck while I waited for sleep to come. When it didn't immediately I picked up the phone Pops had given me, opened my email account and looked at the text transcripts between Tonya Woods and Louis Mallally.

They started hesitantly. Two people who had met by chance, dancing around each other, neither wanting to be the first to voice the unspoken thing between them. He must have been nervous about the age difference. She must have been nervous about the wedding ring.

LOUIS: How's the eye?

TONYA: See for yourself.

LOUIS: That's a nice picture. You look happy. Are you at home?

TONYA: Sort of. Little place I've been renting. I've got Rebbie here. We're watching *Frozen*. AGAIN. It's hard to focus. I've been thinking.

LOUIS: About what?

TONYA: My life. I want to change. I've tried to do it myself for so long, but I think I need help. You picking me up off the street the other day like a ragdoll was crazy. I thought, what the hell am I doing? Why don't I have someone in my life who takes care of me instead of smacking me down?

LOUIS: I'm glad you're staying away from that guy. You don't need that. Not around your kid.

Tonya's texts were all grammatically perfect. Smart girl trapped in a stupid cycle. As I read through the texts in the dark, I saw her falling for him. Not just Louis, but the idea of Louis. The lawyer. The defender. The guy with his life sorted out.

Tonya wanted Louis to influence her. She wanted some of his power and confidence sprinkled about her world. I scrolled forward a couple of weeks.

TONYA: It was so great seeing you today. You're like an energy supercharge. A bolt from the blue. I got home and scrubbed the room. Mopped the floors. I'm going to try to get a crib for Reb so she can sleep in her own bed when she stays here. It's like you said, one step at a time.
LOUIS: You can do this, Tonya. You're a smart, beautiful, sexy woman. You're a good mother. I'm here to help you.

The kitchen fitter stirred, disturbed by the light of my phone. I put it away, thought about Tonya latching on to Louis Mallally, her supercharge. She was a lonely, unhappy girl trying to grab onto a man, trying to feel something. Something that would shake her up, set her on the right path. Right now I was doing the exact same thing. Dragging a man into my life, trying to shake off the numbness that the trauma of my time in prison had brought into my life. It was an easy but unhealthy outlet.

I fell asleep to the sound of his breathing and the rain falling softly on the garage roof.

Chapter 38

'IT WASN'T AN inmate,' Pops said.

I wasn't awake yet. Dressed, yes. Sitting at the kitchen table, visibly conscious. But not awake. He put a coffee down in front of me and the dogs arranged themselves on and around my bare feet. I thought about what he'd said for a long time.

'Why not?'

'The prison was tossed, top to bottom, for the knife,' Pops said. 'But there wasn't one. They found all sorts of things – razors, shanks, home-made picks. But nothing that would have made cuts that wide, neat and deep. So that means it was someone other than an inmate who killed Goldman. No inmate could hide a knife that big for that long.'

'Did you actually see the wide, deep, neat wounds or is this from what Dolly told you?' I sipped the coffee. 'Because I like her but she's as reliable as a cheesecloth condom.'

'I got the idea from what she said to look at the forensic report,' Pops replied. 'Dolly claimed there were three wounds, and blood everywhere. And, from the post-mortem examination, she was right. A big gash here, here and here.' He pointed to the side of his neck, his ribs, his belly, all on the same side. 'Three. Now, that's not a prison shanking, is it?'

'No, it's not,' I confirmed.

'A prison shanking, you go for quantity, not quality,' he said. He wasn't talking to me now, just rambling, walking around the kitchen. 'Prison shanks are long and thin. Toothbrushes, wire, strips of glass or plastic. Easily slid down pants or up sleeves, don't show through the fabric. So with something so narrow, you hit them as many times as you can. Try to get an artery before someone comes and stops you.' He mimed stabbing himself in the chest, his fist moving in short jabs like someone using a salt shaker. He didn't need to tell me any of this. I'd seen one fatal shanking and two non-fatal ones during my four months inside.

'You want to see the autopsy photographs?' he asked.

'Not particularly. Goldie was my friend.'

'That's fine. I looked at them. The wound in the neck was a stab wound, not a gash. We're looking for a big knife. Blade about five centimetres thick.'

'So where did this big knife come from?' I asked.

'The kitchen?'

'There wouldn't have been anyone in the kitchen.' I shrugged. 'It was after breakfast. Lunch is just pre-packaged sandwiches. They wouldn't start dinner prep until the afternoon, and even then, they're searched on the way in and out of the kitchen.'

'But you said there was a riot.' Pops sat down next to me.

'Not a riot, a level-one lockdown. A fight broke out in one of the cell blocks. They escalated it to a level two when they discovered the doctor had been stabbed.'

'Convenient, don't you think: a level one starting just minutes before the doctor was targeted?' Pops was staring at me intently. The fire was in his blood, and it was affecting me, quickening my breath, waking my mind before the coffee had chance to take effect.

'A level-one alert would have diverted guards.' I nodded. 'Tied them all up securing and observing inmates. The killer made sure the hall outside the doctor's office would be clear. All inmates would have been on the ground, stationary. No witnesses.'

'There must be a camera trained on the doctor's rooms, right?' Pops asked.

'If there is, the footage would be with prison officials. And Dolly's lawyer.'

'I'm going to see if I can get it.' Pops looked determined, his brows low over his eyes as though he was already shouting down anyone who tried to stop him. 'My Corrections contacts may be able to help. They're in Long Bay, not Johnsonborough, but they're our best shot so far.'

'I'll try to find out what I can about the level-one fight just before the stabbing,' I said. 'I think I have an idea about someone I can . . . talk to.'

'Why did you say it like that?' Pops gave me a sidelong look. 'You're just going to *talk* to them, right?'

'I'm sure there'll be talking involved.' I got up.

'Oh, Jesus,' Pops sighed.

Chapter 39

I KNEW THE guy was going to try to hurt me as soon as I laid eyes on him.

He was not looking at my car. Determinedly avoiding it with his eyes, like a dog refusing to look at the couch cushions torn to shreds all over the living-room floor. He was in such a hurry that his own car, parked haphazardly at the kerb, still had its driver's door propped open. I spotted him in the rear-view mirror, walking in a straight line towards me between the cars waiting at the traffic lights, ten minutes' drive from Pops's house.

I glanced at the dashboard, the doors of Pops's car, didn't spot a central-locking button. The man's gun was hanging low by his side, but his hand told me he wasn't going to fire it. Finger off the trigger, butt gripped like a club.

I put the car into park, ripped up the handbrake. He opened the passenger-side door and slid in beside me, as I knew he would, the car rocking with the new weight. Big guy. Boxy and solid. In his fifties but still strong. He grabbed a handful of the back of my hair and raised the barrel of the gun to my face.

I heard his long intake of breath as he prepared to bark threats, directions.

Before he could, I fainted.

Chapter 40

TO FEIGN FALLING unconscious, you've got to commit to hurting yourself. When people faint in real life they do all kinds of damage; bite their tongues, smash their faces on the kitchen countertop, drop a glass on the floor and sprawl all over the shards. When the guy grabbed me I went limp in his hands. He wasn't ready for it, so he dropped me, and I fell forward and smacked my face on the steering wheel. I waited. He tried to process this new and unexpected turn of events, probably looked around, panic rising. The traffic light changed and the car behind us beeped its horn. I heard the *clunk* of his gun as he rested it on the dashboard, and that's when I sprang into action.

I grabbed the gun and palmed the guy in the face so that his head hit the window beside him. In the confined space I twisted sideways and clubbed him hard in the head a couple of times with the butt of the pistol, losing the weapon into the back seat as his thick arm came up to block the blows.

He opened the car door and spilled out, and I followed, sliding across the passenger seat. We tangled on the asphalt, a hand as big as my head coming for my hair again, using it like a handle, rolling and shoving me down, grinding my face into the road.

Chapter 41

THE GUY WASN'T going down easy. Drivers, confused and frightened by the fray, leaned on their horns or sped past into the intersection. I caught glimpses of the man's face as we wrestled: ruddy cheeks and a nose that had been smashed flat in the centre, scars on his shaven scalp. He was a bruiser, a bar-room brawler from the smell. I got on top of him, and he grabbed my throat. I ripped his fingers backwards, kept wrenching until the wrist and then the whole arm came with me and he rolled onto his front to stop me dislocating his shoulder. Sharp, angry cries of pain. A knee to the face ended his efforts. His big head smashed into the road and he was out.

At that moment I saw Tox and Whitt standing across the road, watching, doing nothing. They started walking towards me. There was blood running off my chin from the collision with the steering wheel, dripping onto the road that was already warm under the morning sun.

'Oh, gee, thanks, guys.' I threw my hands up as Tox grabbed my attacker under the arms and hefted him up. 'You got here right in the nick of time.'

'You had it,' Tox grunted, his cigarette clamped between his lips. 'Don't pretend you're some kind of damsel in distress.'

I was reminded of Pops's car, still sitting a few metres away at the lights, the gun on the passenger seat and the door open. An old woman sitting in her shiny new Kia behind Pops's Datsun seemed to be reporting everything into a phone, probably on the line with police. I signalled to Tox to meet us in a nearby alley with the guy while Whitt and I took care of the car.

The square-headed bulldog of a man who had attacked me was sitting upright, dazed, against a brick wall when Whitt and I arrived. Tox was perched on a garbage can, watching as the man came to. He tossed me a thick leather wallet.

'Meet Travis Blenk,' Tox said. 'Failed carjacker extraordinaire.'

I looked at the wallet, the driver's licence, at Blenk. He was staring at his chubby fingers, rocking slightly, probably trying to assess if he was dreaming or if he really had just had his arse whooped by his own mark.

'You know this guy?' I asked Tox.

'Heard of him. He used to be a pretty good cage fighter back in the day. I heard they put him in the cage with a bear once. Don't know how true that is.'

'A *bear*?' I looked at Blenk, tried to picture it.

'Californian black bear, not a grizzly.' Tox shrugged.

'Hey.' I nudged Blenk with my foot. 'What's your fucking problem? You don't like lady drivers?'

Blenk's eyes were almost clear. He looked at us each in turn, then reached up and took his left ear off. Checked it for damage, the way a person checks a phone they've dropped on the ground for cracks on the screen.

'Christ,' Tox laughed, squinting at the hole in the side of Blenk's head, the embedded hook where he hung the prosthetic ear. 'Forget it. That's the element of surprise right there.'

'Hey, I asked you a question.' I nudged Blenk again. 'You play this rough with everyone you're sweet on, or is it just me?'

'It's not just you.' Blenk put his ear back on. He spat blood on the ground, felt a tooth to see if it wobbled. 'I have no idea who you are. I was just going for the car, that's all. Nothing personal.'

I glanced at my partners. Blenk was about as convincing as a guy who had been caught in a toilet cubicle with the boss's wife. A block over, at the intersection, I heard police cars arriving with their sirens wailing.

'What do you mean, you have no idea who I am? How do you know I'm anybody?'

'I don't.' Blenk wouldn't meet my eyes.

'Come on, Blenk,' I said. 'You didn't just want the car. You weren't going for the forty-year-old cherry-red Datsun Bluebird when you had a two-year-old grey Kia Sportage right behind it at the lights with a woman older and frailer than me in the driver's seat.'

Blenk didn't answer.

I crouched before the man on the ground, reached up and pulled his prosthetic ear off the side of his head. It came free from the hook fixed to his skull with a *pop*. I held it close to my lips.

'Listen carefully, Blenk,' I said into the ear. 'You know exactly who I am. I'm Harriet Blue. I've been a lot of things in my life. A cop, a fugitive, a killer. But I've never been an idiot. You came for me just now because you'd been following me and you saw your opportunity. And if you've been following me, that means you knew where to find me. And *that* means you knew I was at Chief Morris's house, released from Johnsonborough into his custody. Not even the press know that.'

I threw the man's ear back at him. It hit his chest and flopped into his hands. Two patrol cops stepped into the alleyway ten metres from us. Blenk looked almost relieved at the sight of them.

'Is this about Doctor Goldman?' I asked. Blenk got unsteadily to his feet, started walking towards the approaching cops. 'Did someone send you to –'

'I don't hurt girls,' Blenk muttered. He looked back at me, almost apologetic. I was struck by the comment, wanted to hear more, but the cops were shouting at us, pushing us and Blenk apart.

Chapter 42

WITNESSES HAD TOLD the patrol cops in attendance that Blenk had tried to jack my car, that I'd been defending myself. I was encouraged to make a statement, to follow the cops back to the police station to sort the whole thing out. But Tox, Whitt and I refused to give our names, told the young, adrenaline-filled officers it was all a big misunderstanding. We didn't want Blenk locked up. We knew what that meant – lawyers, silence, hours in custody at a police station. I would have to alert Woods to the attack to get access to Blenk, without really knowing if Blenk had anything to do with Tonya and her child's disappearance. It was far less messy if Blenk just walked away and one of us caught up with him later.

The patrol cops apparently didn't recognise us, were bemused by our willingness to see Blenk walk off down the street without charge. The incident brought nearby shopkeepers and bystanders to a standstill, slowed traffic, filled the air with frustrated car horns. My partners and I untangled ourselves from the police, slipped into a quiet cafe and huddled in a booth, watching the officers outside talking, trying to decide between themselves what the hell was going on.

'Well, that was weird.' Whitt gripped his laminated menu, flicked the corner, thinking. 'Did you get a sense of what he wanted? Was he trying to kidnap you or kill you?'

'I have no idea,' I said. 'I don't think he was going to use the gun. He came up on me with his finger off the trigger, and as soon as I pretended to faint he put it down. If he was going to pop me, that was the time to do it.'

'So he was going to take you,' Tox said.

'Take me where?' I huffed in frustration. 'Jesus. I should have let him do it. I just didn't think.'

'You should not have let him do it.' Whitt frowned. 'You didn't know we were nearby. You could have ended up anywhere.'

'I can handle myself.' I kicked him under the table.

'If Blenk knew where to find you, it must be related to Johnsonborough,' Whitt said, rubbing his knee. 'To Bernadette Goldman's murder. Blenk must have a contact on the inside who saw you being picked up by Pops. It's the only way to explain how he would know where you were so fast. The only person other than us who knows where you're staying is Woods himself.'

'Pops called the prison yesterday.' I said. 'Spoke to my old cellmate, Dolly. Someone could have looked at the call list. Seen Pops's name. Connected the dots.'

'Someone from inside the prison sees you're out, sees Pops pick you up, sees the call from Pops to Dolly,' Tox pondered. 'They found out where you were. Sent Blenk to shut you up about the doctor's murder.'

'Makes sense to me,' Whitt said.

'We'll give him a little while, let him settle down, forget about the botched hit,' Tox said. 'Then we'll go snatch him up and stick ice picks in his nuts until he tells us who killed your quack.'

We fell silent. I screwed up my nose. Tried to fit the pieces together.

'That's not it.'

'It's not?' Whitt asked.

'You heard him at the end there. *I don't hurt girls*. That's a bit of an odd thing to say.'

'He wasn't thinking straight,' Tox said. 'The guy had just got through trying to paint the road with your face. Of course he hurts girls.'

'I'm not a girl.' I put my hands out.

'This isn't the time for a feminism lecture, Harry,' Tox said.

The waitress came and took our order, set a plate of oily, flaky baklava on the table that we hadn't asked for. She winked at Whitt as she turned to go back to the kitchen. I grabbed a baklava and started munching it.

'Think about it,' I said. 'Tonya's, what – twenty-two? Her kid's a toddler. They're *girls*. I'm not a girl. I'm a woman. He's not going to think of me as a girl, first because of my age, and second because I just made a human pretzel out of him in front of fifty witnesses. I don't see it.'

'Bernadette Goldman isn't a girl, either,' Whitt said. 'She was older than you, Harry. I get what you're saying. But the whole response doesn't make sense. You said *Is this about Bernadette Goldman?* and he said *I don't hurt girls*.'

'He was dazed. You'd beaned the guy with your kneecap,' Tox said. 'I don't think we should lean too heavily on what he said. Let's focus on what he did. He tailed you from Pops's house. He knew you were there because someone told him. I'll jump on him when we get the chance and find out what he knows. But for now, we need to talk about this.'

Tox put a baggie of brown tar on the table.

Chapter 43

'THIS LITTLE BAGGIE of smack was found on a guy who came into the emergency room at St Vincent's Hospital a month ago,' Tox said. He tapped the bag with his finger. 'It's a hot shot, loaded with arsenic.'

'So?'

'So the same type of hot shot was found in Tonya's motel room yesterday, hidden under the sink,' he said.

'Where are you getting this information? Who gave you this baggie?'

'I have a source at the hospital who let me see the file, take the sample. It hadn't been picked up for the police lab yet. My contact saw the guy die,' Tox said. 'Pretty bad way to go, apparently. All your organs shut down one by one.'

'A contact, huh?' Whitt gave a wry smile. 'That's what she is now?'

'Who are we talking about?' I asked.

'Chloe Bozer.' Tox rolled his eyes. 'She's a quack at St Vincent's. She's the one who saved my life when Regan Banks tried to punch my card in your apartment.'

'Wooo-*ooooh*!' I made a sound like a little kid finding out about a crush. Whitt tried to make it too but broke into laughter.

'Please.' Tox looked strained. 'She's a doctor. She'd know my sexual history just by looking at me. I've probably got varieties of the clap they haven't even documented in medical journals yet.'

'That didn't stop the entire nursing staff at St Vincent's jumping your bones every twenty minutes for the duration of your stay,' Whitt said.

'This is probably the first and last time I'm ever going to say this.' Tox put his hands on the table. 'But can we please stop talking about my dick?'

I nearly choked on my baklava.

'Let's talk about murder,' Tox continued. He tapped the baggie of heroin again. 'I'm trying to brief you idiots on some very important shit. I think I was wrong about the motel room being a staged abduction. I think it was a desperate search. They trashed the room looking for this. I had a friend of mine at the lab put it through the wringer this morning. It has the same chemical composition as the one found in Tonya's apartment. Whoever made that one, made this one.'

We all looked at the baggie.

'This dead guy was Wendell Hamm,' Tox continued. 'He had a Silver Aces patch on him when he came in. He was a badged bikie who'd just got out of the can. Guess who put him there?'

'Joe Woods,' I said. Tox nodded and leaned back in the booth.

'Woods led the task force that put Hamm and a couple of other guys away for ten years,' Tox said. 'He'd just got out after five with good behaviour. The other guys were already out.'

'I think we just found motive,' Whitt said.

Chapter 44

WE TOOK POPS'S car, but Whitt drove. We had decided to leave Tox behind to chase Travis Blenk rather than have him burn his identity with members of the Silver Aces motorcycle gang. As someone who rubbed shoulders with Sydney's underworld, Tox had a chequered history with bikies. He wasn't loyal to any club, so bikies tended to use him to spread rumours and misinformation to other clubs or to drop hints about the criminal activities of rival organisations. He was also a cop, but he regularly looked the other way on their underhanded deeds in order to take down bigger fish in the worlds of drugs, prostitution and extortion. He was a friend, but not a friend. An enemy, but not an enemy.

I examined my face in the car mirror as we turned onto the M4 motorway, heading west. The bruises from my last prison fight were fading, and Travis Blenk grinding my face into the road had left only minor grazes, the worst of which was a patch on my chin.

'You alright?' Whitt asked.

'Fine.' I flipped the visor up.

'There's something going on with Tox and that doctor.'

'How strange.' I laughed. 'You think he likes her? Like *likes* her?'

'Does Tox Barnes really like anyone?' Whitt asked.

'I don't know!' I slapped the dashboard. 'It's exciting, and I don't know why. I guess I like the idea of him having a girlfriend. He deserves to be loved.'

Tox Barnes was my friend. He'd saved my life, and Whitt's, on more than one occasion, and though he was emotionally arid, infuriatingly stubborn and he blanketed cigarette smoke over everything that came within ten metres of him, I wanted to see him happy.

As a child, Tox had accidentally destroyed his chances of leading any kind of normal life. He and a group of other boys had been tossing rocks off a highway overpass onto traffic, giggling as the stones tinked and clinked off the tops of cars and windscreens, and the drivers honked in anger. The boys had no conception of how dangerous their game was until it was too late. A woman driving home with her young son in the car had been startled by a pebble on her windscreen, swerved, and had collided with an oncoming truck. She and the boy had been killed instantly.

Tox had been a double murderer before he was ten years old. Though his record was sealed due to his youth and no charges were pressed against the boys, I knew Tox did all that he could to punish himself in his everyday life for his crime. He let his colleagues believe rumours about his past that caused them to despise him. He wandered through the world unable to fit in anywhere – not a cop or a criminal, an ally or a foe.

He pushed people away, sabotaged relationships and flaunted the rules of his job, almost daring the brass to fire him and leave him without the only thing that gave him purpose.

Tox lived his life almost exactly the same way I did, and for almost the same reasons. As a foster kid, I'd never fit anywhere. Circumstances in both our childhoods had made a normal life impossible.

But if Tox Barnes could find love, maybe that meant he was overcoming who and what he was. And maybe the same was possible for me.

'Get this,' Whitt said, smiling as he remembered. 'When Tox was telling me about the bikie who died of arsenic poisoning, I made fun of him for going back and talking to Chloe Bozer again, just like you did. He said she'd seen his heart.'

'*What?*'

'Not like, *Oh, she's seen inside my heart and soul*, or whatever. Tox would never talk like that. He meant she's seen his *heart*.' Whitt tapped his chest. 'Chloe Bozer had to jack his ribs open in the emergency room and check that his heart hadn't been nicked by the tip of the blade when Banks stabbed him. She's laid eyes on his actual heart.'

We fell silent. Whitt looked over at me.

'Why did he tell you that?' I asked.

'I don't know.' Whitt laughed, shrugged. 'He just said it.'

'I guess you never get to see your own heart,' I mused. 'Or if you do, you're in deep shit.'

'It was kind of . . . romantic,' Whitt said. 'I guess.'

'Yeah,' I agreed. 'I guess.'

The highway stretched before us, baking in the midday heat. Suburbs thinned as the city shrank behind us.

'I wonder what my heart looks like,' I said.

'It's big, we know that,' Whitt said. The silence grew heavy. Whitt shifted in his seat. A rose colour grew around his neck, near his collar, then faded.

'That was kind of romantic,' I blurted, unsure how to respond.

'I guess.' He laughed.

Chapter 45

YOU CAN'T JUST walk in to a bikie clubhouse. If you call ahead, no one will be there. The place will be locked up tight like a fortress, and snooping around could get you killed. Police in New South Wales had in the past been deterred from arriving unexpectedly on bikie properties by the use of bear traps, punji pits, trip-wire explosives, tear-gas bombs and good old-fashioned warning shots fired from hidden lookouts.

Whitt and I arrived outside the Silver Aces clubhouse on a sparse property in Panuara in the afternoon. There were no buildings visible from the roadside, and much of what lay beyond the wooden boundary fence was disguised by tall yellow grass and harsh scrubland. I got out and stood leaning against the hot bonnet of the car, watching grasshoppers fluttering and frolicking near the fence line. Cicadas were screaming in the trees at the roadside. Whitt stood with me and waited. We knew hidden cameras or lookouts would pick us up and alert the men on the property to our presence.

It was twenty minutes before someone arrived. Long enough for the lieutenants to question everyone inside to see if they recognised us. To discuss among themselves what we might want, hide any evidence of nefarious activities. A man with a bulbous nose, shaved head and a blond beard parked by the gate and emerged from a ute. He walked over to us, not attempting to disguise the almost certainly unlicensed handgun in the front of his jeans.

Whitt put his arms out and so did I, and the guy patted us down roughly, shoving Whitt against the car to do it, trying to send a message to the big guy. I braced to be grabbed on the crotch or breasts but wasn't. Some male criminals think female cops are hero-making sexual conquests, and some think we're poisoned meat.

When the guy spoke it was to Whitt, like I wasn't standing there.

'Wallets, phones,' he said. We handed them over. He took the wallets but opened our car door and tossed the phones in, not caring where they landed.

'What's this about?'

'We want to join,' Whitt said. He jerked his thumb at me. 'This one's been watching *Easy Rider* and now she's hooked, and police salaries are for losers.'

The guy didn't even smirk. He walked back to the ute and we followed, slid inside. No one spoke as we were driven to the clubhouse, a sprawling brick-and-concrete compound squatting in the middle of an overgrown field.

Whitt leaned over and stared hard at the man's forearm for a moment as we rode. When we slipped from the car again I leaned close to him.

'What'd you see?' I asked.

'Guy's got a tattoo of Mitsuko Uchida on his arm.'

'Who?'

'A Japanese pianist.'

'Would you get in the fucking game, Whitt? You're thinking about Japanese piano players and I'm trying to stop us getting murdered here.'

'Sorry,' he said.

There was a hundred metres of gravel spread around the cluster of buildings, peppered with shell casings and broken beer bottles. Approaching this place on foot at night would be impossible for the noise of one's footsteps, and then there were the dogs. A dozen of them rushed at us as we exited the car, a collection of tan and black mongrels barking and howling. They were all mixed breed, but I recognised the shapes of skulls and snouts: Rottweilers, ridgebacks and pit bulls. Older dogs rose slowly from dirty blankets and towels spread around the concrete outside the buildings and barked from where they stood, too tired and frail to cross the gravel and glass divide.

The front of the main building was a parking lot for Harleys, some of them meticulously restored antiques. Beautiful airbrushed designs, big, leather-bound handles. Hogs and flame-emblazoned choppers gleamed in the sun.

Inside the compound, out of sight of any cameras or tele-scopic lenses that might be positioned at the roadside, the guns came out. As we walked into the building, I spotted at least ten guns – some lying casually on tables, some gripped in the hands of the men around us, some pointed directly towards us.

The room was set up like a bar. No natural light. Billiard tables, dartboards, stools, low leather couches. The smell of beer and vomit was like a wave crashing over us. There was a huge mural of the Silver Aces badge spray-painted on one wall.

The only person not looking at us was a man standing behind the bar, pouring frozen chips into the basket of a huge deep fryer.

'You,' the bearded guy said, pointing at Whitt. 'You go through to the back. The bitch stays out here.'

'Forget it,' I said. 'You're not separating us. We meet with the boss together or we don't meet at all.'

'This is a courtesy, us coming all the way out here to this shithole,' Whitt said. 'We can do this in the city, if you'd like.'

I felt a presence behind me, a cloud of human heat. A man sniffed loudly in my ear. He didn't touch me with his hands, but the tip of his nose ran up the side of my neck.

Every instinct told me to twist, clamp onto his face with my fingers, squeeze and bite in with my fingernails until I drew blood, gouged eyes, a one-handed claw attack. I pictured him bending back in pain, screaming, trying to wrench me off. Instead I remained frozen, my jaw locked.

'She smells good,' the guy reported to his friends. 'Sweaty. It must be hot out there. Or are you just scared?'

I wasn't scared. I should have been, but my well-practised numbness was preventing it. There was absolutely nothing stopping these men from overpowering us, holding me down on one of the billiard tables, maybe making Whitt watch, maybe filming it for the enjoyment of other chapters of their club. Whitt and I would end up somewhere on the property, buried deep. They'd dump our car with our phones in it in the desert and be all wrapped up in twenty-four hours, the whole caper a booze-blurred memory.

Was this what had happened to Tonya and her child? Had she asked for a hot shot from a bikie pal to take care of a troublesome dealer or boyfriend, only to find herself in debt to a dangerous crew? Had they come for her at the Oceanside, brought her out here, buried her somewhere on the plains?

Our escort went through to a room at the back of the bar. When he returned we were beckoned forwards.

I glanced back at the men standing around the room as I left them behind. Their eyes were hollow in the dim light.

Chapter 46

IN A SMALL, cluttered office, Whitt and I were seated on two wooden chairs before a desk that had been turned sideways and pushed against a wall. As I took my place I noticed duct-tape marks on the legs of my chair. Someone had met their fate in this chair, sitting as I was sitting before the Silver Aces boss in his private chambers.

Jax Gotten was slumped in a battered leather chair, pricking the surface of the desk with a push pin obviously fallen from the wall behind him. There was a huge corkboard that had probably been covered in maps, photographs and other secret paraphernalia that had been ripped down and stuffed away somewhere when Whitt and I appeared out front. There were more pins on the floor. Framed photographs hung on the wall, of big men with tattoos, gang leaders of times past, some of the frames obviously memorials to those fallen in wars or in prison. The computer beside Jax was humming quietly, an ancient thing I knew Drug Squad detectives would be drooling to get their hands on. Bikie gangs are malignant gatherings of vile criminals pooling their collective aggression towards society, but they're also incredibly lucrative businesses. That Jax had seen us in his office likely meant that the rest of the compound's rooms were filled with far more intriguing material these guys wanted to keep hidden.

'Mr Gotten,' Whitt began. 'I'm Edward Whittacker, and this is Harriet Blue.'

'What?' Jax snorted. 'No Detective Senior whatever-the-fuck? The boys out front said you chumps were cops.'

Jax was one of those people who looked dumber than he was. His face was broad and scarred, and his long, thick arms sported faded blue tattoos of the usual criminal fare – naked girls, skulls, knives, spiders. But he'd identified our weakness already, probably before we'd entered the room, and was hitting us with it before we'd even settled into our chairs.

'We're pursuing a police-sanctioned inquiry right now,' I said.

'Police-sanctioned but not police?' Jax said. 'What does that mean? The cops are so hard up for recruits these days they're asking civilians to do their dirty work? What kind of training do you have to –'

'We're suspended,' I said lazily. 'That's what you want to hear, isn't it, Jax? Whitt and I are suspended for a variety of professional misdeeds.'

He smiled, a small and petty win. I leaned forward, put my forearms on my knees.

'Tell us about Wendell Hamm,' I said.

'We've already been questioned about Hammy by *real* cops,' Jax said. 'They hauled us in when he kicked the can, maybe a month ago.' He jutted his chin at a framed photograph on the wall of a portly man in a Silver Aces jacket.

'When did –'

'They stood all around watching us from the tree line at the funeral and the wake,' Jax said, talking right over the top of Whitt's words, like a train mowing down a kangaroo on the tracks. 'Binoculars and cameras. Got no respect, coppers. Stand there making observations in their notebooks at a fucking funeral. Who does that?'

'Wendell was found to have died from –' I began.

'He was a user, yeah,' Jax cut over me. 'He must have dealt with the wrong guy. Sometimes those dealers in the city spice up their batches with hot shots just to keep business rolling. If the skels hear a few people have kicked it in a certain area then they know where the strong stuff is, and arsenic is cheaper than fentanyl.'

'Mr Gotten,' I said slowly. 'If you interrupt my partner or myself one more time I'm going to take that pin and stick it into your eyeball.'

Jax gave a broad smile, rolling the pin between his fingers. He was starting to like me.

'We understand Wendell Hamm had been released from prison only days before his death,' Whitt said. 'And that he was in prison largely as a result of the efforts of Deputy Commissioner Joseph Woods.'

'He's got a good title, hasn't he?' Jax mused.

'Here's a scenario for you,' Whitt said. 'Wendell Hamm gets out of prison. He starts talking about getting revenge against Joe Woods for putting him inside. He's obsessed with it. Driven. You're a smart guy, and you know targeting one of the highest-ranked police officers in the country is a terrible idea. Bad for business. If the cops get wind of Hamm's plan, they're going to be crawling all over this place, and you don't want that because this is the hub of your business. This is ground zero.'

'You tell Wendell to let it go.' I took over, tagging Whitt with a glance. 'But he keeps on blathering about Woods. He's a user. He talks to whoever will listen. He does something stupid – he gets a hot shot to Woods's junkie daughter. You know the hot shot can be traced back to you. It's your product, and Wendell's spiked the shot the old fashioned way – with arsenic. You know it's only a matter of time before the cops start thinking whoever targeted Tonya Woods was old school. An ex-con. Maybe a bikie.'

'You can't take out one of your own guys without rattling the whole crew, so you give Wendell a taste of his own medicine,' Whitt said. 'You switch out his personal stash with a hot shot. Wendell goes down, and you hope both your crew and the police think it's just another Kings Cross overdose. Wendell's gone: part one of the problem is solved. Part two – you've got to get the hot shot back from Tonya. You go to her room at the Oceanside, try to find the baggie and can't. Tonya and her toddler arrive unexpectedly and you have to pop them both and bury them in the desert.'

Jax was silent. Whitt and I stared at him. I heard the *whoosh* and the bubbling sound of the frozen chips being sunk into the deep fryer out in the bar. While we'd talked, Jax had pushed the pin into the surface of the desk all the way to the plastic stopper and now he was turning it slowly, gouging the wood. His dark eyes settled on my face, and when he spoke the words were so calm and measured he might have been telling us the time of day.

'You've got some balls suggesting I would hurt a kid,' Jax said. 'Just saying something like that makes me wonder whether you two deserve to ever walk out those front doors again.'

Chapter 47

THERE WAS A knock at the door and Jax went to it, brushing roughly past me. I leaned urgently towards Whitt.

'Get me the room to myself,' I breathed. The men at the door were talking quietly.

'What?' Whitt frowned at me.

'I want to look at the computer,' I said. 'Get me the room. Now's your chance. Draw them away from here.'

'Are you nuts? He's never going to –'

'Just do it!' I hissed.

Whitt rose reluctantly and walked to the door behind me. I set my feet, ready to spring into action as soon as the coast was clear.

'Wait a minute,' Whitt said loudly. I glanced back and saw him pushing between the men, trying to make his way back down the hall. 'I remember that guy now.'

'What guy?' Jax glanced back at me, torn. He turned to follow Whitt. A roaming cop in the house was a bigger threat than one sitting quietly in his office.

'There's a guy out here I arrested once,' Whitt said. 'George Bell. He's supposed to be on parole in Perth. Hey! Bell!'

The door to the small office swung closed but didn't click shut. I didn't take the chance of closing it completely. I went to Jax's computer and tapped the keyboard to wake it up. On the desktop was the Silver Aces logo. I opened the only program running, a spreadsheet with numbers, no names, huge amounts of money. I went to the email icon, clicked it open. Another win; Jax kept his email open and ready to go. There were no names in the inbox that I recognised. Without really knowing what I was looking for, I danced through the computer madly, my fingers aching with tension as they tapped the keys and mouse. Down the hall I could hear Whitt's voice.

'You're telling me this guy isn't Bell? You're the spitting image, mate! Are you his brother or something?'

I took a deep breath, tried to focus. Fishing randomly through Jax's personal emails wasn't helpful. I was burning a good opportunity. I went to the search bar and typed a whole-system search for the name Tonya Woods.

Nothing. I tried Joseph Woods. Wendell Hamm. Emails arose with Wendell's name and I scrolled through them, looking at the preview text. Friends emailing to ask about Wendell's release, his funeral. In desperation I spied a folder full of photographs and clicked it open, scrolled through the latest saved images. Tonya Woods had been missing eleven days. I looked through the dates and found there was only one image saved around the time of her disappearance. A picture taken the day after Tonya took Rebel home from Joe Woods's house and wasn't seen again.

I opened the picture. Jax Gotten was standing under a huge, unnaturally blue sky, a shovel in his hand and a smirk on his face. I selected the image, went to Jax's email account and emailed it to myself, went back to searching for anything useful. I had just closed the email application and was poised to type something else into the search bar when I realised the voices in the hall had silenced.

I looked up and saw Jax standing in the doorway, Whitt beside him. They were both watching me.

Chapter 48

THEY TRIED TO separate us again, but Whitt and I knew and told each other with just a meaningful glance that we wouldn't let them do that. If we were going to get out of this alive, we needed to stick together. A guy jammed a gun into Whitt's ribs and tried to push him up the hall. Instead of going the way the man wanted, Whitt backed into the room with me, stood by my side.

'What did you see?' Jax asked me. I said nothing. It didn't matter what I said, and we both knew it. All pleasantries were abandoned. Jax's offsider was looking at him like an expectant dog, waiting for a command. But we were standing in his office, and that gave Jax pause. He didn't want his stuff peppered with bullets and blood.

'You're not going to do this,' I said. Jax looked from Whitt to me. It was clear Whitt was his bigger concern. He'd defied instructions once by slipping back into the room with me. He was sizeable and defiant, and apparently I was not. Underestimated, as I had been all my life.

'You're not going to kill two cops on your property in broad daylight,' I said.

'I'm not?' Jax asked.

'There are too many unknowns. You don't know who we told that we were coming out here. Who came with us. There might be ten guys waiting just up the road, planning an ambush if they don't hear back from us.'

'That's bullshit,' Jax's guy said. 'The road's clear. You think we didn't check?'

'You don't know when we're expected to call in,' I continued. 'It might be an hour from now. Which means reinforcements will be out here before dark looking for us, before you've had time to bury us. You don't know what I've seen. If I'm even a threat.'

'Think about it,' Whitt said. 'Letting us go is smarter than acting rashly. You can keep the car and the phones, even. Delay us getting back. Buy some time to clean up whatever secrets Harry might have just been exposed to on your computer.'

'Shut up, both of you,' Jax snapped. He looked at his man. Seemed to have a silent conversation with him, their eyes locked. 'I need to think. Whatever we do, we can't do it here. Put them in the lock-up.'

The guy grabbed Whitt's arm. He let me follow untouched. A big mistake. Jax walked behind me. We turned right out of the hall and moved through behind the bar area, as I'd hoped we would, past the bartender. There were two baskets of chips sunk into the hot oil of the fryer, bubbling madly. I grabbed one and, in a single fluid motion, lifted it, swept it through the air and smashed it into Jax's face.

Chapter 49

FRYER OIL BURNS at about 370 degrees Fahrenheit. That's 187 degrees Celsius: almost twice the temperature of boiling water. That kind of liquid heat will make your skin blister and bubble, leave scars that might last a lifetime if the wounds aren't treated properly. There was about half a kilo of chips in the frying basket, soaked in oil, and as the basket hit Jax's head it sprayed oil droplets and chips over the bar and the area beyond, a huge arc of searing liquid fire. The closest men were seated at a table nearby. I saw the oil hit them, their whole bodies jolting with shock and pain like they'd been blasted with buckshot. Jax's scream was high and loud, his face and arms soaked and scalding.

Before anyone could react I grabbed the second basket and turned it sideways as I swung it and smashed it on the bar. Chips and oil again sprayed out across the room. There was a wail of surprise, shouting. I dove for the floor as Whitt grabbed the gun of the man escorting him, smacked it out of his hands while he shoved the guy into the bar top, knocking and scattering a collection of bourbon bottles lined up there.

It didn't take long for the men around us to compose themselves. The first bullets hit the mirror behind the bar, then punched through the splashback behind the sink above me, raining shattered tiles on my back. Whitt knocked his escort down and crawled with me to the end of the bar. We got up and ran towards the rear of the building.

The room we found ourselves in was small and made of brick, the door thick steel that swung closed slowly under our hands. The locking bar clunked into place. There was a reason for the overkill on the door. We turned and saw that lining the walls all around us were plastic storage tubs stacked to the ceiling, each laden with bread-loaf sized packages wrapped in plastic. In the middle of the room was a table with a scale, more plastic wrapping, scissors, sorting and mixing equipment. If I hadn't seen anything incriminating on the computer, I was sure getting an eyeful now. There were more drugs in this room than I had ever seen in one place in my entire life.

'Jesus,' Whitt said, momentarily forgetting about the enraged, scalded bikies pounding on the steel door. 'Jesus, Mary and Joseph.'

'We've got to get out of here.' I went to the barred window, looked out. Beyond the compound were empty fields, waist-high grass. Even if Whitt and I could get through the barred window and run for it, we wouldn't make it far. 'We need to act fast before they send guys around the back.'

I shoved the window behind the bars but it was nailed shut. There was an air conditioner in the corner of the room. I dropped and peered between the stacks of storage tubs, found what I was looking for. The vent was a foot high and two-feet wide. The room needed airflow or the men packaging the drugs would be overcome by airborne particles of the narcotics within an hour of sitting down to work.

'I don't want to leave you here,' I told Whitt. 'But I'm going to have to.'

'I know,' he said. 'It's OK.'

Together we set about prying the vent cover off the wall. The sounds of our enemies assembling outside reached us, muffled by the steel door. At first there was furious yelling and screaming, the pounding of fists. Then a gunshot, another scream as the bullet ricocheted off the steel and hit one of the men crowded into the hallway. It was only a matter of time before they thought of sending someone around to the window at the back of the building.

I bent to the vent and looked in. There was daylight on the other side, maybe ten feet away. My best bet was to squeeze backwards into the opening, get to the other end of the vent and kick the door out. Whitt took my hand and helped me to my feet.

'I'll cause a distraction,' I said. 'Stay put. I'll draw them away from you. If I can't make it back I'll –'

Whitt dragged me to him and kissed me hard on the mouth.

Chapter 50

THERE WAS NO time to think about the kiss. My mind was flooded with images of my grisly death inside the ventilation shaft. As I crawled backwards into the hole, my knees and elbows banging awkwardly on the edges of the opening and my boots thudding on the steel, I thought of the bikies bursting through the door and mowing Whitt down in a hail of bullets, bending and doing the same to me as I lay trapped and helpless. I inched my way backwards towards the opening, panic unfurling in my chest as the square tunnel lengthened in front of me. Whitt replaced the vent opening and turned away, his voice echoing back to me.

'Let's talk about this!' he was yelling. 'We can work this out!'

The exterior grille gave way after three sharp kicks. I slid out into the still burning afternoon, bracing myself for the impact of a bullet. But there was no one there. I bolted into the long grass and sprinted in a wide circle towards the road.

I thought about the kiss as I ran for the car. Stupidly, uncontrollably, the feel of it came back to me, Whitt's arm around my back and hand in my hair, his sharp exhalation of relief or excitement or whatever the hell it was. I was running for my life, for *our lives*, and trying to decide if I'd had a momentary lapse of sanity and imagined the event, or if Whitt had just planted one on me without any kind of warning in the midst of deadly chaos. I was feeling something. Confusion at his actions. Terror at the possibility of reaching the car too late, hearing gunshots on the wind and knowing Whitt kissing me was the last thing he would ever do on the Earth. I reached the car, threw myself into it and screeched off the road and through the gates of the compound.

Only one thing was going to draw the bikies away from Whitt. I gripped the wheel of Pops's lovingly restored Datsun, took a deep breath to get me through the pang of regret lying heavy in my chest and floored it towards the building.

The dogs all headed for the grass, as though they knew my plan. At the last second I wrenched the wheel, cut a sharp arc and sent the back of the Datsun smashing into the line of bikes standing on the concrete. The sound of the car swiping and crunching the bikes as it wheeled by was a deafening, crashing explosion. The back window of the Datsun burst with the impact. Sparks flew. I hit the brake and swerved again, almost spun out on the gravel, the nose of the car ending up pointed at the side of the building. I looked over my shoulder.

I had reduced a good number of the bikes to scattered piles of debris. Broken backs of mechanical horses, carcasses piled and leaning against each other. The first men began arriving at the door of the building, mouths gaping, hands gripping hair. I didn't hear their howling, furious cries. I'd spotted Whitt exiting the building through a side door, his gun out, sweeping for danger. I'd drawn the men away from the hall outside the room we'd been captive in long enough for him to slip out and away.

I barely stopped to let him in. The Datsun bashed and banged over rocks and rotting logs in the field as I gunned the vehicle towards the tree line. Whitt gripped the seat with one hand and the dashboard with the other, his jaw locked as we raced to safety.

Chapter 51

TOX BARNES SAT in his Monaro and watched Travis Blenk in his car fifty metres away on the other side of the pretty suburban street. Blenk got out of the vehicle, went to the boot and extracted a small nylon pouch. Tox watched him walk confidently down the driveway of the house he was parked in front of. A few seconds later he appeared briefly, hopping the back fence of the property and dropping into the yard behind.

Tox waited. As he expected, he soon smelled smoke on the wind. Blenk jumped the fence again and ran to his car. Black smoke began coiling from the house beyond, and Tox heard a window blow out. Blenk drove away and Tox followed.

Blenk didn't clock Tox's presence in the car park of the Nicholl Hotel or standing at the almost empty bar. Tox followed him right into the gaming area and stood a metre away as Blenk set his beer down and pulled a Keno card from the stand on the tabletop. The older man only looked up when Tox sat down right in front of him.

'Aw, shit.' Blenk dropped his Keno card and pencil and sat back resignedly on his stool.

'You're not a terribly perceptive person, are you, Blenk?' Tox clicked the hammer back on the gun in his jacket pocket so Blenk would hear it. 'I've been just about stepping on your heels since that house over in Merrylands.'

Blenk said nothing, just worried at the scab on his cheek, given to him that morning in the scuffle with Harry.

'You're setting insurance fires for a dime now? In broad daylight?'

'It's better during the daytime,' Blenk said. 'Most people expect fires to happen at night. I don't know why. The owners are at work. They have an alibi. No one gets hurt.'

'That was your aim this morning, wasn't it?' Tox said. 'Someone hired you to come after Harriet Blue. You agreed because you thought you could do it without anyone getting hurt.'

'That was a misunderstanding.' Blenk glanced at the patrons around them, old men at the nearby tables watching horses racing across lime-green screens. 'I just needed a car.'

'Come on, Travis,' Tox sighed.

'Look.' Blenk put his arms on the table. His pudgy face sagged at the cheeks and below the eyes, exhaustion brought on by years of hard living. 'I needed the money, OK? I'm not the guy in the cage anymore. That stuff used to be my bread and butter, but I'm fifty-eight years old now. It's been a decade since I got behind the wire. The last time they put me with a guy trained in some kind of weird dance fighting.'

'Capoeira?' Tox asked.

176

'I don't fucking know.' Blenk took his ear off with a pop sound and started toying with it. The old men looked over in undisguised horror. 'It was one of those new-age things. He was swaying and bobbing all over the place. I thought it was pretty amusing until the kid snapped both my femurs.'

Tox winced.

'Yeah,' Blenk said.

'So why the desperation for money now?' Tox asked. 'You've put some away over the years, haven't you? Those cage fights don't pay peanuts.'

'That's for me,' the older man said. 'But my sister needs the help. They're hard Christians. She lost her husband last year. Got run over by his own car while he was changing the oil. Popped his head like a tomato right in front of their eldest son. There's six kids altogether. So I'm trying to put together a nest egg that'll help my sister keep her flock together.'

'She'll take your dirty money?'

'I've always told her I'm a whizz at the stock market.'

'Right.' Tox looked at Blenk's smashed and scarred face, his fighter's knuckles, swollen and crooked. 'So you've been taking odd jobs from all comers, or do you work for someone?'

'Look, I don't talk to cops.'

'You've been sitting here talking to me for five minutes,' Tox said.

'Yeah, well, I've got somewhere to be now.'

'You do,' Tox nodded. 'It's in the men's room over there. Your head in a urinal. I won't pull any weird dance fighting on you, but you will come away with broken bones.'

'Man,' Blenk sighed. 'I just can't catch a break right now. I'm trying to be the good guy here, you know?'

'Are you working for someone?' Tox asked again.

'It's just me. I take a blind drop.' Blenk fitted his ear back on. 'All my jobs are like that these days. Someone mails a letter to the bar here, no return address. I put the word out a while back that that's how I want to get work. That way anyone can hire me and I don't have to get into a crew.'

'What happens if you don't want to take a job?' Tox asked. 'What if it's not your style?'

'If I don't want it, I just don't do it. They get the picture after a while that I'm not interested. If I'm willing, I usually get it done within a couple of days and they mail the fee in. Same deal, no return address.'

'So someone hired you to grab Harry?' Tox said. 'How's that possible? She's only been out of prison two days.'

'Well, this time I got a call. Guy called the bar and they called me. It's not how I work but he said it was urgent. It was nothing personal, just like I told her,' Blenk said. 'It was good money. Not my kind of money.'

'You mean the fee was disproportionately generous?'

'It was about ten times what I'd usually charge for something like that.'

Tox took his hand off the gun in his pocket and folded his arms. He thought for a minute, staring at the broken capillaries in Blenk's nose.

'How'd he know where to find Harry so fast?'

'I didn't ask.'

'What was the job, exactly?'

Blenk shrugged. 'Snatch her up, take her to a field out near Eastern Creek Raceway, give her a talking to.'

'About what?'

'Whatever she's working on right now. I was just supposed to tell her to take a break. Go to Queensland. Get a suntan. I don't know. Just make sure she leaves off whatever the hell she's doing.'

'I thought you said you didn't hurt girls?'

'I wasn't going to hurt her.' Blenk held his hands open wide. 'I was supposed to threaten her. I don't hurt girls. I told you. Believe me, I've had good offers. Recent ones.'

'Like what?'

'A month ago, maybe more, I got a blind drop. Another really big fee. Only this time they were asking me to pick up a girl and her baby and I wouldn't do it.'

Tox felt his breath quicken. He put his hands on the table.

'You still have the note?'

'No, I threw it away,' Blenk said. 'I told you, I'm not like that. Had that Harriet person cooperated this morning neither of us would have got hurt.' He rubbed his head. 'There was going to be a return on it, too. Second job, if I did the first one right. Get rid of Harriet, then get rid of her partner. Edward Whitman or something like that.'

'Shit,' Tox said to himself. 'It's not about Goldman. It's about Tonya and the kid.'

'Huh?'

'Never mind.' Tox lifted his head. 'The girl and the baby. That would be the Oceanside Motel in Punchbowl, right? Tonya Woods and her daughter Rebel.'

'That sounds right.'

'What did the guy want done with them?'

'It was bad stuff.' Blenk shook his head. 'I was supposed to take them both out to a river somewhere and drown them.'

Chapter 52

NIGHT HAD FALLEN over Officer Hugh Ridgen's Rydalmere home, slowly bathing the large, empty rooms in pink and purple light before the yellow streetlamps came on. I sat in his recliner in the corner of the living room and waited, drinking one of his beers. The house was barren, a place where he slept between long shifts at the prison, a nowhere zone where he passed the hours before he could go back to work and enjoy the powerful weight of cuffs and a baton on his belt.

With the blinds drawn, I was safe to watch Ridgen's television quietly. I saw a familiar face surrounded by journalists on the steps of the courthouse in Liverpool Street. Louis Mallally was waving the press away, talking as he walked.

'There was no bribe,' Mallally was saying. 'Our position remains unchanged. The story about the bribe is a fabrication, and we'll prove it.'

Mallally seemed to be defending the small, suited man hiding from the journalists in his shadow. The small guy had apparently been accused of bribing a round-faced, rosy-cheeked man who appeared on the screen – something about airport security. Mallally and his defendant scooted away through the crowd as one of his lackeys distracted the press, his arms out like a traffic cop.

I couldn't focus on what was happening on the screen. I hadn't talked to Whitt about the kiss yet. I'd told myself it was a mindless, desperate move by a man staring down the barrel of his own violent death at the hands of a mob of scalded, raging psychopaths. He hadn't mentioned it either, and when I'd dropped him at his apartment we didn't say goodbye. It was easy to compartmentalise what had happened inside my fractured mind, to set the kiss aside for another time. I was being driven by hunger alone: an itching, burning need to know what happened to my friend Doctor Goldman and a survivalist desire to see Tonya Woods and her daughter found safe and well. If I couldn't find Tonya and Rebel, my bail would be rescinded and I would go back to prison. And if I couldn't prove Dolly innocent, a murderer would remain stalking the halls of Johnsonborough while a good woman was punished for their crime. I didn't have the time or the strength to feel anything about what Whitt had done.

Ridgen's heavy, clumsy trudge up the porch stairs was unmistakeable. I stood and slipped into the small space between the front door and the coat rack beside it. As he closed the door behind himself, I raised the butt of my pistol.

'Nighty-night, dickhead,' I said.

Chapter 53

THE BLOW TO the back of the skull didn't draw blood. It didn't even render Ridgen unconscious. I needed him to be awake. He was like a man sleepwalking as I led him to the dining-room chair I'd pushed against the wall of his big, empty kitchen. I duct-taped him into place and he watched, stunned. Within fifteen minutes he was coming to his senses, stirring to the sound of the objects I was clunking onto the kitchen table.

'What the fuck is this? What – what are you *doing* here?'

'Don't flatter yourself,' I said. 'I haven't escaped. If I was a fugitive on the run from the law this hellhole is the last place I'd spend my precious time.'

'What do you – I'm gonna . . .' He was working hard, trying to form threats and deadly promises, but we both already knew that he was never going to report this. A man like Ridgen wasn't going to have his fellow guards telling stories next week about the police cutting him from a kitchen chair, drenched in sweat and shaking, a woman's name on his lips.

'I should probably be surprised, but I'm not,' I said, continuing to lie the weapons out on the table. 'You have basically no furniture here. No knick-knacks. No pictures on the wall. Everything is functional. So when I went looking for things to play with, I had to scratch around. The one thing I come up with? Knives. Lots of knives. Of course a predator and a creep like you has a huge knife collection.'

Ridgen and I looked at the knives on the kitchen table. I'd found the weapons lovingly displayed on the wall of the garage, where a normal man might have hung tools. The garage itself had been converted into a half-hearted man cave, with another recliner, a big-screen TV, a bar fridge and the knife rack. Ridgen lifted his eyes from the knives to me and tested the duct tape binding his wrists to the arms of the chair.

He drew a huge breath, ready to bark and bluff.

'I'd keep it down if I were you,' I said, selecting a small, thin knife from the collection. 'I need my focus. I'm not trained. I'm just an amateur.'

'Not trained?' he exhaled. 'Not trained in what?'

I walked to the other side of the kitchen, lifted the knife by the blade and threw it with all my strength at Ridgen's head.

Chapter 54

THE KNIFE SHUNTED into the drywall a foot to the right of Ridgen's left ear. He bucked in his chair, his eyes squeezed shut.

'Jesus Christ! What the fuck are you doing?' He cowered, looking at the handle of the dagger sticking out of the wall. 'You're insane. You're going to get put away for the rest of your life for this!'

I selected another small knife.

'I have some questions about the murder of Doctor Bernadette Goldman.'

Ridgen stared at me. He was wide awake now, sweat blossoming in the fabric at the front of his uniform shirt.

'Just go now. Go and I won't tell anyone about this,' he blurted.

'You're not going to tell anyone about this anyway. You're a man of little pride. You're not going to sacrifice it for me.'

'My girlfriend's going to be here in fifteen minutes. She . . . her whole family. They're coming over for dinner.'

'You don't want me laughing my arse off, Ridgen. It will affect my aim.'

I threw the knife. It buried itself in the wall fifteen centimetres above Ridgen's head, making a *chunk* sound that shook his whole body.

'Fuck!'

'A few minutes before Goldman was killed, there was a fight in E Block,' I said. 'Was the fight connected to the killing? Did someone start it to draw resources away from C Block?'

'I don't know!' Ridgen snarled.

'Well, you better get knowing fast.' I picked up another knife.

'It wasn't . . . No, it can't have been. The two fighters had been beefing for months. Claudia Pittman and Nadia Cowell. It was a gang thing, and the fight was a long time coming. There was no set-up over Doctor Goldman. Dolly Quaddich was the killer. She went into the doctor's surgery and snapped, and stabbed her. It was just coincidence that –'

'Dolly didn't kill the doctor,' I said.

'You don't know that.'

'Yes, I do.' I weighed the knife in my hand. It was heavy, an ornate dagger. 'Whoever killed her did it with a knife as thick as this one. It wasn't something that could easily be obtained or hidden. That means a guard was involved. A guard let the killer take it out of the prison kitchen, or brought it into the prison themselves. The fact that it wasn't found in the shakedown after the killing means it was either returned to the kitchen – during lockdown – or taken back out of the prison.'

'I don't know what you're talking about, you stupid bitch!'

'Yes, you do,' I said. 'Goldman would have been a juicy target for a guard for a number of reasons. She had easy access to drugs. While guards bringing drugs through the front doors of the prison have to spin the roulette wheel with random searches, Goldman could have just ordered them in bulk and sold them on to inmates. A guard like you, someone known for supplying drugs to inmates, might have wanted a piece of that action. Goldman said no.'

'Please.' Ridgen huffed a huge sigh. 'Listen, I just –'

I threw the knife. It embedded itself into the drywall close enough to Ridgen's head to pin some of his hair to the plaster.

'Oh fuck! Fuck!'

'Yeah, fuck.' I laughed. 'That was close. I'm getting better at this.'

'Look. I pushed Goldman for drugs,' Ridgen confessed, gripping the arms of the chair until his knuckles were white. 'I did it, OK? I nudged her a little. Made her upset once or twice. But I didn't kill her and I didn't put a hit out on her with an inmate.'

'Did any other guards hassle Goldman for drugs?'

'Of course they did!'

'Who?'

'Everyone. Everyone had a shot at it at some point. If Goldman had been on board the place would have been raining cash. But without her we had to go to extreme measures. Guys have been bringing coke in up their butts.'

'So who killed her?'

'I don't know! I don't know! *I don't know!*'

I picked up a knife.

'It might not have anything to do with that! I heard the doctor was fucking some crazy bitch in ad seg.'

'Anna Regent?'

'Yeah, the kid-killer.' Ridgen sniffed. 'Goldman was always taking a special interest in the worst of the worst. She was one of those serial-killer groupies, you know? She and Anna had lots of meetings in Goldman's office, and people saw Goldman on the phone in her office all the time, laughing, chatting. Not work calls. Maybe Regent would call her through the prison's internal line.'

I remembered the document on Goldman's home computer. *Sexual Boundaries: Guidelines for doctors.*

'Goldman got Regent a cushy spot at Long Bay,' Ridgen said.

'I know. And that doesn't fit with your theory. If they were in a relationship, why would Goldman get Anna a placement at another prison? They'd never see each other. No more of those perks she enjoys so much in solitary: wandering around out of her cell, using the phone. Even if it meant Anna would get out and be free again one day and she and Goldman could be together, we're still talking decades.'

'I don't know, for God's sake!' Ridgen snapped.

I stood silently, trying to put the pieces together. I threw another knife at Ridgen for good measure. It shunted into the wall an inch from his sweat-slick jugular. I was too deep in thought as I left the house to pay much attention to the furious shouts following me from the kitchen.

Chapter 55

THERE WAS A man standing in the dark at the back entrance to Pops's house. I recognised the big frame and stooped shoulders. Cigarette smoke on the wind. Joe Woods was pacing back and forth across the narrow street, watching as I parked Pops's battered car a few metres away. He stopped as I approached, examining the car's condition in the street light.

'This damage has to do with the bikie thing,' he concluded.

'As they say in the classics, *I can explain*,' I said, holding my hands up.

'I'm very interested to hear the explanation.' Woods exhaled smoke at me. 'You've been on this case forty-eight hours and all you've managed to dredge up is a bikie boss claiming grievous bodily harm. Jax Gotten says you and Whittacker raided his property without cause and attacked his crew with hot oil. He's got second-degree burns on his face, neck and arms.'

Whitt had messaged me to say that Nigel Spader and his officers had picked up Gotten at Cowra Hospital. Nigel's team had raided Gotten's property, finding only twenty-one dogs at home. The uninjured members of the Silver Aces crew and the drugs we'd seen had disappeared into thin air.

'Did he tell you I smashed up about four hundred thousand dollars' worth of their bikes?' I asked.

'He did,' Woods said. 'Between that and the burns, you've almost certainly got a hit out on you now. Whittacker too.'

'I'm not worried,' I said. 'He's only making noise about the assault because he wants you to go away. He won't follow through. He won't want you to look very closely at that property, because you'll find it has been the headquarters of probably the nation's biggest drug operation. The drugs are gone, of course, but a sniffer dog would keel over a metre inside the door.'

'Harry –'

'He's not going to press charges,' I said. 'You back off, he'll back off. That's how it works with these guys.'

'What about the lawyer, Mallally?' Woods asked. 'Are we done with him?'

'Not completely. He has an alibi for some of the night Tonya went missing. He was in his office, consulting with a client, and then he went out for drinks with a few other lawyers. Nigel's people have been asking her friends and associates if the relationship with Mallally was ever abusive or violent, and it seems it wasn't – he spoiled her. Took her out riding around in the BMW. Nice, private, expensive lunches. But we've hit on something strange. We haven't been able to locate any communication between the two after the initial three-month period in which they texted and called. There are no records of calls or texts between Mallally and Tonya on either of their phones after a sudden stop around that time.'

'None at all? No emails either?'

'No. They've never emailed.'

'So how did they organise their meet-ups?'

'Mallally says they had a standing arrangement. They'd meet every week at the courthouse, Tuesdays, four in the afternoon.'

'That doesn't sound right.' Woods rubbed his nose.

'Nigel has got his people on Mallally round the clock,' I said. 'If there's a second phone and he dumps it, we'll get it. But getting into his house is a bit of a nightmare. After Whitt and I showed up unannounced, he's dragged out every legal precedent he can find about authorities visiting and searching a property without a warrant. He's threatening to sue everyone even remotely connected to the New South Wales Police for everything they have. He's going to have our station cleaners living in their dumpsters. He does not want people wandering around his house.'

Woods gave a heavy sigh.

'Everybody's doing their best here, Woods,' I said. 'You need to step back and stop micromanaging.'

Woods grabbed a fistful of my shirt and dragged me towards him. He was a tall man, so his reach pulled me up on my toes. Only this close to him could I detect the alcohol on his breath.

'Listen here,' he said. 'All this bullshit about lawsuits and goddamn phone records – your best isn't cutting it right now. You're not moving fast enough. You smell that?' He inhaled deeply through his nose. 'That's free air. I would advise you to suck it in. If you don't get your arse into gear and stop messing around, you're going to spend the next ten years in a fucking cell.'

'Let me go,' I breathed. It had taken so much resolve not to reach up and smack Woods in the face that I'd barely comprehended what he'd said. I staggered a bit as my weight fell away from his grip.

The city hummed, distant and glowing between the trees across the street. Suburban sounds punctured the silence. Dogs barking. Televisions playing.

'You ever touch me like that again and I'm going to make sure some unlucky morning jogger finds pieces of your body in a park, I swear to God.'

Woods stood with one hand covering his eyes. His cigarette was smouldering, lying on the pavement between us. I watched his silhouette, trying to decide if he was holding in tears or rage.

'Where are they?' he asked. He dropped his hand and looked at the stars, let out a chest full of air. 'Where the hell are they?'

I watched him as he recovered slowly, rubbing his eyes.

'Do you think it's possible Tonya has just run off?' I asked.

Woods looked at me sharply.

'You were sick of taking care of the baby,' I said. 'You're an older man. A young kid's got to cramp your style. You wanted Tonya to step up and take control of her life. She was trying. Borrowing money to buy baby stuff. Maybe you thought if you gave her a little push she'd realise things needed to change. So with you pushing her, and bad people hanging around in her life, maybe she decided to get away.'

'I wasn't sick of taking care of the baby,' Woods said. 'Rebbie is the light of my life. That kid was born into the worst circumstances. Unwanted, unloved. And she's just a delight. You wouldn't believe it. Look.'

He took out his phone, scrolled to a video he had no trouble finding, something he must have played often. Tonya's little girl was sitting on a yellow rug, turning a stuffed toy fish over and over in her hands. She was chubby, apple-cheeked. Little toes wiggling idly as she played. She was a beautiful child, sunny and carefree-looking, blessedly and tragically unaware of the chaos of her early life.

'*What's that?*' Woods's voice asked on the video. A big hand appeared, pointing at the toy fish.

'*Doo Bee!*' The toddler gave a gummy grin, fat dimpled cheeks.

'*He's a fish, Rebbie. Little fish. Fishy fishy fish.*'

'*Doo Bee! Doo Bee!*'

'She calls the fish Doo Bee.' Woods sniffed. I looked at him. The white light of the phone flickered in the tears clinging to his lower eyelids. 'I don't know why. I can't get her to say fish for the life of me. It's always been Doo Bee.'

I tried to tell myself not to lose focus. That all kids that age were cute. But my throat was tight.

'I'm going to find them,' I said.

'I hope she has run off,' he said. He closed the video. 'That would be the best outcome.'

'Get out of here,' I told him. 'Go home. You need sleep. Wherever they are, they need you to keep it together for as long as you can.'

Woods glanced at me with eyes shining in the dark, then he left, brushing past me, trailing the smell of desperation.

I unlocked Pops's back door and went into the gym. I was tired, but I knew the adrenaline dump from Woods grabbing me would leave me twisting and turning in the sheets. I strapped up, flicked a light on over the middle of the boxing ring and dragged a heavy bag in with me, hung it from a hook in the ceiling.

I hadn't boxed in prison, or in the months before I'd been incarcerated, running from the law and chasing a serial killer. My body seemed to awaken under the strain in my shoulders and arms as I smacked the bag, dodged and weaved from its motion, bobbed and smacked it again. My heart was hammering and my body was dripping with sweat when the knock came at the gym door. I sighed. Woods again, surely. He had probably walked up to the pub on the main road, sunk a few bourbons and was now back for round two.

When I opened the door, the fluorescent light from the gym flooded onto the sandy-haired kitchen fitter from The Workers. A wave of silent humour passed over me, half shallow desire, half embarrassment that I'd never asked his name and it was far too late to do so now. He looked at my sweaty body, strapped hands, the boxing bag beyond.

'I've been thinking about you.' He squinted at me sceptically. 'I think I've figured it out.'

'Oh yeah?' I leaned in the doorframe.

'You're fresh out of prison, aren't you.'

'Good guess,' I said.

'That's . . . kind of hot,' he said.

We smiled at each other.

'Get in here,' I said, and held the door open for him.

Chapter 56

DESPITE THE EXERCISE, I couldn't sleep. The phone Pops had given me was again an escape to another place, an electronic world of distractions. I went into the living room of Pops's house, tiptoeing through darkness and a silence punctuated only by his snores from the front room, and settled on the couch.

Anna Regent was on my mind. Seeing Woods's chubby little grandchild had got me thinking about children and the evils done to them, and I felt I needed to try to understand what might drive a person to commit an act of violence against someone so small and vulnerable.

I had made many assumptions about Anna Regent, based on our meeting in solitary and her reputation around the prison as a quiet, lethal, lumbering giant who was to be avoided at all costs. But the Anna Regent who appeared in the Google Images shots was a wholly different creature. Anna was pictured leaning on the defence table at her trial, talking to a lawyer, her strong, muscular legs showing beneath a skirt suit and her hair in a soft and stylish low bun. She was wearing make-up, eyes big and worried, her hands captured mid-gesture as she spoke. She was apparently a Bachelor of Engineering student at the time of the murder. A hot-rod enthusiast. A quick scroll through the article previews online told me Anna had killed her nephew not in some blind, sadistic rage, but because he had seen her with a bag of cash in the garage of her home and she'd snapped, trying to protect herself from being implicated in a theft.

'Theft?' I scoffed. I was frowning hard. Clicking through to an article, I saw Anna in a casino-worker's outfit. She had been a floor manager at The Star casino, a 'pit boss' as they were called in the industry, watching the tables in a sharp red blazer. 'What the . . .'

I read on through the articles covering the trial.

Over several weeks, Regent is said to have skimmed sums of cash from the casino count room and stored them in a location on the casino grounds before shifting them to her home in Seven Hills. The prosecution alleges Regent was moving these same funds from one location inside her garage to another in preparation for a family visit when her nephew, having arrived to the gathering early with his mother, stumbled upon . . .

I clicked a video, watching Anna come to life on the witness stand at her sentencing.

'What I have taken from my family in my atrocious act against little Jeremy is immeasurable. I can't hope to ever atone for it. All I can hope is that . . .'

'This isn't right.' I shook my head. The Anna Regent I was seeing on the phone screen wasn't the one I had seen in Johnsonborough – slow-talking, inarticulate, fixated, it seemed, on the senseless violence she had committed. Anna Regent, casino pit boss and cunning thief, had to be sharp enough to keep an eye on multiple gaming tables at once, on would-be thieves and scammers inside the casino. She would have had to be smart enough to work out how to skim floor counts without being noticed, move the cash safely off the premises, avoid falling under suspicion if the theft was ever discovered. The Anna Regent I was reading about hadn't killed because she was a monster. She'd killed in a panic, trying to save her skin.

It was possible Doctor Goldman had been right. That Anna was saveable. She hadn't killed out of a hideous evil desire for violence against a child, as I'd assumed. She was complex, multi-layered, a chimera. Had her performance in solitary been an act, then? Had she wanted me to underestimate her, or had she been drugged? Had prison life driven Anna, as it had many other inmates, into the arms of addiction?

I saw an article about Doctor Goldman's murder, in which Anna Regent was listed as one of the notorious inmates housed where the doctor had been killed. In the dark, I looked away from Doctor Goldman's smiling face, the shining eyes of a woman who never gave up, even on the worst people. I wanted to find who had killed her, but I was beginning to feel like I hardly had a grasp on the kind of predators who had surrounded her at the prison.

Chapter 57

'WHAT THE HELL happened?'

Pops's wail snapped me out of my sleep. I slid out of the channel I'd been sleeping in, the kitchen fitter's naked body making a wall on one side of the bed and the fluffy dogs piled on the other. I threw on some clothes and found Whitt, Tox and Pops standing around the ruined Datsun in the street behind the house.

I hadn't had a chance to look properly at the damage until now. The rear quarter of the car was substantially crunched, and long gouges travelled along the side and back of the car. The only surviving glass was the windscreen and the driver's window. Even the wing mirrors were cracked.

The three men looked at me.

'I'll fix it,' I said. 'It still drives fine. It's aesthetic damage.'

'Yeah,' Tox said. 'That'll buff right out.'

'It's half my fault.' Whitt put a hand up. 'I'll throw in for repairs.'

'Oh, good,' Pops huffed. 'And when can I expect this generous offer to come to fruition? I happen to know for a fact that neither of you is gainfully employed.'

'I'll sell my prison memoir and Whitt will hire himself out as a lap dancer at bachelorette parties,' I said.

Pops groaned at me. I patted his shoulder in consolation. The street around us was filled with the smell of bottlebrush trees, wet in the morning dew, droplets falling as lorikeets crawled in the branches across the road.

'We need to talk about your friend from the carjacking yesterday,' Tox said to me. He sat on the undamaged bonnet of Pops's car. 'He was hired to kill Tonya and Rebel.'

'Jesus,' Whitt said. 'So you've brought him in?'

'No,' Tox said. 'He didn't do it.' Tox explained the blind drop system at the Nicholl Hotel, the request for Blenk to dispose of Tonya and Rebel Woods.

'So there's no way we can tell who wrote the letter?' Whitt asked. 'What could he tell you about it? Was it handwritten? What was the tone?'

'The whole point of the blind drop is to leave the employer anonymous.' Tox shrugged. 'Blenk said the notes usually come in typed up and basic. He didn't remember much about the letter targeting Tonya and Rebel, and neither did the bartender who passed the envelope on.'

'What about the phone call asking Blenk to pull Harry aside?'

'Blenk says it was from a payphone,' Tox said. 'Guy told him so, in case they got disconnected.'

'Is that bullshit?' I asked.

'I don't know. He's not a terribly acute guy, Blenk,' Tox said. 'And all this happened a couple of days ago. He said he read the letter and discarded it, and there was only the one phone call. But he did mention it was big money both times. Too big.'

'The Silver Aces have big money to spend on hits,' Whitt said. 'We saw their drug operation out in Panuara.'

'But they didn't know I was on the case until we went out to chat to them,' I said.

'That's what we assumed,' Whitt said. 'But maybe they did and they were playing it cool. Maybe they knew exactly who we were and what it was all about before they even saw us out there.'

'Whitt and I will go talk to Gotten again. I'm sure he'll be delighted to see us,' I said. I took my phone out of my back pocket and opened my email. 'I want you to see what you can do with this.'

I texted Tox the picture of Gotten in the desert with the shovel. He looked at it on his screen.

'You want me to see what I can *do* with it?'

'Yes.'

'You got any ideas?'

'I don't,' I said. 'Be creative. And fast. If that's a picture of Gotten standing proudly over someone's grave, then I want to know where it is before he thinks about checking his sent emails folder and realises I've got the picture. His crew will move the bodies. We could be talking about Tonya and Rebel here. The picture was taken the day after Tonya was last seen.'

'We could be talking about a guy who's buried a dead dog,' Tox said. Whitt was leaning over him, looking at the picture.

'Or a guy who's just really proud of his new shovel,' Whitt said.

'Tox, would you just –'

'Meh.' He waved a dismissive arm, walked off towards his car.

Whitt and I walked towards Whitt's car, parked two down from the partially destroyed Datsun.

He slid into the driver's seat, put his hands on his thighs.

'We need to talk,' I said.

Chapter 58

WHITT WAS MOTIONLESS in his seat. We watched Pops standing in the street ahead of us, examining his ruined vehicle.

'It was a stupid move,' Whitt said.

'Probably,' I said. 'Kissing a woman while you're trapped in a bikie drug den with a dozen of them waiting behind a steel door to murder you is not the smartest way to spend your time. We probably could have used those extra three seconds for something more productive. Anything.'

'It was a moment of madness,' he said. 'I was sure I was going to die.'

'I thought so.'

We sat silently.

'It wasn't . . . *inspired* by that moment though,' Whitt ventured. 'I mean . . .'

'What?'

'I've thought of doing it before.' He stole a glance at me. 'I've thought about it for a long time. It was just . . . being in the situation we were in. I thought it might be my last chance to actually do it.'

I said nothing. His hands were in his lap, his eyes on Pops.

'So what does that mean?' I asked. There was a strange tightness in my throat.

'I don't know,' he said.

The back door of Pops's garage swung open in front of us. The sandy-haired kitchen fitter was there with his boots in hand. He looked at Pops, waved awkwardly, bent and pulled the boots on and started walking up the street towards us. He didn't see Whitt or me sitting in the car. Pops watched the man go with a cocked eyebrow and then went back to his work.

The expression on Whitt's face was unreadable. He put the keys in the car's ignition and started it up.

Chapter 59

JAX GOTTEN WAS not pleased to see us. We reached the interview room where he was housed after passing through halls, offices and walkways full of officers and detectives similarly annoyed by our presence. The bikie boss sat with his big arms folded, arms that were, like his face, patched here and there with bright white bandages. His left eye peered out from beneath a white awning made from a bandage over his brow.

'You're going to die, Harriet Blue,' Jax said.

'Wow, straight out of the gate with the death threats.' I laughed as I sat down before him.

'It's not a threat, it's a fact. You don't touch a man's bike. You don't so much as *scratch* it. I'd watch your back if I were you, because some of the bikes you trashed yesterday have been with those men's families for generations,' he said. 'They're like family members.'

'You sound more pissed about the bikes than you do about your face,' I noted.

'I am,' Gotten said.

'Priorities.' I glanced at Whitt. 'What can I say, Jax? I wish I'd had time to reverse up and give it another crack. I loved those smashy, crunchy sounds. Metal twisting. Glass shattering. And then there was the girly screaming you were all doing in the house when I flung the oil at you. The whole afternoon was music to my ears.'

'What kind of police force arranges for a victim be confronted in a locked room by their attacker?' Jax asked. 'Should I add emotional trauma to my assault charge?'

'I don't know. Should I add triple murder to your drug trafficking rap?'

'There will be no drug trafficking rap.' Jax smirked. 'The cops went out to the property and had a good look around, waving a half-arsed, judge-bought warrant. There's no evidence of any illegal activity on the premises. The evidence of your attack? That's all over the place. All over my face. I can see why a pair of balls-out psychopaths like the two of you had your badges taken away.'

'You're not putting up an assault charge, Jax,' I said. 'Let's be real. Whitt and I might be very unpopular with our fellow police right now but if you keep this up you'll have every available copper from here to Panuara breathing down your neck for the better part of six months. Officers popping by unexpectedly to see how your recovery is going. Officers pulling your car over because they haven't been able to get you on the phone. Officers visiting your friends and relatives to interview them about your emotional state.'

'I don't know anything about any murders.' Jax's words were clipped, his teeth flashing as he spoke. 'Not Wendell's, not the junkie's, not her kid's. You're barking up the wrong tree here.

All you have is a hot shot in a motel room that might not even be hers, and certainly isn't mine. This is bullshit.'

'It's not bullshit,' Whitt said. 'The hot shot from Tonya's room was chemically linked to the one that killed Wendell. That ties Wendell and Tonya together. And Joe Woods put Wendell away. That ties them together, too. Whoever killed Wendell Hamm set out to kill Tonya.'

Jax sighed. 'And what? You think that person is me?'

'You're the boss, aren't you?'

'I don't know what you're talking about.'

'Did you attempt to farm the job of killing Tonya and Rebel out to Travis Blenk?' I asked. 'It would have been a smart move. Rub out Wendell, rub out Tonya and the kid, get the job done without looking like you're a leader who hits men in his own crew, and little girls.'

'No comment.' Jax shrugged.

'If the girls are still alive, now's the time to tell us,' Whitt said. 'You're circling the drain. It's not too late for us to pull you out before you get flushed.'

Something flickered in Jax's features. I stared hard, trying to decipher it, but his eyes shifted to the door as it burst open and a man entered the room.

'Alright, that's enough,' the guy said. He was wearing a navy pinstripe suit with a bright red shirt and red satin tie. 'My client and I will need the room immediately to confer. He has nothing further to say. You and you – get out.'

I looked at Jax. He showed no recognition of the man standing over him. He was examining his blond-tipped hair and waxed eyebrows with the surprise and distaste of someone who had not seen them before. I left the room with Whitt and we stood in the hall. Across the office, a group of young detectives was eyeing us and whispering.

'He'll clam up now,' Whitt sighed. 'That's the best we'll get, and it's nothing.'

'I don't know.' I shrugged. 'I thought what just happened was rather interesting.'

'Why?'

'Because that lawyer in there works for Louis Mallally.'

Chapter 60

TOX AND OFFICER Caroline Forage leaned on a large stainless-steel bench in the Forensics lab, their faces inches away from a photograph of a man standing in the desert. Caroline's fingers were long and slender, her nails acrylic, so that when she put her hands on the tabletop the nails clicked loudly. She straightened the photograph between them.

'I think this is the clearest we'll get it,' she said.

Tox grunted his affirmation.

'So that'll be all?' she asked. 'We're square?'

'Are you kidding?' Tox said.

'Oh, come on,' she sighed. 'I rushed that baggie of heroin through for you yesterday!'

'Hey, you don't want to pay a guy back for his services, don't call me in the first place.' Tox shrugged. 'When the loser ex-boyfriend starts up again, hanging lacy panties on your doorknob, calling you sobbing like a wuss in the middle of the night, showing up at your office with puppies and following your mother to her doctor's appointments, don't call me.

I'm happy enough to spend my weekend *not* hanging guys off the sides of buildings by their ankles.'

Caroline sighed. 'I think you're exaggerating.'

'What kind of puppy was it?' Tox asked.

'A schnoodle.'

'Sounds boutique,' Tox said. 'Expensive.'

'What do you want, exactly?'

'Use the photo to tell me where he is.' Tox tapped the image.

'What?' Caroline squinted.

'Use your science.' Tox shooed his hand in the direction of her computer. 'Your special technical wizard science.'

'You're out of your mind.' Caroline looked at the photograph. 'It's a guy standing in the desert with a shovel. It could be anywhere on Earth.'

'It's not anywhere on Earth,' Tox said. 'It's a hundred kilometres, maybe two, outside Panuara, western New South Wales.'

'How do you know that?'

'Because bikies are lazy,' Tox said. 'They're creatures of habit. Old school. They don't drive around scouting out various safe kill-and-dump spots to do their dirty work in, like, say, Lebanese or Armenian mobsters do. They make a chop shop at home in their clubhouse where they do all their other dirty deeds and they bury people a reasonable drive from home. As far out of the nest as practicality calls for and no further.'

'OK.' Caroline widened her eyes. 'Good to know.'

They leaned over the photograph again.

'My *special technical wizard science*,' she groaned, 'identifies a few things we can work with.'

'I knew it would,' Tox said.

'I assume you've arrested this guy and you know how tall he is?' she said.

'He's six foot five.'

'Right.' Caroline nodded. 'So we have that. Then there's the shovel in his hands. We can do a search, try to find out what brand it is. That'll give us two measurements. Then we've got these.' She tapped the edge of the photograph. The endless blue sky behind Jax Gotten was hooked and ridged by huge steel towers disappearing into the distance. 'These are two hundred and seventy-five kilovolt transmission towers. Telstra can probably give us the exact building specifications of those, so we can determine their height and width. There'll be a map of their locations. Then there's this peak. A little hill in the distance. Probably granite. But I can check with the geography guys. We could maybe have one of our botanists look at the scrubland in the picture. Try to see if they can confirm a region.'

'I saw that,' Tox agreed.

'We can draw a perimeter two hundred kilometres around where you say this bikie clubhouse is. Once we do our calculations on the shovel, the guy, the transmission towers, we might be able to come up with a plus or minus for elevation. We can look at a geographical survey map and see if we can find some possible landscape markers that might fit the little granite rock hill within the estimated proximity of the towers.'

Tox clapped his hands together once in excitement, a noise that made Caroline wince in the quiet lab. She straightened, cracked her neck.

'Don't get excited,' she said.

'Why not?' Tox asked. 'All that stuff, everything you just said, it sounds great.'

'It's not,' Caroline said.

'It's not?'

'No.' She shook her head. 'This isn't science we're using here. It's guesswork. You're guessing it's a body you're looking for. You're guessing it's within two hundred kilometres of desert around Panuara, and not anywhere in the other millions of hectares of desert that make up the continent. Approximately a third of Australia is desert, and you're deciding to ignore all that because you have a theory that bikies are lazy.'

'I am,' Tox said. 'They are.'

'Then there's the photograph.' Caroline gestured to it. 'We don't know how accurate the camera is. What the upload of the image onto the computer and then onto the printer has done to its dimensions. We don't know how tall the photographer is, or how high he's holding the camera, or whether the six-foot-five subject was measured properly. Was it by a doctor? Or was it by some half-asleep patrol cop with a bashed-up measuring tape improperly affixed to the wall? Was he wearing boots when he was measured, and is he wearing the same boots in this picture? We don't know what time of the day this picture was taken. You're tallest in the morning when you first get out of bed, and then you can shrink up to two centimetres by the end of the day. The shovel is probably fine, if it's brand name, factory assembled, fairly new and never repaired. But then there are the transmission towers. They expand and shrink depending on the climate and so do their concrete housings.'

Tox stared at Caroline, one hand on the stainless-steel tabletop beside him, the picture lying flat, inches away. Caroline stared back at him, the silence between them punctured by the printer suddenly whirring to life, spitting out a sheet for someone else in the building.

Tox raised an eyebrow, said nothing.

Caroline sighed and snatched the picture from the table and went to her desk.

Chapter 61

PAINT COVERS ALL manner of ills. Johnsonborough prison was an enormous rambling institution of concrete and steel, which, without paint, might have resembled something too Orwellian to pass inspection, with its low ceilings and narrow walkways, lack of natural light and the pervasive smell of human bodies. Thick plasticky layers of paint were splashed over everything, the same colour sliding up from the floor to the bench I sat on, up the wall, across the ceiling and down the adjacent wall of the intake desk.

I had only been out of prison mere days, but this life seemed an eternity ago. The starkest thing was that no one was watching me. Once I had been searched and admitted to the prison, guards looked away, went back to their tasks, talked and laughed with each other. Guards look at you all the time when you're an inmate. Study your eyes, your hands, your walk. The prison inmate is always hiding something, planning something. I felt like an imposter, a terrorist wandering through an airport with a bomb strapped to their chest.

The front-of-house staff weren't familiar enough with me to know I had once lived here.

I sat with the families waiting for visitation time, watching toddlers playing with Lego on the dirty floor and someone's elderly mother sleeping open-mouthed in the corner of the room. I stood now and then to read the posters about sexual assault and drug trafficking in the prison.

The duty officer came in and read off the list of visitor names. Everyone in the room stood. My name was not read out. The officer lolled her head as she looked at me at the back of the line. I realised she was the officer with the barbed wire tattoo and short white hair who had rapped my knuckles in solitary. Steeler.

'Wait there, Blue,' she said as the visitors filed past her. 'The warden wants to see you.'

'I don't care what the hell he wants. I'm here to visit Dolly Quaddich. I'm perfectly within my rights to –'

Steeler left and I sat back down on the bench. For three hours I waited, getting hungry, receiving nothing but hostile glances from behind the desk when I tried to enquire about what was happening. I drank a Coke from the vending machine, then bought two big chocolate chip cookies. By the time the guard came back I was $14 down, halfway through a tube of Mentos and feeling queasy.

I was led to the warden's office. He was a surprisingly young man, in his thirties at most, in a snappy suit. Bald, glasses with plastic frames. The desk was bare but for a keyboard, a computer monitor and a mug with a big red Porsche logo on it.

'Dolly Quaddich,' I said, sitting in the chair before him.

'Detective Blue, good morning.' He stood from his big leather desk chair and offered me his hand. 'It's good to have you back in the facility, certainly in a different capacity to when we saw you last.'

'When you saw me last?' I said. 'You didn't see me at all. I've never laid eyes on you in my life, Mr . . .' I looked at his gold-coloured name plate. 'Parkinson. You know, most wardens like to take a tour of the facility every now and then, if not to convince the officers they're not a puffed-up pencil-pusher then to give the inmates a fair shot at flinging a cup of urine at them.'

'It used to be that way, back in the old days,' Parkinson said. 'But most of what I do at this facility is personnel management, believe it or not. It's the officers who run the place. I'm just here to make sure they're happy and they have everything they need to succeed.'

'Uh-huh.' I rolled my eyes.

'And I can see everything perfectly well from here.' He turned the computer monitor on the desktop towards me. It was split into a dozen small coloured screens. I saw the yard, a row of cells, some classrooms.

'It was from this screen that I watched you assault Officer Hugh Ridgen and set fire to classroom 5A,' he said.

'Oh, right. Well, you must have seen Ridgen attempt to sexually assault an inmate in that room, then,' I replied.

'The camera was malfunctioning and didn't capture Officer Ridgen, who I believe was supervising you and Inmate Chambers.' Warden Parkinson smiled. 'It was proper procedure for Ridgen to separate you and Chambers, both notoriously violent inmates, from the rest of the prison population if he felt you might –'

'I'm bored,' I interrupted. 'Can I see Dolly now?'

'Well, see, Inmate Blue. Sorry, *Detective* Blue. That's why I've brought you here. The prison is a private facility. You can think of it like a cafe. Members of the public come in and go out at certain designated times. And during those times, I – the operator – can refuse anyone entry, for any reason I see fit.'

'You're not going to let me see her?' I gripped the arms of my chair. 'Why?'

'Well, like a cafe owner,' Parkinson said, 'I don't have to state my reasons for refusal of entry. But I will, in this case. While you were incarcerated here, you demonstrated a lack of concern for the welfare and safety of my staff and a willingness to treat our physical resources destructively. The damage you caused to classroom 5A has run into tens of thousands of dollars, and allowing you to return to the facility would surely be a violation of our insurance policies. I can't, in good conscience, subject my staff or my facility to that behaviour again.'

I stared at him. He stared right back, unblinking, a cyborg in a suit.

'What's happened to Dolly?' I asked. 'You won't let me see her because the guards have done something to her. Is she OK?'

Parkinson clasped his hands together, patiently, on the desk.

'If anything has happened to her . . .' I said carefully.

'Inmate Quaddich was moved to the infirmary last night,' he said. 'She's under suicide watch.'

'She should have been under suicide watch from the beginning.' I felt my jaw click hard as my muscles locked. 'What happened to her? Did one of your guards string her up?'

'Detective Blue.' Parkinson opened his hands. 'I've been more than generous with my time here today. But you know

I've got a big job to do. Hundreds of inmates, dozens of staff. I can't sit here and shoot the breeze all day, no matter how enjoyable that might be.'

He stood and gestured to the door. Officer Steeler was waiting for me. I walked ahead of her back down the stairs, out of the visitation intake entrance and into the long diamond-wire tunnel that led to the gates.

I stopped walking and turned around. She grabbed the radio on her shoulder in preparation to call for backup.

'Problem?' she asked me.

'Yeah,' I said. 'I want to get the word out among Johnson-borough staff. If anything else happens to Dolly Quaddich they'll have to deal with me.'

'You really like your threats, don't you, Harry?' Steeler asked. 'You're just full of them. Thing is, you're out there, and we're in here, and so is Dolly. There's nothing you can do to us. Your words are empty.'

'You think so, huh?'

'I do,' she said. 'Now run along. As you would know, it's almost lock-up time. I've got stuff to do.'

I looked her hard in the eye and then at her name badge one last time before I left. Steeler. I added it to a mental list as I walked back towards the gates, a list that was long and that I had been adding names to for as long as I could remember.

Chapter 62

A HAND LANDED on Chloe Bozer's shoulder, hard and sudden, making her yelp with fright in the hallway outside the locker room. Tox Barnes gave a husky laugh that rippled off the walls of the basement level of the hospital.

'Have I told you lately that I hate you?' Chloe shrugged her backpack back on where it had slipped to her elbow in shock. 'You're not allowed to wander around in the staff area.'

'Staff area, public area.' Tox shrugged. 'This whole place feels like home to me. Are you just starting your shift?'

'I'm just finishing. I've been on the floor eighteen hours.' She swiped at a lock of sweaty hair. 'But you knew that. That's why you're here.'

'I'm here to tell you that the arsenic thing might be key to finding that missing mother and her kid,' Tox said. They walked together slowly towards the lifts. 'Wendell Hamm's death might be linked. I'd like to get a copy of the rest of the files on his death. Everything you have, in case we need it for trial. Things tend to disappear as soon as you need them.'

'Don't tell me they've found the girl and her daughter poisoned with arsenic,' Chloe said.

'No. It's complicated. Let me tell you all about it down at Jack's.' He punched the lift button, and before Chloe could protest the doors opened and her emergency-room supervisor appeared.

'Oh,' the man said. 'Chloe. Just the woman I was looking for. Who's this?'

'A friend,' Tox said confidently.

'That's a bit of a stretch,' Chloe murmured.

'Director wants to see you, Chloe.'

'What?' Chloe felt a wave of exhaustion roll over her. 'Right now?'

'Right now.' The supervisor held the door open for her.

'What's it about?'

'I've been advised to bring you upstairs. That's it.'

'I'll go.' Tox got into the lift with her. 'I'll catch up with you –'

'You can come along too.' The supervisor looked Tox up and down with a superior gaze. His lip twitched. 'In fact it might be best if you did.'

Chapter 63

THEY RODE TO level eight of the hospital in silence. The supervisor walked ahead of them, his shoes clacking on the linoleum. Chloe didn't even notice Tox take the strap of her backpack and slide it off her shoulder. The relief when the weight lifted was minimal. Dread was pounding like a hammer at the back of her skull.

'This must be about the Woods records,' she whispered. 'I'll be sacked. You can't give out medical documents like that without approval.'

'I'll take the rap,' Tox said. 'It was my fault. I pressured you.'

'It wouldn't have mattered if you'd held me at gunpoint. It's protocol.'

'Fuck their protocol.'

Chloe heaved a sigh. She was already thinking about disciplinary hearings, job applications. Maybe Prince of Wales had an opening. She could try Concord Hospital, though the commute would be a nightmare.

'If the guy tries to sack you I'll put his head in a bucket of concrete,' Tox said.

'Oh yeah, that'll help matters.'

She prepared to turn into Director Gallagher's office when the supervisor carried on walking ahead of them.

'He's in the boardroom,' he said, gesturing up the hall.

'This is worse than I thought,' Chloe whispered.

Chapter 64

THE SUPERVISOR HELD the door open for them and Tox and Chloe walked ahead into the huge, brightly lit room.

'Surprise!'

The word rose in a roar from twenty or more people. Chloe looked behind her at Tox for some sign of collusion, but he seemed as confused as she was. Everyone was there – Director Gallagher, all of the section heads, some of the emergency-room night crew and a smattering of day nurses. The long boardroom table was cluttered with plates of food, cakes and stacks of paper cups. Chloe's supervisor clapped like the rest of them, a room full of faces turned towards her, beaming.

'Oh, no way.' Chloe spied the little display at the head of the table, a certificate and trophy. 'Oh, no. It can't be me.'

'It's you.' Director Gallagher, a huge pot-bellied man in a salmon-pink shirt, came and shook Chloe's hand so that her whole arm wobbled. 'Well done, Chloe. Very well done.'

'What the hell is this?' Tox asked through the commotion around them. 'Is it your birthday or something?'

'No, no, no.' Chloe already felt her cheeks aching with a wide smile of pride. 'A few months ago the hospital nominated me for an award. It's an industry thing. The Royal Australian College of Surgeons. I . . . I must have won. I can't believe –'

She was swept away into the hugs and congratulations of her colleagues. Into the sudden, terrifying limelight as everyone turned to her and the director gave a little impromptu speech. A cup of wine was thrust into her hand, and more people slid into the crowded room, dashing past on their way home or before they started their shifts. Chloe examined the certificate in the light of the boardroom. She held the trophy and thanked everyone and blathered on about her surprise. The exhaustion of the day's shift, the relief that the director hadn't been about to strip her job away from her, the sizzling joy of seeing her name carved in the trophy swept her up so that when she finally remembered Tox Barnes, she found that at some time during the celebrations he'd slipped away.

Chapter 65

SHE DISCOVERED HIM sitting at the bar at his usual spot, under a vintage candelabra adorned with little green lamp-shades. He was tapping an unlit cigarette on the felt bar runner, reading his phone as though he'd never left. The same bartender from her first visit nodded at her and reached for a bottle of wine from the shelf.

'What are you doing here?' Tox asked. 'You should be out celebrating.'

'I'll celebrate,' she said. 'Right now I've got about half an hour left in these shoes before my feet fall off. I'm saving the party for when I can enjoy it properly.'

She set the trophy on the bar in front of them. It was white marble, cylindrical with a wide, flat base, like an upside-down torch. In gold lettering, etched into the stone, was her name and award.

'Excellence in Clinical Practice,' Tox read. 'So that's it? They just give it to you? There's no ceremony or anything?'

'Oh, yes, there will be a big awards night,' Chloe said. 'A banquet, where all the other awards are presented.'

'What?' Tox frowned. 'So why did they spoil it by telling you early that you've won? Why not tell you on the big night so you can be all surprised and make a gushy speech?'

'Well, they want to make sure you go to the banquet, I guess,' Chloe said. 'Surgeons are busy people. When we're not working we're sleeping, and those banquets are long and full of boring speeches.'

They both looked at the trophy in appreciative silence.

'It's a nice trophy,' she said. 'It looks maybe a little bit . . . ah . . .'

'Like a tombstone?' Tox asked.

'I was going to say . . .' Chloe gripped the smooth stone cylinder, slid her hand up and down its shaft.

'Oh my God.' Tox shook his head. She rocked back in her chair, laughing. She laughed so hard people at the low tables at the back of the room looked over in their direction.

'I thought it looked familiar,' Tox said, gripping its girth.

Chloe giggled. 'I guess it was probably designed by a man, for a man. I'm only the second woman ever to have won it.'

'Well, don't win it next year,' he said.

'Why not?'

'If you win two years in a row they give you a big set of stone balls that attach to the bottom of it.'

He watched her laughing, handed her a napkin when tears started leaking from the corners of her eyes. He seemed content, sitting looking at her, one elbow resting on the bar. They were almost like two people just enjoying each other's company, Chloe thought. Two people who had just met, whose lives weren't inescapably and terribly tangled. For a moment, in the warmth and quiet of the bar, she was able to forget completely about what had happened to link them many decades earlier.

'Fresh air,' he said, taking his cigarette packet from the bar top. 'Want to come?'

In the street he tucked the cigarettes away and instead drew her to him. They held each other and kissed in the dark.

Chapter 66

THE LITTLE DOGS mobbed me when I arrived home. Pops was in the kitchen, lit by the glow of the range hood over a big pot of what smelled like very good Irish stew. He was bopping along to jazz as much as his bad knees would allow, pointing the wooden spoon at me as I appeared in the kitchen like Frank Sinatra singling out a fan in the casino lounge between verses.

'It's kind of nice having someone come home at dinnertime,' Pops said. 'I can say things like "How was your day?" and "Can I pour you a drink?"'

'You can talk to the dogs,' I said.

'Yes, but then all I get to say are things like "Stop licking me" and "Don't put your nose there."'

'Some men would pay anything to spend their whole day saying things like that,' I said. 'But in any case, the answers to your original questions are "Crap" and "Yes".' I slumped into one of the chairs at the kitchen table. He poured me a glass of wine. 'They've got Dolly on the rocks.'

I explained the warden's refusal to let me into the prison. Pops pushed open the laptop that was sitting on the table beside me and clicked on a video file.

'It gets worse,' he said. 'I got this from the contact I was telling you about.'

I watched. It took a moment to realise what I was seeing. The video was a black-and-white view of the outside of Doctor Goldman's surgery, a slice of door and wall before a stretch of hallway and a corner. As the video progressed I saw Goldman's elbow come into view through the glass window in her door, pointed downwards like she was holding something to her ear. The phone call. She opened the door of the surgery room and walked out, disappeared around the corner.

She didn't lock the door behind her as Dolly had said she did.

As I watched, Dolly appeared, limping on her twisted ankle. She turned and followed Doctor Goldman around the corner, a lean black object gripped in her fist.

Chapter 67

I WATCHED THE first half of the video seven times without speaking. Pops stirred the stew. He was no longer dancing.

'She said she stayed down on the floor the whole time,' I said.

'Yeah.'

'She said Goldman locked her in.'

'She did.'

'Both of those are lies,' I said.

'All is not lost.' Pops gestured to the laptop. 'Watch the second half of the video.'

I watched. Goldman reappeared on the screen, staggering, smearing a bloody handprint on the wall that was a dark grey in the video. Dolly was with her, holding her up, an arm around her back and a hand clutched with Goldman's hand over the wound in her neck. Goldman collapsed on the floor in the doorway of the surgery, dragging Dolly down with her. The two bloodied women held each other as Goldman kicked and shivered and died.

I put my head in my hands.

'She's helping the doctor,' Pops said. 'That's plain as day on the tape. Why stab a woman and then help her get to safety? Hold her while she dies? That doesn't make sense.'

'Why lie about leaving the room if all she did was go and help Goldman?'

Pops shrugged.

'Are there any other angles of it?' I asked. 'Something looking down the hall where the attack occurred?'

'Nope,' Pops said. 'That would be too easy. The camera with the perfect angle down the hall beside the doctor's rooms was malfunctioning.'

'Of course it was,' I sneered. I held my head, burning with frustration. 'Of *course* it was!'

'It doesn't look good, the tape,' Pops said. 'Dolly said she didn't follow the doctor out into the hall, and she clearly did. If she's told the prison staff this, then she's lied in an official statement. And she's carrying something in her hand. Gripped in a fist. It's long and thin, whatever it is, and it's gone by the time she comes back. I'm seeing if we can have the tape cleaned up, of course.'

I watched the video five more times. It was a sequence only one minute and forty-five seconds long. By the time I was done Pops was slipping slabs of garlic bread under the oven grill.

'She's in the infirmary now,' I said. 'They pulled her out of ad seg for a supposed suicide attempt. She'll be strapped to a bed in the hospital wing.'

'So?' Pops said.

'So if we want to call her, the prison would be expecting us to phone the ad seg line,' I said. 'Inmates can only receive calls in the prison in two areas: the general-population phone bank, and the ad-seg phone bank. If I can get Dolly on the phone in the infirmary, whatever we say won't be recorded.'

'Will they even transfer an outside call to the infirmary?'

'They don't have to. I know all the extensions.' I smiled.

'But what are you going to say? They're not going to give her the phone for a quick chitchat,' Pops said.

'Yeah,' I said. 'They're not going to let *Harriet Blue* call.'

Chapter 68

THE PHONE RANG. I slipped off my shoes and wriggled my toes underneath the belly of one of the dogs. Pops was staring at me, our bowls of stew and plates of garlic bread steaming on the table before us.

'This isn't going to work,' he said.

I held a finger to my lips. He sighed and picked up his spoon.

'Infirmary.' A male voice. 'Officer Darender.'

'My name is Adriana McKinty, QC,' I said, glancing at the bookshelf near the entrance to Pops's kitchen and snatching an author's name. 'I'm calling to speak to an inmate named Dolly Quaddich.'

There was a moment of silence while Officer Darender assessed the situation.

'I . . . uh . . . You've got the wrong line, Ms McKinty. This is the prison infirmary, and you've called well outside the permitted hours for –'

'Yes, I realise it's late,' I said. 'I've just been patched through from the switchboard. I've got approval from the warden to speak with my client. It's regarding a matter of some legal urgency. I need verbal affirmation from Ms Quaddich to release some documents pertinent to her case and that has to occur within the next hour.'

'The warden?' Officer Darender baulked. 'But the warden went home at five.'

'Officer Darender.' I sharpened my tone. 'I'd be happy to describe in excruciating detail the various leaps and bounds I've made trying to get in contact with my client tonight, a veritable jurisdictional and administrative gauntlet that I've not experienced in all my years at the bar. But the clock is ticking. I'm sure you realise that not only is restricting my client's access to legal counsel a breach of professional conduct by Johnsonborough staff, but if I can't speak with my client in the next –'

'Jesus, just hang on, will you?' Officer Darender sighed. We waited. Pops was smiling over his stew, shaking his head.

'Hello?' a familiar voice said.

'Dolly, it's Harry,' I said. 'Don't say anything. I'm pretending to be your lawyer so they'll let us talk.'

There was silence on the line.

'Is the officer listening in?' I asked.

'No, he walked away,' Dolly said.

'Good,' I said. 'What are you doing in the infirmary?'

'I can't talk about that,' Dolly said. 'There was a fight, that's all. In my cell.'

'With other inmates or with the guards?'

'The guards,' she said.

'That's not a fight, Dolly. That's a beating.' I could hear the rage in my own voice. I gripped the edge of the table and tried to breathe evenly. 'Listen, Doll, we need to get you out of there. You're not safe. We don't have much time to talk, so listen up, OK? I need to know what you saw the day Doctor Goldman was stabbed. I know you followed her out of the medical room and around the corner into the hall. Did you see who attacked her?'

'No,' Dolly said. 'I didn't see anyone else. Just her.'

'Why did you tell my friend Trevor Morris that you'd stayed in the doctor's room when the attack happened?'

'Huh?'

'You said you lay down at the sound of the alarm. But you didn't. You followed the doctor out not long after she left.'

'I don't know, Harry.' Dolly's voice was hoarse with tears. 'I was so scared. It was bad stuff, man. It was so bad. I've never seen anything like that before. I'm from the country, you know? We're, like, simple kind of people. You don't get stabbings and that sort of thing out there.'

'You had something in your hand when you left the medical room.'

Dolly said nothing.

'Do you remember what it was?'

'The guard's on his way back, Harry.'

'Listen to me,' I said. 'I want you to get yourself into the doctor's room tomorrow night. Seven o'clock. That way you'll get the night doctor.'

'What?'

'Tell the guards you're sick or something. You've got sharp pains in your belly. I don't know. Just get into the surgery and I'll talk to you there.'

'But how can you –'

'Just do it, Dolly,' I said. 'Seven o'clock.'

There was a rattle, a shuffling sound. I heard the officer telling Dolly her time was up, and the line went dead.

Chapter 69

I COULD STOP this now, she thought.

The thought came even as they rode the lift in her building together, as her hands held him against the stainless-steel wall, his hands gripping her hips, their bodies locked together. His breath was sweet from the Scotch and ashy from the cigarettes, foreign and yet strangely familiar, a body she had known under different circumstances, scared and helpless and wounded, now furious and forceful with passion. Chloe had to drag herself away to get to the door, drunk on the wine in the boardroom and at Jangling Jack's, and dizzy with excitement. She dropped her keys at the foot of the door, laughing as she scooped them up. They didn't turn the lights on, staggered over a stack of library books in the hall, fell onto the couch together.

I should stop this now, she thought.

He dragged her into his lap, ripped her shirt open and shoved it off. He popped her bra clip so quickly she was drawn out of the spell by it, by how perfectly he executed the manoeuvre, because of course this was what he did – he seduced nurses and filled the hospital hallways with big-breasted callgirls worrying after him, turned up wherever and whenever he liked because he could charm women into letting him through doorways and into restricted areas. She was suddenly strangely angry, but then she was laughing again because he had scooped her off his lap and growled like a caveman and carried her in the dark towards her bedroom, somehow knowing exactly where it was.

Chloe thought about putting a stop to it all even as he stood above her in the dark, pulling his T-shirt over his head, slices of light from the blinds illuminating the scars and tattoos she had already seen and a face she'd first looked at when she was a little girl.

I've got to stop this, she thought, even as she pulled him to her and wrapped her legs around his, locking him to her, their breaths and rhythms matching in the darkness.

Not him, she thought. *Anyone but him.*

Chapter 70

WHITT WAS ABOUT to get out of his car when the side gate of the Mallally house opened across the street and Shania stormed out of it. He paused, then started his car and followed the BMW down the hill and into Bondi. She parked at an askew angle and sat in the car for a long time outside a little hole-in-the-wall bar. He got out and waited in the shadows by the window of the sunglasses store next door, becoming increasingly horrified by the prices on display, until eventually he went to her car window and tapped gently.

'Oh God!' she squealed.

'I'm sorry!' Whitt held his hands up. Even in the dark of the car he could see her mascara was running, see the tension in her throat as she suppressed sobs. 'I'm Detective Whittacker. Remember me?'

Shania Mallally held the steering wheel for a long moment, staring straight ahead, her body now and then shuddering with tears. She got out of the car and stood with him, the sound of the roaring ocean reaching them from a few streets over.

'I can't – do this – right now,' she cried like a child, unable to catch her breath. 'I – just –'

'Who told you?' Whitt asked. He chanced putting his hands on her arms, giving them a squeeze.

'One of – the – other detectives.' She glanced around, probably wary of people she knew in the streets. 'Spader. He just – He just – He just –'

'He just came out with it,' Whitt said. 'Laid it on you.'

Shania nodded.

'Yeah, he's not really the empathetic type.' Whitt rubbed the woman's arms. 'But it would have been a real shock either way, I guess.' She fell against his chest unexpectedly and he held her. As he did so he wondered if she was hiding her face from a young couple who passed, the tall bearded man giving Whitt a look of solidarity as he went.

Inside the bar he sat rigidly, refusing to look at the wine list at his elbow while she explained it all. She didn't even notice when he didn't order himself anything, gulping her martini like medicine between sobs. They were the only people there, and the bartender made himself scarce.

'I've seen her,' Shania Mallally said. 'The girl. He brought her around the house *while I was there*. He said she was a client. They had meetings. I suppose she was looking around the place and imagining herself moving in. Sunbaking in the pool area. Making lunch for the girls and sending them off to school. He might have been fucking her in the upstairs office while I watched television downstairs. Oh, Christ.' She wiped at her eyes. 'Detective Spader wanted to know if Louis had a second phone that he'd used specifically for the affair. As if I'd know!'

'A second phone is pretty common, for affairs,' Whitt said. He was finding himself scratching around for something comforting to say to Shania. 'The police wouldn't need the handset exactly. Just the number.'

'Listen to you,' Shania sniffed. 'Looking for clues. You're trying to find her too. She's probably shacked up with some other wealthy lawyer. Found a bigger goldmine to dig.'

Whitt pursed his lips. The bartender was watching them from the other end of the bar, polishing glasses, intrigued by Shania's harsh tone.

'My understanding is that this girl is a long-term drug addict. That she has a baby she frequently loses custody of.'

'That's right,' Whitt said.

'Addicts.' Shania sniffed, wiped her eyes again. 'They're weak people. Louis used to deal with them early in his career. They never really straighten out.'

Whitt shifted uncomfortably in his chair, slid the wine list away from him down the bar. 'I think you might be stereotyping, Mrs Mallally.'

'It is true that the current lead on her whereabouts is bikies from the Outback? I mean, are you serious?'

Whitt could smell the martini on her breath. There was a siren in his head, ringing louder and louder as the minutes passed, wailing his need for a drink.

'I've barely seen him in weeks, you know.' Shania drained her martini. 'I thought it was this huge case tying him up. Now I know the truth.' She gave a rueful laugh.

'The corruption thing?' Whitt grasped at anything that might distract her from the affair. 'I've seen some of it on the news.'

'It'll be his biggest-paying defence to date. It was supposed to change everything. I suppose it will. I'll fight for half of whatever he gains from it in the divorce.'

She explained the case. The company was called VISKO, an Australian-grown security firm that had begun its life providing on-site security to shipping warehouses and marinas around Sydney Harbour. VISKO's CEO, a petite, well-dressed up-and-comer named Antonio Santarelli, was the Aussie migrant dream realised – he'd worked in his father's shoe shop to put himself through business school. Through his twenties and into his thirties, Santarelli had grown VISKO security from a fifty-man team to a fifteen-thousand-man empire that watched over warehouses, shopping centres, universities, stadiums and small airports all over Australia.

'So what's Santarelli charged with?'

Shania held up a finger, paused before she recited. '*Section 249B(1) of the Crimes Act prohibits an agent from corruptly offering or receiving any benefit from another person as an inducement, a reward, or on account of doing or not doing something, or showing or not showing any favour to any person in relation to the affairs or business of the agent's principal.*'

She broke into laughter. 'Are you impressed?' Shania slapped Whitt's knee. 'This is my second martini, you know.'

'Actually I believe it's your third.'

'I was in law school but I dropped out.' She sipped her drink. 'That's where Louis and I met.'

'So Santarelli paid a bribe?' Whitt asked.

'Sydney Airport was due to renew its security licence with a company called Wake Services. It was a big, big contract. All Australia's other airports tend to follow Sydney with their food and cleaning and security services. We're talking tens of thousands of jobs, specialist teams on the metal detectors and the baggage handling and parking and the tarmac. Everything. Santarelli wanted the job, so he paid a guy, the CEO of the airport. Drew Bortfield, I think his name was. Weird name, Bortfield.' Shania was growing bored, her mind wandering, her gaze becoming sadder as she looked at her empty glass. 'Anyway, Bortford got caught by the anti-corruption squad. He flipped on Santarelli. Bort*field*, I mean.'

'Something like that could take down Santarelli's whole business,' Whitt mused. 'It would be a big case. Your husband's probably looking at millions of dollars in legal fees.'

'Yes. What a waste.' Shania smoothed her hair back and looked Whitt right in the eyes. 'All that money, and he'll blow it on flowers and jewellery and nice cars for his little junkie girlfriend. She'll probably snort the whole lot up her nose, if she's not dead already.'

'OK.' Whitt stood. 'I think it's home time for you, Mrs Mallally.'

'No way.' She stood with him, tried to grip the hand that was passing his credit card over the bar. 'We're not going home. You're coming with me. I know the night manager at the Park Hyatt. We could get a cab . . .?'

'I'm driving you back to your house and seeing you to the door, Mrs Mallally.' Whitt put an arm around her, guided her to the exit of the bar.

'What the hell's the matter with you?' She shrugged his arm off. 'I'm offering myself to you. Don't you think I'm beautiful?'

'You certainly are,' he said.

Shania stopped him in the street just before they reached his car. Her eyes were big and wet again. 'Don't tell me. *Your heart belongs to another*, or some bullshit like that?'

'You could say that, I guess.' Whitt smiled.

Chapter 71

SOME PARTS OF the Australian desert are just sand, miles and miles of it, red and peaked and valleyed by wind like the Sahara. Someone told me once that there are even herds of feral camels out there in the vast empty middle, making their strange, wide tracks across the landscape. But the desert I stood in with Whitt the next morning was not empty. It was crawling with life. From where we stood I could see some kind of sandy lizard flattened on a rock in the sunshine, a collection of red ants working on a mound, and dust-coloured rabbits on the faraway rise hopping in and out of bushes that had razor-pointed edges. The land fell gently away from us, rocky and spiky and treacherous, and then rose to a small hill. I could hear the nearest transmission tower humming. It was strangely loud. I wondered if I was soaking up cancerous rays both from the tower and from the boiling sun on the back of my neck.

Tox Barnes was standing on what remained of the searing blacktop, holding the photograph of Jax Gotten against the skyline like a surveyor.

'This can't be it,' I said.

'Why not?' he asked. 'Looks like it to me.' He came over and showed me the photograph again, pointed to the little hill in the distance.

'If this was a bikie body-dumping ground, the Silver Aces crew would be crawling all over it, trying to move their evidence,' I said. 'Look at our tyre tracks. There's an inch of dust on the plain. No one's been out here in weeks.'

'If they have a body-dumping ground at all,' Whitt chipped in.

'Jax Gotten must know by now that I've got a copy of that photo from his computer,' I said. 'He'd have thought to check his sent items. He's not going to let us come and discover whatever it is that he's buried out here.'

'He may not know yet,' Tox said. 'And if he does know, he might figure there's no way for us to identify where the site is.'

I folded my arms, not convinced.

'The bikies wouldn't be crawling all over it,' Tox continued, sitting on the hood of Whitt's car. 'They'd be taking care to stay as far away as possible. Nigel's team is tracking them, and they'd know that. They're going to be on their best behaviour, and that means staying away from their body dump sites.'

'Didn't you say that the woman in the Forensics lab said it's a million to one you can match that image to an actual spot on the planet?' Whitt asked. 'With all the variables?'

'She did.' Tox nodded. 'But I think we're onto something. I can feel it.'

'You can feel it?'

'Yep,' he said.

'How is Tox Barnes the most optimistic one of us out here today?' I asked Whitt. In the distance, a Forensics van and a canine-unit truck were creating a dust cloud as they headed towards us.

'He's in a good mood. He's had an appointment with Doctor *Luuurve*,' Whitt said.

'Oh, yes.' I grinned at Tox. 'He's juiced up on her sweet, sweet medicine.'

'Diagnosis: extreme infatuation,' Whitt said.

'Prescription: vigorous bed rest,' I said.

Tox didn't bite. He was holding the photo up to the horizon again.

A crew of Forensics officers and a dog handler assembled at the side of the road, unhappy faces, eyes downturned to their work. There was an expected muttering of dissent as the men from the Forensics van unloaded bags and boxes of equipment on the dirt road and the dog handler wrestled a crate with a beagle in it down from the back of her car.

'I thought beagles were drug dogs,' I said, trying to make conversation. It was clear to me from the team's faces that they knew who I was and didn't want to work with a suspended cop who should rightfully have been in jail. The presence of Tox Barnes, the New South Wales Police's favourite punching bag, wouldn't have helped matters. But I've always found that a hard job is best started with a cheerful attitude, even if it eventually must dissolve into misery and spite. The dog handler gave me a heavy, bored sigh as she shut up her truck.

'Any breed of dog can be a cadaver dog. Training and attitude, that's all there is to it.'

'Are we really working off a photo?' one of the Forensics guys said. 'We heard Caroline at the Surry Hills lab basically had to throw a dart at a map to get Barnes off her case.'

'This is a waste of time,' another said, wiping sweat off his neck with the collar of his shirt. 'If I get heat stroke I'm claiming compo.'

'Let's send the dog out first.' Tox walked over to the dog handler. 'We'll do a grid, check off this area. There are a couple of other spots along the line of transmission towers that Caroline said we should search. Right elevation, right ground conditions. Shouldn't take until nightfall to get it all completed.'

I looked at my watch. It was nine in the morning. It was going to be a hellish day in the heat. The dog handler bent and unlocked the dog's crate, and the beagle trotted out importantly, did a lap around Tox's ankles, tail wagging. We watched it walk off the dirt road to the edge of the desert, maybe a metre into the wilds and no more.

Then it sat, hard and fast, like a little soldier snapping to attention. Butt slammed on the ground. Chest out, head up, tail dead still.

The dog handler looked bemused. She glanced at the sprawling desert before us, collecting a dog leash in a spool in her hand.

'Alright, Sprocket. Let's go. Time for work.' She pointed at her boots. 'Come, Sprocket.'

The dog sat, facing the desert. It turned its head and looked over its shoulder at her. The men and women around me waited in silence.

'Come, Sprocket,' the handler said again, tapping the heel of one of her boots against the toe of the other. The dog looked at her.

'What's he doing?' Tox asked.

'He's . . .' The handler squinted at the horizon, shielded her eyes from the glare. 'Well, he's alerting. He's supposed to sit like that when he hits on remains. But I haven't even started the search yet. I haven't even told him to start looking.'

The little dog sat and stared at the landscape ahead of it. We all watched it.

In time, Tox picked up a shovel that had been leaning against his Monaro and walked off the road into the desert.

Chapter 72

MY PHONE RANG at midday. I had just got into Whitt's car and turned the engine on, blowing dust and sand off my clothes as I jacked the air conditioning up to maximum. My clothes were damp with sweat. Everyone's were. We had been working tirelessly in the desert sun for hours, each of us infected with an energy and determination that defies personal grudges and dark histories and the threat of heat stroke. Outside the car window, the Forensics team were sticking flags in the sand, gesturing towards their truck, arguing about what to do when they ran out of flags.

'Spader,' I said. 'What do you want?'

'I'm hearing things about a gravesite,' Nigel said.

'You heard right. We've called in more resources,' I said. 'Tox had a hunch about a photograph we took off Jax Gotten. We came out here looking for Tonya and Rebel's graves, maybe. Instead we've found a mass grave. There are . . .' I looked out the window, shook my head. 'There are so many bodies out here. Maybe a dozen so far. All skeletal. Tox walked into the desert and stuck a shovel in the ground and turned up a radial bone, first fucking shot. I've never seen anything like it.'

'Explains why Gotten has bolted,' Nigel said.

'He's *what*?'

'He's bolted.' Nigel sounded depressed. 'We've got a manhunt on here.'

'Your team was supposed to –'

'Don't start,' he said. 'Just don't.'

'Well, don't let Louis Mallally bolt, will you?' I snapped. 'He's not off the hook yet. There's a reason we can't find a second phone. And one of Mallally's associate lawyers was defending –'

'Just shut up, Blue,' Nigel said. I opened my mouth to blast him but he cut over me. 'Get in your car and come here. I'm going to text you an address.'

'I can't go there. I've got a mass gravesite. Did you not hear me?'

'Uh-huh.' He sounded distant. 'Just leave Tox and Whitt there and get to where I'm telling you to go, *right now*.'

'You sound weird,' I said. 'What's wrong with you?' I was starting to feel a strange shakiness creeping up from my fingers into my arms. This was the first conversation I'd had with Nigel Spader, perhaps in my entire career, in which he hadn't tried to shoot me down me with some pathetic insult.

'They found Tonya,' was all he said.

Chapter 73

I DROVE LIKE an insane person, veering onto the wrong side of the road to overtake trucks on the highway with my teeth gritted, heading for a marker on a map in the Western Sydney suburb of Toongabbie. As I passed through a wide, tall gate heading towards boom gates and a weigh station, I read a sign that said *Suez Waste Management*. The smell coming through the car's air conditioning was suddenly sour and sweet, the familiar reek of garbage I'd thankfully encountered only a few times in my career.

I'd trawled waste disposal sites for evidence before. Knives, photographs, guns, handbags thrown into city skips following rapes and murders. I prayed as I drove through the boom gates and parked between two police cruisers that I'd be looking for such an item again. But as Nigel Spader spotted me from a huddle near one of the large sorting buildings, I knew from his face what was happening. He was wearing gloves and forensic booties. He peeled the gloves off, pocketed them and lit a cigarette on his way to greet me at the car. I watched him approach in the rear-view mirror, unable to move, hoping somehow that if I stayed where I was the awful truth might stay where it was too, in the unknown future.

I popped open my door and he leaned on the frame. I looked at him hopefully. He shook his head.

'The baby?' I asked.

'We're still searching.'

Chapter 74

A LIGHT RAIN started falling, misting, swirling in by Nigel's breath. There were flecks of shredded paper in the mud everywhere under my boots, like fallen snow, little letters and numbers discernible on some of the tiny pieces. I got out of the car, threw my phone back on the seat. My shocked brain's hyper focus on tiny details and the cool, cloudy sky in contrast to the searing heat I'd been in only hours ago made the whole situation seem unreal. The men standing by the corner of the sorting building were actors in a play waiting for me to join them. *Harriet Blue enters stage right.* They looked at me sadly, the usual hatred gone. Death does that. Makes everyone equal.

'Does he know?' I asked.

'He's been in a meeting for the past three hours,' Nigel said. 'We didn't want to disturb him. Needed time to figure out who'd be the best person to tell him. No one wanted to do it.'

'I wouldn't want to do it,' one of the guys said. He shook his head. 'No way in the world.'

'We got his brother,' Nigel said. 'He told him. They're on their way out here now.'

'*Here?*' I looked around. 'He can't come here. This is . . . No. What condition is she in?'

'There was no stopping him.' Nigel shrugged. 'He's a cop, Harry.'

'Oh no.' I went to a patrol car parked nearby and opened the boot. I began to shiver under the rain, my skin raised in goose-bumps. I pulled on some gloves and booties. I'd need a whole suit to attend the scene properly, but I just wanted to look. To see if there was anything I could do. A part of me knew there wasn't going to be. That nothing could soften the horror of a father seeing his daughter's murdered body. I walked past the gathering of men and women outside, into the huge warehouse, where there were dozens more officers milling around, making phone calls, taking photographs and measurements, standing, talking.

There wasn't much to see. Tonya Woods was buried in the trash, lying on her side, one pale arm slung up and over the handle of what looked like an old pram. I saw her long dark hair, a glimpse of her ear. Bruises on her neck. Probably strangled. My eyes wandered over the things she was buried in, wanting to record everything. There were papers, empty food tins, small plastic bags of wet and lumpy items, cleaning-product bottles and cardboard boxes. The rubbish had been dumped alongside a long, wide trench running the length of the warehouse, where it would be sorted and carried away on huge conveyor belts. Tonya must have been spotted as the truck pulled up to the trench, and instead of dumping the load for sorting the driver had dumped it on the ground to get a better look.

I felt his presence. The low voices of the men and women around me snapped off as though a switch had been flipped. The sound of trucks rumbling and machines grinding and the pattering of rain on the warehouse roof seemed to dim. There was a ringing silence as Joe Woods approached and stood next to me.

I watched his face, trying to decide what might come next. He could have any kind of reaction. I'd seen the families of homicide victims burst out laughing at the sheer absurdity of what they were seeing. I'd seen them scream and faint and close in on themselves, blank, numb, the shutters pulled down to protect the mind. Walking zombies.

Joe Woods didn't do any of those things. His eyes fell dark, his jaw clamped shut, and he seized my arm, almost lifting me off the ground. He turned and marched me towards the door.

Chapter 75

THE HAND ON my arm was like a vice. I knew simply from his grip that Woods was going to put all his rage at the situation onto me. That was confirmed when I tried to resist. He slammed me onto the ground outside the sorting building. The breath left me. I could only lie there while he ratchetted cuffs onto my wrists. Nigel and his group of officers were watching, motionless. I sucked in a lungful of air painfully.

'Nigel, help me, you arsehole!' I managed. But he didn't. He couldn't, and I knew that. There was a man standing by the row of cars, big and broad like Joe, probably his brother, watching the arrest with his mouth open.

Woods hauled me up and shoved me towards a patrol car so fast my feet dragged in the dirt. I fell into the back seat and he slammed the door behind me and got in the front. I looked around and saw that everyone from inside the warehouse where Woods's daughter lay had come outside to watch me being taken away.

'Woods,' I managed. 'Just —'

'You had your chance,' he snapped. His voice was unrecognisable. Low and dark and gravelly, a sound that made my blood run cold. 'You could have saved them. You could have stopped this.'

He pulled the car out of the space it was parked in so fast and hard I fell sideways on the seat. When I righted myself we were driving towards the highway.

I let some time pass. The cuffs were so tight I couldn't feel my fingers. Woods's knuckles on the steering wheel were white, his palms wringing the leather, making grinding sounds. I searched for words, but there were none. He was taking me back to prison. I had failed to find his child safe, and he was going to make sure I had nothing to do but think about that failure while I stared at the blank concrete wall of my cell for the next decade or more.

I sat back in my seat and watched the suburbs roll by, perhaps for the last time in a long time. I was so consumed by my own thoughts that I didn't notice we had missed the road that led to the highway. Woods turned the car into a street I didn't recognise, full of houses, gardens. Empty of people.

Woods parked the car neatly on the side of the road and pulled the handbrake on, turned the ignition off.

Then he put his head in his hands and cried.

Chapter 76

I LISTENED FOR a long time. He cried hard and desperately, not caring, or perhaps having forgotten completely that I was sitting there. Joe Woods was not a nice man. He had, in the past, endangered my life and the lives of my friends, thrown me in prison, threatened and abused and manhandled me. But the pain in his voice brought tears to my eyes. All the numbness I'd had left after leaving prison was gone. I wiped my eyes on my shoulders and sat quietly until Woods was done. He put his head back against the headrest of the driver's seat and stared out the windscreen.

'Woods?' I said from the back seat.

He didn't answer.

'Look, I'm just going to talk,' I said, shuffling forward. 'You can listen if you want. I hope you do.'

He was still and silent.

'Somebody else in my position right now would probably say all kinds of nice things,' I said. 'About being sorry for what happened to Tonya. About how you did the best you could and there's nothing you should have done differently and all that sort of stuff. But lots of gentle, supportive people are going to come and say that to you in the next few weeks, so I'll leave it to them. It wouldn't mean much coming from me, anyway. We've always hated each other's guts. I'm not one of those gentle supportive people, and I'm on the clock here. I've got a killer to catch. So I'm going to plead my case instead, OK?'

Woods turned his head slightly.

'You hired me to do a job,' I said. 'Throwing me in prison will mean I can't do that.'

'What does it matter now?' Woods asked. His voice was so small I could barely hear it. 'They're gone.'

'It might not matter to you at this very second,' I said. 'But it's going to matter soon. We don't know that Rebel is back there. She might still be alive. And you will want whoever did this brought to justice. You're going to want your time with him, and I can give that to you. We are within reach of finding your family's killer, sir. Don't throw it all away now because you're angry.'

He didn't answer. I shuffled again, pressed my face against the steel mesh separating us.

'I can do this, sir,' I said. 'Give me one more chance.'

Deputy Commissioner Woods sat quietly for a long time. Then he got out of the driver's seat and opened my door. He dragged me out of the car by my elbow and dumped me on the wet road.

The handcuff key tinkled as it hit the asphalt. I sat up and watched him climb into the vehicle and drive away.

Chapter 77

SHE SMILED WHEN she opened the door, and he was watching for the little sparkle of surprise and delight when she saw it was him. The smile quickly twisted into confusion, maybe a little disgust, as she took in his clothes, hair, face. Like a monster from the wilds turning up to ruin a pristine family picnic. She was all clean and beautiful, her hair falling in a single perfect roll on her shoulder, her make-up done. She was even wearing heels. In her own house.

In contrast, Tox had been in the desert all day, and the back of his neck and his forearms were scorched red. His hair was thick and coarse with dust, his nails blackened with dirt, and he almost certainly had microparticles of bodily remains on him from digging and turning up bones, pulling leather biker jackets and boots with foot bones still in them out of the sand. He was like a death dealer standing there after a long hard day collecting souls from the Earth, returning to an angel in her spotless apartment.

'Turning up unexpected and unannounced is a bit of a thing with you, isn't it?' she asked, the smile slowly returning.

'It keeps people on their toes,' he said. 'But I see you have guests.'

'They've just gone,' Chloe said.

'I think I just passed them at the lift. Two pretty ladies.'

She nodded. He stood there in the hall and she stood in the doorway, both of them smiling, remembering what they had done the last time they were together. Taking a moment to enjoy the anticipation of what they would do now. He stepped in and she led the way to the shower, unzipping her dress as she went.

Chapter 78

THE GYM WAS full of young people. A pair of boys were sparring in the ring while Pops stood at the ropes shouting directions, other kids were working a circuit through a row of bags hanging from the ceiling. I stood and watched from the door to the house as the boys on the bags dropped at the sound of a buzzer and did a round of sit-ups, and then flipped into push-ups at the next buzzer. There was a young girl shadow-boxing in the mirrors by the roller door and another girl strapping herself up to enter the ring. Pops spotted me and came over, and we went into the house together.

'I'm going to take a nap,' I said, pointing to his bedroom.

'Jesus, Harry, what the hell happened?' he asked.

'What do you know?'

'I know they found Tonya Woods's body and Woods dragged you off, and that's it,' Pops said. 'No one has seen you since.'

'Wrong.' I went to the freezer and took out an icepack, pressed it against my ribs. 'The first two people to see me after

Woods dumped me, handcuffed, in the middle of suburbia, were a very frightened Russian couple.'

Pops stared at me, wide-eyed.

'Woods decided he'd arrest me because I didn't find Tonya in time,' I said. 'Then I talked him down, so he tossed me out of his car, threw a handcuff key after me and bolted. I heard the key hit the road but I didn't see it, and when I looked all around I couldn't find it. I think it must have bounced down a drain or into the grass somewhere.'

Pops's mouth fell open.

'So there I am in some street I don't recognise, without a phone, handcuffed and alone. I went to the nearest house and kicked on the door but no one answered. Took me three houses before I found someone. A Russian couple. No English. I tried to explain who I was and what had happened but they weren't buying it. So I shoved past the guy into the house, trying to indicate that I wanted to use the phone, but he just kept shouting and she just kept screaming. Eventually they locked me in their laundry and called the police, and a couple of young patrollies came and picked me up.'

Pops laughed an exhausted, sad laugh and covered his face. 'Oh no.'

'They didn't unlock my cuffs until they got me back here,' I said. 'Dickheads.'

'Oh, Harry.'

'So now I'm going for a nap, and then I'll call Dolly,' I said. 'You'd better get back in the gym. You've got a lot of teenagers in there. If you take your eye off them for too long they'll start drinking beers and making out.'

I turned towards his bedroom. His voice stopped me in the doorway.

'They haven't found the baby yet,' Pops said. 'There's no sign of her.'

I thought about that, nodded. There was still hope.

Chapter 79

THE COLDNESS CAME over her as she lay beside him after-wards on the bed, their bodies still damp and hot from the shower, the sheets and coverlet kicked into a pile on the floor. He was lost to her, staring at the corner of the ceiling, thinking, dozing now and then. At home. He had said little to explain his state. A desert, she knew. Bodies. Bikers. The girl and her daughter who were missing.

The coldness that fell softly on her skin wasn't the breeze coming from the open window but the passion easing away, realisation hitting her. That they were really doing this now. They were *together*. He was going to keep showing up and sleeping with her and she was going to keep thinking about that in the moments when he wasn't around, having imaginary conversations with him, remembering the feel of his big, hard hands on her. She was going to think of him and wince privately at the sharp plunge of her stomach. If they kept on through this phase, it would lead to other things. She could see it in the way he looked at her. There would be dinners. Presents.

Weekends away. Friends meeting. Anniversaries. Promises. More lines crossed.

It couldn't go on like this. She wanted it to, so badly, but there was pain and ice at her core.

He kissed her on the mouth as he slid over her, stood and grabbed a towel from the floor and wound it around his waist. She heard the shake of his cigarette packet and looked up at him as he drew one from the pack.

'Do you want me to go?' he said.

'No,' she said. It was the truth. 'Stay here again tonight.'

He looked pleased with that. He walked out and she heard the door to the balcony slide open.

She slept, mere minutes. And then something snapped her awake. A change in the air, maybe. Electricity. It was impossible that they could be connected that way after such a short time together, she knew. But she could almost feel the horror rushing through him, sizzling through the air to her. She got up and slipped into a robe, went to the living room and found him standing at the bookcase.

'Oh, God,' she heard herself say.

The picture was tiny. An egg-shaped silver frame that had been tucked behind some knick-knacks on the middle shelf. She'd forgotten it was there. When Chloe wanted to look at pictures of her dead mother and brother she had a whole album of them hidden away in a cupboard that she leafed through. Tox could only have found the small picture frame when he wandered in from the balcony and started perusing her shelves. He was holding it now, and she could see from where she stood that his hands were trembling. He lifted his eyes to hers and she knew.

He knew.

Chapter 80

'WHAT . . .' HE BLINKED. Looked at the picture again. 'What . . .'

She couldn't find the words. For a moment they just stood there in the light from the apartment building across the street, breathing hard, minds racing.

'Anna Peake,' Chloe said. 'And David Peake.'

'I know who they are,' Tox said. His eyes were big and glassy, full of something. Fear or rage, she couldn't tell.

'My mother and my brother,' Chloe said.

Tox exhaled hard, looked around like he suddenly didn't know where he was.

'I'm sorry,' Chloe said. She took a step towards him. Just one. 'You couldn't have known. I changed my name years ago, to her maiden name. I should have said something. From the beginning. I just . . .' She felt tears beginning. 'I knew when you came in that day. When you came into the emergency room. I looked down at you and I knew who you were, even with the new name. The other boys from the bridge, I know what their new names are, too. I've sort of kept an eye on you all, over the years.' The words were rushing out of her. She wiped her face. 'One of them's dead. One has a family up the coast.'

He wasn't saying anything. He was just looking at the picture.

'But I knew your face, too,' she said. 'I saw you in the paper once. And I remember the day it happened. You ran past me. All of you. I was crossing the bridge walking home, and I heard the crash and smelled the smoke. Didn't know what it was. Then you all ran past. You were the last one. We looked at each other.'

Tox said nothing.

'I should have told you from the beginning,' Chloe said.

Tox put the picture back where he'd found it. He strode rigidly to the bedroom, dressed and walked out of the apartment, closing the door quietly behind him.

Chapter 81

LESS THAN A third of the inmates at Johnsonborough Correctional Complex were women. So at night, there was no dedicated doctor servicing the female section and the doctor on roster for the male sections would be summoned if necessary. When Dolly complained of stomach cramps at seven that night, she was taken from her bed in the infirmary to the empty doctor's surgery and chained to the table.

The guard left her there while they waited for the doctor to come across.

She sat for a while, then reached over as far as her chain would allow and dragged the jar of jelly snakes towards her, extracted two. She pocketed one and chewed the other carefully. Her teeth had been rattled when the guards came for her in ad seg. They had rained blows down on her while she curled in a ball on the floor, and when she had thought they were done, she lifted her head to watch them exit the cell. They hadn't been done. One of them had kicked her in the jaw. Dolly had been taking beatings since she was a kid, in her home, in group homes, and then on the street. Now and then she got impatient and broke form too early. She'd learn, one day, she supposed.

She was excited about seeing Harry. Harry had said she would talk to her at seven in the doctor's surgery. Dolly didn't know how Harry was going to get into the prison to do that, exactly, but Harry was pretty clever. Dolly waited, sucking on her snake, reading the labels on the drawers in the cabinet across the room from her.

At five minutes after seven the phone rang on the counter beside her. Dolly looked at it, then looked away. Inmates weren't allowed to answer the phones of prison staff. Dolly listened to the ringing, thinking after ten rings that whoever was calling the night doctor was pretty persistent. She figured he would be on his way now, walking over from the male section to see her. She wondered if the caller would ring back.

They did. The phone fell silent for thirty seconds, and then the ringing started again. Dolly huffed, kind of annoyed by the sound of it. She wondered when Harry would get there. What the doctor would say when she arrived. It certainly wasn't visiting hours. Perhaps Harry would be disguised as a guard, as the night doctor himself, even. Dolly looked out the window at the empty hallway and winced at the ringing that was vibrating around her bruised skull. She scratched her head and sighed. The ringing kept on and on.

On the third call, Dolly picked up the phone.

'Hello?'

'Dolly?'

'Um, yes?'

'Christ, Dolly, what took you so long!' Harry blasted.

'Har . . . *Harry?*'

'Yes! My God, who the fuck else would it be!'

'How did you get this number?' Dolly looked around. 'I . . . I thought you were coming here. Are you coming here?'

'Am I – oh, Jesus – Dolly, I'm not coming there,' Harry huffed. 'You've got to pay attention. I'm going to give you some instructions and you're going to have to try to really focus. We haven't got much time. The night doctor is probably on his way over right now.'

'Oh. OK. Right,' Dolly straightened. 'What do you want me to do?'

'Listen carefully,' Harry said. 'Do exactly what I say. OK? I want you to hang up the phone, and –'

Dolly put the phone back in its receiver.

Chapter 82

THE PHONE RANG. Dolly picked it up.

'Hello?'

Dolly could hear a clicking sound, like teeth grinding. Harry's voice was low and dark. 'Dolly. I meant. After. I've finished. Giving. You. The instructions.'

'Oh,' Dolly said, nodding. 'OK. Sure.'

'I want you to write down a number,' Harry breathed. 'When I say "Go", I want you to hang up, and then pick up the receiver and dial those numbers into the phone, and then hang up again. Have you got a pen there? There should be one on the desk.'

Dolly looked around. There was a pen at the furthest edge of the tabletop. With difficulty she threw a leg up onto the counter, knocked the pen onto the floor and pulled it towards her.

'OK,' she said, 'I'm listening.'

Harry read her a list of numbers. Dolly wrote them on her ankle.

'What do you mean, star?' she asked. 'How do I dial star?'

'There's a star button on the phone,' Harry said.

'I don't see one.'

'There's. Dolly – It's there, I'm telling you. Look. Use your eyes. It's . . . it's next to the zero. On the left.'

'There's an asterisk?' Dolly said. 'Do you mean that?'

'Dolly . . .' Harry said. 'I am going to straight up murder you.'

'You always say that.'

'It's the truth.'

'When are you coming back?' Dolly asked. 'Are you in gen pop now or are you still outside?'

'No, I'm not in gen pop, I – Just, just focus, Dolly. OK? Focus on what we're doing. We haven't got time to chat.'

'They're taking me to the Bay tomorrow, Harry. For a psych assessment.'

'That's a good thing, Doll. While you're in Johnsonborough you're in danger. The people at the Bay won't know you,' Harry said.

'I don't want to go. I've heard about that place. That's where they send all the mentals. The skin-eaters and baby-killers. If they decide I'm crazy I might never get out.'

'Dolly, we can't talk about this now. We have to do this thing with the phone.'

'This is all a bit complicated, Harry,' Dolly whined. 'Can't you just come here and do it?'

'No,' Harry said. 'But you can. Do it now, alright? If it works, I won't be able to call you back.'

'What's all this about?'

'It's about helping you, Dolly. So just do it before the night doctor gets there.'

'If you say so.' Dolly shrugged. She put the phone receiver down, picked it up, dialled the number and the asterisk and put the phone down again. She waited. Nothing happened. She heard the night doctor and the guard buzzing through the gate at the end of the hall. She looked at the ground and remembered Doctor Goldman lying there, dying, her blood spreading out over the linoleum.

Chapter 83

I CLOSED MY eyes and exhaled long and slow. Teaching Dolly to divert the phone in the doctor's surgery at Johnsonborough had driven me to furious levels of tension. If she had keyed in the numbers correctly, dialling the surgery number would now send the call to Pops's mobile, which was sitting on the bedside table at my elbow.

Hoping silently with every fibre of my being, I reached over and picked up Pops's landline phone, dialled the Johnsonborough female section doctor's surgery. Pops's mobile rang. I pressed the answer button on the mobile and listened to the silence, eased air through my teeth. Now that I had the surgery phone line under my control, I took Pops's landline and dialled into the surgery's voicemail. I knew there would be no pin code on the prison phone system, precisely so that any officer would have access to the voicemail of other officers anywhere in the prison in the event of an emergency. Sometimes the prison couldn't use the PA system to direct staff, because then prisoners causing riots or trying to escape would know their movements. If the radio system went down, or the prisoners got hold of a radio, officers calling each other and not getting through during a crisis needed to be able to leave messages telling one another what was going on.

A charming female voice came on the line.

'*You have – three – unplayed messages,*' it said.

I listened hard.

'*Message from February twenty-five, at one sixteen pm:* Hi Goldie. Marie at the front office here. You've got a package. Thanks.'

I waited.

'*Message from February twenty-eight, at seven forty nine am:*' There was silence on the line. A click. The hope was draining from me. The messages were weeks old. Perhaps Goldie was too busy to check them.

'*Message from March thirteen, at twelve twenty-one pm:* Hey, it's me, babe.'

I sat up sharply on the bed.

'The Corolla was making weird noises this morning. I'm going to have the NRMA come out and look at it today. But if it won't go, can I get a ride home with you? You can call me back in the staff room – I'm having lunch and finishing those cell search reports. See you later.'

I smiled, played the message again, listened to the soft lilt in the man's voice as he signed off the message.

See you later.

See you soon, I thought.

Chapter 84

WHITT KNOCKED ON the door of the Mallally house at five in the morning. The sun had not yet risen over the sharp, dark-blue edge of the distant sea. The slope towards Bondi was cluttered with mansions with darkened windows. He had to push the doorbell four times before he heard padding footsteps inside the house.

Louis Mallally opened the door in a red satin robe. His hair, unstyled, fell in a crown of oily ringlets over his head and behind his ears. He squinted in the dim light.

'What the hell is this?'

'We need to talk,' Whitt said.

Mallally lifted a finger, pointed it at Whitt's face like he was chastising a dog. 'No. *No*. You're not doing this.'

'Doing what?'

'Starting a program of harassment,' Mallally said. 'This is what you cops do. You get desperate, and you herd anyone even remotely involved with a case and you start pushing and pushing to see who'll fall off the cliff first. This is an inappropriate time to come to my home and disturb me, Detective Whittacker. And as I have been constantly telling your colleagues, this house will not be entered by the police against my will without a warrant.'

'Just give me the second phone,' Whitt said. 'You must have had a phone that you used to communicate with Tonya to organise your meetings. Give it to me, and I'll review the messages between you, and we'll be done.'

'No,' Mallally said. 'There is no second phone. You have not a shred of hard evidence that suggests there ever was a second phone. I've got detectives following me up the fucking street, standing in my driveway, taking my trash out of the bin every night. They haven't found a phone.'

'There's no recent communication with you on Tonya's phone,' Whitt said. 'And no communication with her on yours.'

'Yes, and discovering that was a blatant invasion of my privacy.' Mallally pointed again. 'I have not viewed a warrant to access my personal phone records.'

'Our investigators don't have to justify themselves to you, Mr Mallally,' Whitt said.

'No problem.' Mallally shrugged. 'They can do it to a judge in my civil lawsuit against the department.'

'No communication between you and Tonya on your personal phone tells us that you must have bought –'

'– I've explained how Tonya and I –'

'– *must have bought* a two-pack of burner phones and given her one.' Whitt held his hand up. 'I don't need hard evidence to know that. It's common sense. The idea that you met at the courthouse every Tuesday and didn't find a secure way to communicate with each other outside of that arrangement is bullshit. Unless you communicated through telekinesis, a second phone is the only sensible way –'

'I'm asking you to leave these premises, Detective Whittacker,' Mallally said.

'And I'm asking you what you and Tonya discussed that was so incriminating that you won't surrender your phone.'

Mallally rubbed his brow, leaned in the doorway. He was fighting back, but he was not fully awake yet. Whitt knew that when he came to completely he would be spouting deeper, more damaging legal threats. Whitt needed to hit hard, and keep hitting, before that happened.

'Why is your colleague, Elliot Prince, acting as Jax Gotten's lawyer?' Whitt asked, changing tack.

'I don't choose Elliot's cases for him,' Mallally said. 'He has an obligation to take a certain number of pro-bono cases in order to fulfil his requirements as an associate at my law firm. He chose Gotten because the case interested him.'

'Bit of a coincidence, don't you think? With Gotten suspected of killing your ex-girlfriend?'

'My colleague didn't know Tonya was my ex-girlfriend until Detective Nigel Spader told him,' Mallally snapped, his eyes dark and blazing. 'And neither did my wife! Do you people have any kind of training in confidentiality in your line of work? Can you even *spell* the word?'

'What's Gotten going to say about you when we find him, Mallally?' Whitt asked.

'I don't think I'll be his major concern.' Mallally shrugged sharply, making the shiny satin of his robe flash in the morning light. 'From what I've seen on the news, the guy's running from mass murder charges. There were seventeen bodies in the desert, is that right? An entire rival bikie crew killed and dumped in a mass grave?'

'Do you know Jax Gotten, Mr Mallally?'

'No.'

'Did Tonya ever mention him?'

'I'm telling you for the second time now, I want you to leave my property.' Mallally grabbed the edge of the door.

'Submit your house to a search,' Whitt said. He stepped forward, put a foot in front of the doorjamb. 'If there's no phone, then let our officers confirm that. Show us you've got nothing to hide.'

Mallally tried to slam the door but it bounced off Whitt's boot and smacked back into his hand. The two men heard a little whimper at the sound of the scuffle. Mallally turned, and they saw one of his small daughters standing at the foot of the stairs, looking frightened, her hands clutched under her chin.

Whitt slid his foot out of the doorjamb and felt the whoosh of air as the door slammed shut in his face. He took out his phone and scrolled to find Tox's number.

Chapter 85

TOX BARNES WAS standing in the waiting room outside the emergency department of St Vincent's Hospital, watching the television screen in the corner of the room, like everyone was. There was aerial footage of the mass grave outside Panuara, shot the day before, rotating slowly above scrolling headlines. A news anchor was speaking, her words flashing on the screen in black-and-yellow closed captions.

It has been an extraordinary 24 hours for New South Wales Police, who have confirmed the discovery of a mass grave just outside the town of Panuara in the state's central west. Early reports indicate the remains may belong to members of outlaw motorcycle gang the Road Rabbits, who . . .

Tox was hardly taking in what he was seeing. In his mind he was a small boy running across a highway bridge to the safety of the bushland beside the road, trying to keep up with his friends, a girl he didn't know walking towards him, confused by their terror, meeting his eyes as he passed.

. . . second incident playing out in tragic scenes last night. The body has been identified as Tonya Woods, the 22-year-old daughter of Deputy Police Commissioner Joseph Woods. Police have not yet confirmed the whereabouts of missing two-year-old Rebel Woods, and are asking the public to . . .

Around him in the emergency waiting room people shuffled, murmured, sighed and looked at the clock. Tox had come to the hospital planning to do what he had been doing a bit lately: walking through the emergency-room double doors, turning left through the fire door, taking the stairs to level five and walking down the hall to Chloe's office. She had the midnight-to-midday shift that day, he knew. He needed to find her. He needed to understand. But his feet were stuck, as though magnetised, to the scuffed linoleum floor. It was rage that paralysed him. Fury at himself, at the stupid boy on the bridge, a boy who grew into a stupid, blind man. He should have known something was wrong when Chloe Bozer came into his life. People like her didn't hang around people like him. They sure didn't love people like him. And yet somehow he'd entertained those fantasies, whispered promises of what they might have. He'd seen it in her smile in the doorway. Felt it in her arms as she held him, breathed him in. It was all a lie he'd chosen to believe. That life was not for him, and he needed to understand why she'd let him believe it was.

He was about to leave when she came through the doors into the waiting room. She was wearing pink scrubs, and her eyes had the hardness of someone prepared to look upon death and disfigurement all day. But they softened as she approached him, deliberately, like she was shaking it off.

'I'm quitting,' she said.

Chapter 86

HE DIDN'T KNOW what to say to that. They walked together to a small alcove near the triage desk. The activity of the waiting room seemed to fall away. Tox wanted to take her hands, but he stuffed his fists into his pockets instead.

'What the hell are you talking about?'

'I wanted to say before you left last night,' Chloe said. Her voice was smaller than he'd ever heard it. 'I wanted to say meeting you has made me realise that I can't do this job anymore.'

'That's . . .' Tox shook his head. The rage re-emerged suddenly, never far from the surface. 'That's unfair. That's unfair to me. I made a mistake as a kid and you're punishing me by making it so that I've ruined something so perfect, so right, as you being in this job. You're not going to run into anyone like me ever again around here, Chloe. It's a horrible coincidence.'

'You don't understand.' She wiped a tear from her cheek. 'It's not you. It's not what you did. It's me.'

He couldn't look at her. She leaned in close.

'When I was standing over you in the operating theatre, and I saw who you were I . . . I *decided* to save you.'

'Of course you did. You're a good person.'

'No. It's not like that. It's not supposed to be a decision at all,' she pleaded. 'It's supposed to be automatic. I do my best for everyone who comes in here. *Everyone*. I'm a doctor. My job is to go to every effort to save the murderer or rapist or paedophile on my table just as if it were my own child lying there. And when I saw it was you, for a split second I stood there and thought about not helping you.'

Tox looked away. He could hardly speak. 'But you made the right decision.'

'Yes, but I hesitated.'

A nurse walked briskly past them, carrying an armful of papers. There was stillness in the waiting room.

'I don't know how this happened.' Chloe rubbed her brow. 'After I saved you I thought that would be it. I . . . I'd done the right thing. I'd hated you for so long, but that hatred didn't win out against what I knew was the right thing to do in the operating theatre. And then it didn't win out against wanting to see you again after you showed up here. It didn't win when I balanced it against wanting to kiss you that night outside the bar.' She shrugged. 'It just seemed to get weaker and weaker. And I kept crossing lines,' she sighed. 'And then it seemed impossible to tell you.'

'Chloe.' He held her face in his hands. 'Please don't quit. You're a good doctor and a good person and you deserve to be here. Forget about me. You won't ever see me again, so none of this will matter. If you really don't hate me then you'll let things go back to the way they were before I came in and ruined everything.'

She fell into his arms. He held her briefly. Then he had to walk away.

Chapter 87

TOX STOOD IN the car park and put his head in his hands. When his phone rang it was a welcome distraction from the hurt. He took the call from Whitt without speaking at all, his memories rolling through that moment on the bridge, the sound of car tyres squealing and the gasps of horror from the boys around him as the impact boomed from the road, up the struts of the bridge, into the concrete beneath their feet.

'Jax Gotten is in the wind,' Whitt was saying. 'There's nothing we can do about that now. But I want to clamp down on Mallally while we can. The guy's life is in ruins. If he's connected to Jax Gotten, if he knows anything at all about what happened to Tonya and the baby, he'll be worried about what Jax is going to say when police catch up to him. We need to get into Mallally's house and find that second phone.'

Tox said nothing. He stared back at the automatic doors to the emergency room.

'I've tried to get a warrant and so has Nigel. We're coming up empty. The judge likes Jax alone for the murder, and Mallally's probably got him in his pocket anyway. Tox, if you have any ideas about how we can get into Mallally's place without –'

Someone tapped Tox on the shoulder. He hung up on Whitt and looked down. A familiar face. Pretty, wide-set eyes and a small mouth. One of the nurses. Tox couldn't remember her name. He knew she'd been the one to sneak him mini bottles of Jim Beam when she started her shift every night.

'Hey, handsome,' she smiled. 'Something I can do for you?'

'There certainly is,' Tox said.

Chapter 88

TERRY LANCER WAS smaller than I'd imagined. Wiry and toned, where most of the guards at Johnsonborough were jacked into broad, bulky giants by spare hours spent in the staff gym. He was sitting in his car in the parking lot of the McDonald's just outside Sydney Airport, watching dirty brown ibises picking through the trash. I came alongside the car and put my cup on the roof, tapped the window, holding the paper bag in front of my chest so he wouldn't notice that I wasn't wearing the uniform. The McDonald's hat I'd bought from a teenager arriving for work was pulled low over my brow. Lancer rolled down the window.

'Sir, your breakfast,' I said.

Lancer reached for the bag of trash as I'd hoped he would. When he turned to set it on the passenger seat I reached in and grabbed the keys from the ignition of the car and put them in my pocket.

'Hey, what —'

I took the McDonald's coffee cup from the top of the car, held it over his lap, my elbows and forearms resting on the windowsill.

'This cup is full of boiling water,' I said, easing off the plastic lid. 'I can feel how hot it is, even through this special cardboard liner. It's hurting my fingers. The staff behind the counter will give you a cup of boiling water for free. Did you know that? It's so nice. Anyway, you're going to answer some questions for me or I'm going to dump it right in your lap.'

Lancer stared at me, open-mouthed. He looked at the cup in my hand, then his lap below it.

'Think carefully,' I warned. 'Don't try to grab the cup. I'll hurl it in your face. If you try to shift sideways and get out the passenger door I'll toss it on you, too. And don't think I'm bluffing. You'll actually be one of more than a dozen people I've grievously burned this week. I'm on a bit of a streak.'

'Just take my money.' Lancer's hands were gripping the knees of his uniform trousers. 'My wallet is in my back pocket. I can get it. You can take the whole car.'

'I'm not mugging you,' I said. 'I'm here to talk about your girlfriend, Bernadette Goldman.'

Chapter 89

LANCER WAS YOUNG in the eyes, desperate-looking. He glanced around me at the parking lot, the big stalking ibises and the morning commuters pulling in, pulling out. To anyone else, we probably seemed like two people having a friendly morning chat through the car window. The water in my hands was so hot it was steaming the windscreen, adding to the sweat at Lancer's temples.

'Who the hell are you?'

'I'm Harriet Blue.' I extended a pinkie finger carefully from around the cup. Without knowing what else to do, Lancer reached up and shook it delicately, grimacing as the water moved in the cup. 'I'm actually a former Johnsonborough resident.'

'Of course,' he sighed shakily.

'We haven't got a lot of time before the real waitress comes out with your meal,' I said. 'And I want my answers before the water cools down. So let's get moving, alright?'

'OK.'

'I'm investigating Goldie's murder,' I said. 'I know you two were in a secret relationship in the prison. Rumour had it that she was seeing an inmate, Anna Regent, but that's bullshit. People saw Goldie giggling and laughing on the phone in her office and they saw her unusually empathetic approach to someone as horrendously violent as Anna Regent and they did the math. But actually her secret squeeze was you. Secret, because it's frowned upon for prison staff to be in a relationship with each other.'

'It's not just frowned upon,' Lancer said, eyes on the cup like it was a gun. 'It's a fireable offence. You sign a contract when you're hired at Johnsonborough that you'll disclose any intimate relationships with other staff members.'

'That so?' I said.

'Yeah. It's a safety thing.' He eased a breath in and out slowly. 'They don't want couples breaking policy and trying to keep each other safe when a major incident goes down. If an inmate takes your loved one hostage, you're going to do what the inmate wants to free them, right?'

'But you and Goldie broke policy,' I said.

He sighed, gripped his knees. He was on the edge, stressed at the trap I'd set for him and bottled-up grief was rising quickly onto his features. 'I loved her,' he said. He bit his lips and looked away from me. I saw a waitress with a bag and a coffee cup in a tray heading directly for us.

I made a decision. I stepped away and dumped the boiling water on the ground. Lancer looked up and saw that he was free from my trap, but didn't have time to react before the teenage girl was thrusting his breakfast through the window.

'Your breakfast, sir,' she said. Lancer looked at me, and I waited for him to scream for help. But instead he just took the bag and coffee and thanked the girl. I crossed the front of the car and got into the passenger seat beside him.

We sat in silence, watching the birds. Seagulls were mingling between the ibises, padding over the asphalt in search of stray chips.

'I cared about her too,' I said. 'Doctor Goldman was kind to me. She didn't have to be.'

Lancer wiped the sweat from his brow with the sleeve of his shirt.

'You can eat your breakfast,' I said.

'You want some?' He opened the bag shakily. 'I don't usually have much room for the hash brown.' He reached into the bag and offered it to me.

I snorted. 'You don't have to give me half your breakfast. I just threatened to boil your balls.'

'It's alright,' he shrugged. 'Your reasons were, like, noble.'

I took the hash brown and we ate in silence for a while.

'You could have just asked me,' he said. 'Without the cup.'

'I haven't found Johnsonborough staff very accommodating to my enquiries thus far.'

'I'm not mad. I get worse threats at the prison every other day.' He smiled to himself. I could see why Goldie had fallen for Lancer. He was gentle, forgiving, sweet. I sat sideways in the passenger seat and sipped his coffee now and then.

'How long had you and Goldie been going out?' I asked.

'Oh, maybe six months.' He looked at me. 'An inmate threw a chair at my head and the doctor in my section was at lunch so I went in to her surgery to get a couple of stitches. I'd never met her before. I work over in male housing. We kind of knew from the start that we had a thing for each other.' He smiled sadly to himself, remembering.

'She must have had ten years on you,' I said.

'Twelve.' He laughed. 'She called herself my cougar.'

'No one at the prison knew about your relationship?'

'No.' Lancer looked at me. 'At least I didn't think so. But you said you were an inmate there.'

'I only found out about you two yesterday,' I said.

'Where from? From inside the prison? I need this job, man. I . . .' he sighed. 'I can't have people knowing.'

'No one at the prison knows,' I said. 'I heard a message from you on Goldie's voicemail. You sounded familiar with each other. Intimate. Beyond work buddies. You didn't say your name but you mentioned a Toyota Corolla so I went to the prison this morning at about 3 am, caused a distraction and nabbed the manifest from the car-park guard booth. Security's not huge on the prison parking lot. There were only three Corollas. Two owned by married men. I thought I'd try you first. Called in a favour to run your plate and followed you from home this morning.'

'Jesus. You're really serious about this,' Lancer said. 'You're not just a former inmate trying to find out who killed her friend, are you?'

'No, I'm not. I'm a cop. Well, sort of.'

'Sort of?'

'It's a long story. Look, Bernadette was researching sexual guidelines between doctors and patients on her home computer,' I said. 'Was there anything to her relationship with Anna Regent? Anything more than a keen interest in Anna's rehabilitation?'

'No way.' Lancer shook his head. 'Sex between prison staff and inmates actually classifies as rape, because at the end of the day they're the prisoners and we have the keys. It's a non-consensual act, even if it looks like the prisoner is into it.'

'You're saying the only reason Bernadette wouldn't have gone there is because it was rape?'

'No, no, she wouldn't have gone there at all,' Lancer said. 'She wasn't gay. At least, I don't think so. Because we . . . you know . . .' He gestured awkwardly to himself.

'Tell me about the rest of Goldie's life. She bumped up her home security system in the weeks before her murder,' I said. 'You know anything about that?'

'Sure,' Lancer said. 'Guards had been hassling her about over-ordering her drugs, spreading them around the prison a bit, making some extra cash. No one ever turned up to the house, but someone called her home number once, a few months ago, to discuss it. She didn't like that. She liked to sleep soundly at night. Didn't want to worry about unexpected visits.'

'Were they threatening her, these guards?'

'No, just being persistent, I think. Asking her over and over. Trying to make her understand how much money they could be making,' Lancer said. 'But look, they already found out who killed Bernadette. It was some crackhead inmate.'

'No,' I said. 'The crackhead inmate, as you so tactfully put it, is innocent.'

'What?' He looked at me.

'And she's not a crackhead, she's a stoner, for the record.'

'So who did it?'

'I'm trying to find that out,' I said.

'Well, I didn't do it.' He shifted in his seat. 'I . . . Bernie, she was my . . .'

'I don't think it was you,' I said. 'You don't seem the type.'

Lancer exhaled.

'But my gut instinct tells me Dolly Quaddich is innocent, too,' I said. 'She was there, but she didn't see what happened. Goldie got a phone call, and then she left the surgery and walked around a corner and was hit. And the camera covering that section of hallway was conveniently malfunctioning.'

'I don't know about conveniently,' Lancer said. 'The cameras malfunction all the time. The prison's a million years old. All the electrics are shot. There are power surges. Blackouts. But the phone call right after the alarm, that would have been from me,' Lancer said. 'Just what the management were worried about. I heard the level-one alarm go off. It was the second one that morning. The first thing I did was call her to see if she was OK.'

'Did she say what she was going to do? Why she went up the hall?'

He stared at the dashboard, thinking. 'I'm pretty sure she said she was going to arm herself,' he said.

A cold chill tingled up the back of my arms. I shifted closer to the young man in the driver's seat. 'What do you mean?'

'Bernadette wasn't a guard,' Lancer said. 'She wasn't required to walk around with a weapon on her belt, like we were. But she had the option of having a weapon assigned to her, if she wanted it. She'd been trained with it, of course. It was in the C Block armoury.'

'So you told her to get her gun that day?'

'I don't think so. I think it was her idea. But I was going to suggest it. I think I remember she was kind of spooked, because it was the second alarm that morning. She said she was going to get her weapon, just in case, and I said that was a good idea.'

'Where's the C Block armoury?' I asked, sitting back, trying to think.

'It's around the corner from her office,' Lancer said. 'Right where she was attacked. But they already checked the armoury, straight after the lockdown. Everything was still there, right where it should be.'

Chapter 90

IT WAS A crew Tox had used before. Tommy Mercer was driving the ambulance while Tox rode in the back with Mercer's guys: Ryan, Jelly and Sticks. The thugs looked strange to him in the paramedic uniforms he had borrowed from the staff lockers. Tattooed and hardened, the crew's minds were on the job like this was going to be one of the smash-and-grab escapades that had made them infamous. The unshaven faces and scars, and Jelly's big hairy belly stretching the front of his uniform to its physical limits, made them seem what they were: actors taking on a role. Most great criminals Tox had known were also great showmen, and this lot would need to be convincing, at least initially. The props would help. The nurse who'd helped with the uniforms probably hadn't banked on him taking one of the ambulances, but he was hoping to have it back in good time.

The first time Tox had seen these guys they'd been trying to blow the door off a double-walled iron safe in a gravel quarry in Greystanes. He'd watched them with binoculars as they fought for three hours to make a dent in the thing before he announced his presence. The crew had been grateful for Tox looking the other way, and since then he'd used them for a few minor criminal tasks, always in pursuit of bigger and better collars for himself. The last time he'd hired them, they'd stood guard over a paedophile suspect Tox hadn't had the legal precedent to question, but whom he'd wanted to get answers out of anyway.

As the four of them swayed and rocked in the back of the ambulance, Jelly perusing the little drawers all around him for treasures, Ryan spoke.

'What's wrong with you?' He jutted his chin at Tox. 'You look pissed off.'

Tox shrugged. 'I'm just overworked and underappreciated like every other cop on the planet.'

'There's a baby missing,' Sticks said, picking his nose. 'Cops hate that. The worst crimes are the ones with babies. Ain't that right, Barnsie? It's because they know they gotta find the kid but they're not sure if they really want to.'

Tox sighed.

'It's not that. It's a woman.' Ryan sat back, folded his arms. 'Face like that? It's got to be a woman. Don't worry, Tox, mate. Women are like buses. One goes, and another comes along.'

'Hey, I like that.' Sticks took his hand away from his face long enough to slap Ryan on the chest. 'You heard this one? I like my women like I like my oranges: with the skin peeled off.'

Everyone looked at Sticks in silence.

Tommy Mercer leaned back in the driver's seat. 'We're here.'

Chapter 91

THEY CAME THROUGH the front doors, a crowd surging, fanning out, big guys with big voices. Jelly and Sticks shoved the gurney into the foyer. It had rattled angrily from the back of the ambulance, frighteningly close to a yellow Maserati parked in the driveway and through the security gate into the house. Tox followed the noisy brigade and watched as Tommy pushed over a lamp, just to add to the chaos, the heavy porcelain base splitting on the marble floors with a sound like a gunshot.

Louis and Shania Mallally were in the entryway to the living room, mouths open and faces hard like they'd been arguing. They froze, doe-eyed and lost in the noise and movement.

'Where's the patient? Where's the patient?'

'Ma'am, step out of the doorway, please! Give us space!'

'Get back! Get back!'

Jelly was making fake reports on a radio on his shoulder, wheeling the gurney with one hand, letting it crash into a big credenza standing against one wall, rattling glasses inside.

The scene was like an improvised sketch on a big stage, the Mallallys the only people who didn't have the script.

'Unit two, code six, we've got the patient sighted,' Jelly said. 'Assessing the situation. Stand by for report.'

'What the –' Shania backed up, hands raised to her head as if to block out the noise bouncing off the walls of the foyer. 'What the hell is this?'

'We've received a call saying there is a man at this address acting aggressively, possibly undergoing a psychotic episode, who is experiencing life-threatening cardiovascular symptoms,' Mercer barked at Shania. He backed her into a wall while Ryan and Sticks grabbed Mallally by the arms. 'Ma'am, I'll need you to stay clear and let us work here.'

'This is – I'm not – I – Jesus Christ! Get your hands off me!' Mallally tried to struggle out of the arms of the men shoving him towards the gurney. 'There's been a mistake!'

'Ma'am. This is an emergency situation! Is your husband under the influence of any narcotics? Are you yourself under the –'

Tox turned, glancing back at the tangle of bodies in the living room doorway as he headed for the stairs. He jogged silently to the second floor and headed straight for Mallally's office. He'd discounted the bedrooms, guest rooms, bathrooms and children's rooms immediately. Mallally would want somewhere safe to talk to his girlfriend. Somewhere legitimately off limits to the wife.

A desk. Papers and folders making crooked staircases towards the ceiling. Boxes labelled with dates, surnames. He shoved boxes aside, pushed books off shelves, ran his hands over the tops of high cabinets and under furniture. There was no point trying to disguise his actions. The paramedic ruse would last mere minutes. It *was* a smash-and-grab, in a sense. Tox went to the desk and dragged the chair out, searched underneath the seat, dumped drawers of stationery from the desk onto the floor.

A fish tank stood in the corner on a cabinet. Some big, spiky, probably rare fish eyed him from behind the glass. Tox opened the cabinet beneath the tank and raked the contents out. There was a big cardboard box at the back of the shelf that purported to hold fish food. He heard it thump as it hit the carpet.

That was some heavy fish food.

He shifted back on his haunches and ripped the box open. Twelve phones of various shapes and sizes tumbled onto the carpet.

Of course there was more than one. Mallally was a defence lawyer. He needed to be in contact with secret witnesses, private investigators, dirty cops whose communications might damage a defence case if Mallally's phone records were ever brought into evidence.

Tox started shoving the phones into the many pockets of his paramedic's uniform. Downstairs, the noise was carrying on. He could hear Mallally's voice.

'– come blathering in here like a bunch of morons, terrorising my family, damaging my property –'

'Sir, we've got to respond to critical incidents when we're given them, and this address was listed as –'

'I don't want to hear your excuses! Get out! Take your things and get –'

Tox walked into the hall and nearly ran into two little girls, who must have just come out of their bedrooms. They stopped and stared at him, shuddering with frightened sobs. He was reminded suddenly of what Sticks had said in the ambulance, that cops hated cases with babies. Hated learning what had happened to them, those dark fears realised, when the case found a resolution. He knew from experience it was almost never a good outcome. That it was unlikely, with her mother dead, that Rebel Woods would ever reach the age of the little girls before him.

He patted their heads as he passed, slipping quietly down the stairs and out the front door.

Chapter 92

DETECTIVE NIGEL SPADER listened to Whitt's story in an empty conference room on the second floor of the Sydney Police Centre in Surry Hills. He then called in five of his special operations men, and they sat on tables and in chairs around him and listened to Whitt explain his theory again. There was a long stretch of silence, before Nigel folded his arms and sat back in his chair and laughed. It was a low, mean sound.

'So let me just try to get my head around this,' he said, working his brow with his stubby fingers. 'I've got half the New South Wales Police force out looking for Jax Gotten in every corner of the country, and you think you know where he is because you saw a tattoo on one of his guys.'

'I don't know where Gotten is, but I think I know how we can get to him,' Whitt said. He picked up the *Wanted* flyer he'd taken from a stack in the station staff room, crowded with the faces of the Silver Aces crew. He pointed to the blond, bearded man in the bottom right-hand corner. 'Edgar Romtus isn't just one of Jax's everyday guys. He's a lieutenant at least.'

'Uh-huh,' Nigel sighed.

'Romtus isn't just a bikie,' Whitt said. 'He has exquisite taste in music. The tattoo that I saw on his arm was a portrait of Mitsuko Uchida, a very famous Japanese pianist.'

'You sure it was this Uchida dude and not some other guy?' one of the special ops guys asked.

'I'm certain,' Whitt said. 'It was Uchida. And she's a woman, actually. She was nestled in there among the skulls and spiders and naked girls you'd usually expect to find tattooed on an outlaw biker. Romtus probably hasn't told his fellow gang members what the tattoo means, who she is. I don't think they'd really respect it.'

'Tell me again what this tattoo has to do with where Jax Gotten is?' Nigel snapped.

Whitt leaned forward, put his elbows on his knees, his hands out, appealing. 'I looked into Romtus. I was intrigued. A bikie and a classical music fan? That's weird, right? Well, it turns out Romtus isn't just a fan. He's a musician. His parents put him into music school when he was four. He studied in Vienna as a teenager. He composes. He has quite a following on YouTube, under an alias, of course. I guess he couldn't have his criminal and creative lives clashing.'

'Are we trying to find a serial-killing bikie and possible baby murderer or are we trying to write a biography on this piece of shit?' someone asked.

'A couple of years ago,' Whitt said, his jaw tightening as he tried to remain patient, 'Romtus purchased a 1984 Bösendorfer Baroque semi-concert grand piano. One owner, matching bench. High-gloss walnut finish. The piano was in showroom condition. He had to have it shipped from Amarillo, Texas. It cost him about $320,000,' Whitt said.

'Three hundred grand? For a fucking piano?'

'Before shipping,' Whitt added.

'Get to the part where we find Jax Gotten,' Nigel said.

'Romtus wouldn't leave his piano,' Whitt said.

There was silence again. The men around Whitt stared at him, unblinking.

'I know your theory is that Jax Gotten and his whole crew are scattered to the wind because of the mass grave we found out in Panuara, and our suspicions about Tonya and Rebel Woods,' Whitt said. 'Your guys are looking for them in every hiding place they know of, and they're right to. Most of Gotten's guys are probably on their way north, to Cairns, to hide out in the wetlands or to try to hitch rides to Thailand. It would be madness to stay here in Sydney, right? But I think Edgar Romtus has stayed. I think he'll be near his house somewhere, waiting for all this to die down. He has an apartment in Erskineville where he stays when he's not out in Panuara.'

'That's where the expensive piano is,' Nigel said. 'The piano he's risking life in jail to stick by?'

'The piano was the heart of the Jewish household in pre-war Germany,' Whitt said. 'Many victims of the Holocaust were taken from their homes because they left their escape too late. While some fled, others stayed behind trying to find transportation solutions for their pianos. It wasn't just an instrument or a . . . a piece of furniture. It was a family member. Romtus won't want us coming around and trashing the piano looking for signs of where he is in his apartment. He'll be trying to organise the piano's safe removal.'

The men around Whitt looked at each other.

'If we find Edgar Romtus, put the heat on him, we can find Jax Gotten,' Whitt said.

The men got up from their seats and started heading towards the door.

'I can't go after Romtus myself,' Whitt called after them. 'I'll need backup.'

'How about this,' Nigel said as he stood to leave. 'You find Edgar Romtus, one of the country's most wanted men, sitting in his house playing his piano. You do that and I'll not only give you as much backup as you want on any case you ever have from this day forth, but I'll also give you my badge.'

Chapter 93

THE MEN STORMED into Crazy Connelly's Phones and Accessories in Bondi Junction shopping centre, a fast-moving mass in navy-blue paramedic uniforms. Their stride was so determined that the elderly couple perusing iPhone cases on the wall left the store immediately. The clerk, a thin teenage boy with a fluffy moustache, straightened his lime-green shirt and met them at a display cabinet full of Samsungs.

'Welcome to Crazy Connelly's, where telecommunications excellence is our –'

'Chargers,' Tox said, cutting off the kid. He started heaping phones on top of the cabinet. The men around him watched as twelve phones emerged from various pockets: Samsungs, cheap, battered Nokias, some brands Tox had never heard of. The store clerk picked up the nearest phone and looked at the men.

'What is all this?'

'They're phones, kid.' Tommy Mercer put his big arms on the display case, making the glass creak in its frame. 'You look new on the job, but not that new. We want chargers to fit all these phones, and we want to plug them in here and now. Most of the phones are out of battery, and those that aren't have passwords. You're going to find a way around the passwords and get us into the phones one by one as they charge up.'

The young store clerk looked up as he heard the metal shutters at the front of the store sliding down. Jelly was pulling them into place, blocking the view of confused patrons sitting in the food court, their forks hovering over their buffet Chinese food.

'Uh, I have chargers for some of these models,' the clerk said. 'But . . . but I can't bypass a phone's security, not without identification from the handset purchaser. And, sir, I have to ask you to open the doors. My manager –'

'Kid,' Tox said. 'Take a deep breath.'

The clerk did as he was told. He held a lungful of air until Tox nodded for him to let it out. Ryan went around the counter to unplug the store cameras.

'I'm your manager now,' Tox said. 'There will be no identification from handset purchasers. Unless you want a bunch of real paramedics racing in here in fifteen minutes to try to reassemble your body parts, you're going to get the chargers. All of them. Even if you have to call other stores. You're going to bypass the security on these phones and hand them over. That's the reality of the situation. It might go against the employee handbook, but it's happening and there's not a lot you can do about it.'

The store was suddenly very bright and very quiet. The store clerk listened to the buzzing of the fluorescent bulbs above him, looked at the faces of the men in paramedic uniforms.

He picked up the nearest handset and examined its charging port, then went to a cupboard at the side of the room.

Chapter 94

POPS AND I sat at the kitchen table together, the phone between us, the screen lit. I could hear familiar sounds coming through the speaker. Doors buzzing and shutting, clanging noises bouncing down hallways. Women having shouted conversations between cells. Footsteps. The sounds were making my stomach twist, and Pops knew it. He picked up one of the fluffy dogs from the floor and handed it to me. I stroked the warm, panting creature as we listened some more.

'Where are you?' I said finally, when I could stand the silence no longer.

'I'm heading up the fire stairs in C Block,' Terry Lancer said. Doctor Goldman's lover sounded nervous, his voice muffled, probably as he tried to hide the earpiece running from his ear down his collar and into his shirt, connected to the phone in his pocket. 'This is insane, you know that? What am I going to say if one of the supervisors comes along and I'm rifling through an armoury in the female section. How do I explain this?'

'Don't get caught,' I said, 'and you won't have to explain it.'

'What's the theory here?' Pops asked me. 'An inmate was trying to break into the armoury and steal a gun to make their escape, and Doctor Goldman interrupted them?'

'Maybe,' I said. 'I don't know.'

'How were they hoping to get into the armoury?' Pops asked. 'Surely its locked up tight. Seems like a failed mission even before Doctor Goldman's appearance put a stop to it.'

'Maybe the inmate had keys,' I said.

'Highly unlikely,' Pops said. 'If they had a set of keys, wouldn't they have just let themselves out of the prison?'

'Maybe they didn't have keys, but they were hoping Goldman would go for her weapon after the second lockdown. They figured Goldman would unlock the armoury. They met her there and stabbed her.'

'And then didn't take anything?'

'I don't know, Pops,' I said. 'I'm clutching at straws here.'

'I'm at the armoury,' Lancer said on the phone. 'Shit. Shit. There's another officer coming. I'm going to keep walking, circle back.'

I realised I was holding my breath. If Terry Lancer got caught helping me investigate Doctor Goldman's murder inside the prison, he'd be fired. I'd have burned my only source of access to the murder scene, to the armoury, to anything I might need inside the walls of the institution to prove Dolly's innocence. I listened to his footsteps, pictured him turning the corner on C Block's second floor, pacing in front of a row of cells before he turned back. Pops lifted his head as we heard the footsteps stop and a buzzer sounding.

'OK, I'm going in,' Lancer breathed. I heard the armoury door closing. 'I don't have a lot of time. I'm not going to get caught here, OK? I'm looking at the rows of guns. They're all here. Twelve pistols, twelve rifles, twelve bean-bag guns, twelve tasers.'

'Count them,' I said.

'I don't need to count them. They're sitting in racks with padlocks on them. There are only forty-eight slots. They're all full.'

'Count them anyway, Lancer,' I snapped.

Pops and I listened to the young guard counting under his breath.

'They're all here. I told you, this armoury has been checked a dozen times since . . . since the murder. They'd have noticed a missing gun, Harry,' Lancer pleaded. 'Now I gotta go.'

'What else is in there?' I asked.

'What?'

'You said it yourself. They'd have noticed a missing gun. What would they not have noticed? What else is in there?'

I heard items shifting on shelves. Boxes sliding. 'Uh. I don't know. Jesus. There are handcuffs. There's a rack on the wall with batons. Cords. Papers. Gun cleaning stuff. Documents.'

'What papers?' Pops squinted.

'Mostly records of who's done the armoury checks. Weapons cleaning schedules and instructions.' Lancer sighed hard. 'There are two fire extinguishers and a rack of mace.'

'Mace?' I sat up in my seat, thinking fast.

'Twelve mace guns. They're all here.'

Pops was watching me. Lancer's breathing was rattling the microphone attached to his phone.

'I've got to get out of here.'

'Wait,' I said. 'The mace guns. They're the small ones the guards attach to their belts, right? Black tube, about six inches long. They're the same as the police riot squad gets. Finger ring and trigger lever at the top.'

'So?'

'So those mace guns need ammunition,' I said. 'There's the gun itself and then there's the canister that goes inside. They're refillable.'

'OK.' Lancer's tone made it clear he wasn't following.

'So the small aerosol canister that goes inside the gun,' I said. 'Are they all there?'

Pops and I waited. I heard metal tubes clanging between Lancer's breaths.

'All the guns have canisters,' he said. 'And there's a box of refills. They're all here, too.'

'Goddamn it.' Pops put his face in his hands. 'I thought you had it.'

'Lancer,' I said. 'Scratch the canisters.'

'What?'

'Scratch them with your fingernail or your keys or something.'

'Why the hell would I do that?'

'Because it's possible one of them has been painted.'

'Painted?' Pops and Lancer spoke the word at the same time.

'Those aerosol canisters of mace,' I said. 'They're about the same size as the can of aerosol deodorant you get when you arrive at Johnsonborough. Wait here.'

I ran to the garage and retrieved the deodorant I'd brought home from prison.

'Remember this?' I asked Pops as he took it from me. 'The deodorant is aerosol because it can't be tampered with. If you mess with the canister at all the spray won't work. All a guard has to do in a shakedown is press the plunger, see if it sprays. The roll-on style deodorant, you just take the ball out and fill it with –'

'This is insane,' Lancer snapped. 'Someone is going to find me here!'

'Someone might have swapped out a can of deodorant with a can of mace,' I shouted over him. 'The mace cans are plain black, aren't they? It would be an easy paint job. There were women working on wrought-iron chairs in the workshop at the prison. Painting them black.'

'This is a hell of a long shot, Harry.' Pops put the can down. 'How the hell is an inmate going to get access to a can of black paint without anyone noticing?'

'They got access to a kitchen knife,' I said. 'They might have had access to the armoury. Just scratch the cans, Lancer. Do it now before I jump down the phone and throttle you.'

I gripped the dog in my lap too hard. It wriggled out of my hands and jumped to the floor. Pops and I watched each other's faces as the sound of Lancer shuffling around in the armoury came through the line. Agonising seconds ticked by. Sweat was rolling down my sides beneath my shirt.

'Oh my God,' Lancer said finally. 'Oh my God.'

'It's there?'

'It's here.' I could hear the sound of metal on metal as Lancer scratched at the can. 'It's fucking here. It's blue underneath. I can see writing.'

'OK,' Pops said. 'Someone stole a canister of mace. Why do that? Why kill the doctor just to do that? You're never going to escape the prison armed with just a canister of mace.'

'Lancer,' I said, 'I want you to leave the armoury. Go to the front office. Find the transport roster.'

'What do I do with it?' he asked.

'Tell me who's leaving the prison today.'

Chapter 95

WHITT STRUMMED HIS fingers on the steering wheel, watching Edgar Romtus's apartment block while he listened to the tactical channel Nigel had taken command of for the day. Hour by hour, the strike teams looking for Jax Gotten all over the state checked in and gave their reports as they smashed their way through known bikie safe houses, checking locations off an exhaustive list. The teams hit Jax's mother's house, and the houses of family members and ex-wives of all the Silver Aces members. Whitt knew that in Queensland, similar raids were being conducted. The airports were being watched, especially the small rural ones. There was no one looking for Jax's men here, at the apartment of one of his right-hand men. For any member of the crew to stay in their own home would be ludicrous.

But still, Whitt waited.

At midday he could wait no longer. He crossed the road, spying a mother trying to wrestle both her toddler and its stroller through the front door of the building. He held the door open and then slipped in after her, trying to affect an air of confidence as they took the lift together.

Whitt got out on the third floor and walked to apartment eleven, then crept the last few metres to apartment twelve. He stood listening, heard nothing, then knelt and looked under the crack of the door.

A movement. But it could have been anything – light shifting through the windows, a plane passing, heading towards the airport. The flicker of shape was not accompanied by sound. Whitt would have to make himself known. He put his hands out, drew up a foot to stand and got no further.

A hole was punched in the door two feet above his head, right where his centre mass would have been if he'd been standing. Splinters of wood fell all around him. The blast was like hands clapped over his ears, vibrating his eardrums. Whitt scrambled sideways and grabbed his gun from his belt, flattened instinctively on the carpet half a second before another hole blasted through the chipboard wall above his head, only an inch too high this time. He sprang into a standing position, stepped back and kicked the door in. He fired rapidly into the open space, creating cover for himself, enough for him to slip in the door and duck behind a couch.

Chapter 96

THERE WERE A number of strategies available to him. Whitt crouched, sweating, and reviewed them in the ticking silence. There were no fire escapes on the east side of the building. Romtus was trapped. If Whitt simply waited, covering the door, backup would come, alerted by triple-zero calls from residents in the building. But he could also charge forward, cornering the bearded bikie, cutting off any strategising the man himself was doing. It was possible Romtus was arming himself with something more substantial than whatever had blasted the holes in the apartment's entry. Whitt had known bikies to carry hand grenades and pipe bombs, a rocket launcher once. He had also known cornered suspects to take their chances with third-storey leaps onto concrete as a means of escape, and he needed Romtus conscious enough to tell him where Jax was hiding.

Whitt was moving towards the end of the couch, where he could hear heavy breathing coming from around the corner near the kitchen. Then he heard shuffling at the other end of the apartment, near where a beautiful walnut piano was reflected in a mirror hanging on the wall.

'Who else is here?' Whitt called.

Whitt thought he saw Jax Gotten step out from behind the wall near the piano. He didn't have long to look before a hole was blasted in the couch behind which he was hiding, tearing the padded arm clean off.

'Guys, this is not the way to do this,' Whitt ventured. 'If there's still a chance we can save Rebel Woods, your cooperation now would turn everything around. Just tell me where the baby is. I'll back off and we can get a negotiator in here.'

'We didn't do this,' Romtus called. 'Tell 'em, Jax. Don't let them pin it on –'

'Shut up, Ed!'

'Look, mate. A rival club is one thing,' Romtus continued. 'We're going to go down for wiping out the Rabbits crew. We can't get out of that. But if they stick us with the Police Commissioner's daughter and grandkid, we won't make it to the intake cell alive. They won't risk us getting into the prison yard where the other crews will protect us. The cops will put us in a cell and we'll be carried out in a body bag, Jax.'

'I said shut up!'

'Tell 'em,' Romtus said. Whitt listened to his heavy, panicked breathing as it was slowly consumed by the sound of approaching sirens. 'Tell 'em about the lawyer.'

Chapter 97

TOX HAD BEEN through five of the phones himself. The men around him in the store were reading the others as best they could, but Tox couldn't count on their ability to discern information important to the Woods case, or indeed their ability to read at all. He picked up a newish Samsung as the nervous teenage store clerk set it down, having just tapped his jailbreaking code into its secure page. He opened the messages folder and felt a bolt of energy sizzle through him as he noted there was only one collection of texts there, under the letter 'T'.

He opened the most recent message from 'T' and read it aloud.

I don't want to play games. It's a simple exchange. The money for the tape. You can afford this, Louis, and you know I need it.

'What does that mean?' Jelly asked.

But Tox didn't answer. He was rolling up the sliding door of the phone shop and slipping away into the crowded shopping centre.

Chapter 98

ABOVE 130 KILOMETRES an hour, travelling by car is all just fast and loud. I took Pops's long-suffering Datsun to its limits around corners and through intersections, heading for Lane Cove. Whenever corrections staff transport prisoners, they tend to take the most discreet and secure routes, even if it means making a longer trip and subjecting their human cargo to soaring temperatures in the back of the vehicle. I knew the truck heading out of Johnsonborough that morning was going to take the Lane Cove tunnel, north of the facility, then head south through the Harbour Tunnel, staying underground all the way to the airport.

The Datsun screamed up behind buses and trucks, the steering wheel shaking in my grip. There seemed to be a million hazards on the road before me. Slow-moving semis spewing smoke, old ladies wheeling walking frames over crossings, groups of teenagers carrying schoolbags spilling out onto the asphalt. Terry Lancer's words on the phone rumbled through my head as I cursed the traffic.

A truck left for Long Bay ten minutes ago. Three inmates, three guards. The inmates were Dolly Quaddich, Susan Wu and Anna Regent.

I had been wrong about Doctor Goldman's murder from the outset. I ground my teeth with regret as I sped through the traffic. All along I'd assumed that such a brutal and vicious killing must have been related to the kind and sweet woman somehow. Because that was how it went in my job – the victims were so often people who had listened or risked or given too much to bad people and been cut down for their efforts. But it was starting to look like the person who had killed Doctor Goldman hadn't done so because she was so willing to cross the line into the territory of those irredeemable souls. And she hadn't been killed because she wouldn't smuggle drugs into the prison, or because she broke the rules and fell in love with a colleague.

Doctor Goldman's death had been one step in a long and complicated plan, and I now had to interrupt that plan.

Or a woman who should never again walk among the innocents of society would take her first steps to freedom.

Chapter 99

'WHAT ABOUT THE lawyer?' Whitt called.

There was silence in the apartment. In the hallway, Whitt could hear residents leaving, running, talking frantically about the source of the blasts. Jax Gotten didn't speak. It was Romtus who continued.

'The lawyer, Mallally. He came to us,' Romtus said. 'He'd already tried to hire someone to knock off the girl. Some button man for hire in the city, I don't know. Either the guy fucked it up or refused to do it. Mallally was paying big money, so we thought we'd play it easy and give her a hot shot. A simple way to do it, you know? No violence. She would take care of it herself.'

'And that didn't work?' Whitt asked. He was watching for Jax Gotten in the mirror. Now and then he could see a slice of shoulder as the man paced in the short hall.

'She didn't take it. People said she was trying to get clean. We don't know what she did with it.'

She hid it, Whitt thought. *In her filthy motel room.*

'After a week Mallally asked us to go in,' Romtus said. 'Do it right.'

'You need to shut the fuck up,' Gotten warned.

'I'm telling him we didn't do it!' Romtus protested. 'Listen, man. We didn't do it. We got there and saw she had a baby. He didn't tell us nothin' about that. We don't do kids, man. No amount of money is worth that. You won't find a crew in Sydney who does kids. That's a specialist deal.'

'So what happened?' Whitt asked. He crept to the blasted-up end of the couch to see if he could get a better angle on Gotten, but the man had disappeared.

'We pulled out,' Romtus said. 'The lawyer was saying we didn't need to do the kid. Just go in there and pop the mother, whatever. But it was just getting too complicated, man. He was leaving shit out. Not being real with us. There was too much communication, too many trails. We don't work like that.'

'Did Mallally –' Whitt began. But he spied Gotten at the bedroom door, directly to his left. There must have been a passage through the bathroom into the bedroom, a loop in the apartment that meant Gotten could sneak up beside him.

Whitt turned and raised his gun, tugged the trigger, as two bullets impacted like punches in his chest.

Chapter 100

A DAY TRIP was exciting for Dolly. She usually got at least one during her stints at Johnsonborough. The last time she'd been banged up for participating in a burglary, and she'd scored a trip to see the ear, nose and throat specialist at the Prince of Wales Hospital. The guards had even bought her a vanilla thickshake from Hungry Jacks on the return journey to prison.

She sat now in the back of the transport truck, gripping the rail that ran along the inside of the vehicle and watching the highway roll by, cars passing beneath her. She stood to catch a glimpse of Sydney Harbour before the truck dipped into the Harbour Tunnel, blackness lit by orange lamps enveloping the vehicle. She tried to think if there were any Hungry Jacks restaurants between Johnsonborough and the Bay. The trip home, after the guards had dropped off Anna The Spanner and the mystery woman, was a good bet for a treat, if Dolly asked nicely.

She took her seat on the bench again, her ankle chains rattling on the steel floor, and looked at the great hulking mass of Anna Regent on the bench opposite. The violent inmate was counting silently, her lips forming regular, familiar shapes, and Dolly watched for a while, wondering what she was counting down or up to. There was one female guard seated beside her, dwarfed by the kid-killer's bulk, and two male guards in the front, chatting behind the steel grille that separated them from the prisoners' area. The third inmate was a woman Dolly hadn't seen before, another ultra-violent freak, judging from the paleness of her skin and her exhausted look. She'd probably spent her entire stint at Johnsonborough in solitary, where there was no sun and no sleep, and the fact that she was going to the Bay permanently meant she was crazy to boot.

Dolly was just thinking about asking the guard what the chances of a quick stopover at Hungry Jacks on the way home might be when Anna stopped counting. She slid her hand into her prison-transport jumpsuit and brought out a bundled-up white undershirt.

Dolly watched, perplexed, as Anna wound the shirt around her nose and mouth.

Chapter 101

I SPOTTED THE Johnsonborough transport truck from nearly a kilometre away, breaking free of a tangle of vehicles and heading down into the Harbour Tunnel, hitting eighty kilometres an hour. I floored it, the Datsun's temperature gauge soaring and the vehicle smelling of burning oil, praying for the little car to make gains on the truck before Anna's plan was initiated.

I knew I was too late when the truck swerved. It was a sudden, shallow move, a jolting that was corrected immediately, but the truck immediately sped up as though the driver was trying to flee the trouble inside his own vehicle. I heard the engine roaring as it climbed quickly to over a hundred kilometres an hour. Then I watched helplessly as the truck swerved again, harder this time, the side of the cabin throwing up a shower of orange sparks as it hit the concrete barrier that ran along the wall of the tunnel.

The truck overcorrected, turned at a jarring angle and toppled over. I saw the front of the vehicle tear away from the cabin, bouncing off the side of the tunnel like a pinball and smashing through two other cars, as the back half crashed onto its side and skidded to a halt.

I wedged the Datsun in as close to the crash as I could, shoving an old man back into his car as he tried to get out to help. Black smoke was thick in the air, but as I neared the scene I felt a familiar stinging in my eyes and throat, a tightening pain, like tiny razor blades being sucked into my nostrils and windpipe. As I ran between the cars, horns blaring all around me, the fire extinguisher system deployed from above, hard rain falling, making it impossible to see.

I staggered blindly forward, glimpsing the broad, hard shoulders of Anna Regent hunched as she ripped the handcuff keys from the belt of a female guard sprawled on the floor of the van. Anna was free in seconds. She emerged through the smog at the truck's torn side, spraying mace wildly back into the vehicle as she went.

Chapter 102

I COULD CATCH a killer, or I could save my friend.

The hissing of engine oil hitting the asphalt was like a clock ticking down to the engine of the truck exploding. Flames licked and swirled from the cabin, where a guard emerged, coughing, clawing his way free. I pushed my way into the back of the truck and grabbed the guard in the blackness and choking heat, recognising the feel of her buckles and belt as I searched. I dragged the unconscious guard out onto the roadside and went back in for Dolly. An inmate I didn't recognise was kicking at the back door handle, unable to get to the torn piece of the truck's side, cut off by twisted metal benches. Her face was awash with blood. I stumbled over Dolly, picked her up and tumbled out of the vehicle as the inmate named Susan Wu broke through the dented doors of the truck.

Dolly was limp and small in my arms. I glanced at the bloodied, unnamed woman as she got her bearings in the crowd of people and vehicles.

'Don't,' I warned, holding my friend against my chest. But the woman gave me a defiant half-smile and took off limping, scattering gawkers as she disappeared in the opposite direction to Anna.

I'd thought Dolly was unconscious but she gripped my shirt with a bloody, chained hand as I set her down a safe distance from the truck. Her shoulder looked dislocated and there was a gash the length of my index finger in her forehead. I lay her flat and let the water from the sprinkler system fall on her face, trying to wash the mace and blood out of her eyes.

'I've got you, cellie,' I said. 'You're alright now.'

'She maced us,' Dolly exclaimed, her chained hands shaking as she gripped me. 'How . . . how rude! I don't even know Anna The Spanner!'

'She knows you. You took a murder rap for her,' I said. 'Don't worry, Doll. I'm going to drag her back here by her hair and make sure she pays for what she did.'

'I . . . I was waiting for you to call again,' Dolly said. 'I think I remember what I was holding. In the hallway. When I came out of –'

'Dolly, just –'

'I had one of Goldie's snakes. Those jelly snakes. They're really good.'

'I've got to go, Doll,' I said.

'I'll just wait here.' Dolly put her head back against the road surface. 'I'm staying put. I think my leg is broken.'

People from the cars around us were gathering at my side. A young man in a courier's outfit knelt over Dolly and started giving her gentle reassurance as he placed a jacket under her head. I knew she was in safe hands.

I got up and sprinted in the direction Anna had fled.

Chapter 103

TOX ARRIVED BACK at the Mallally house just as a red-wine-coloured Chrysler Pacifica was pulling out of the left-hand door of the double garage. He saw the whites of Mallally's eyes as the man glanced towards the approaching Monaro, jerked the wheel and sped away up the hill.

Tox cursed and used his phone one-handed as he drove. Nigel Spader picked up in one ring.

'I've got the lawyer for the Woods killing,' Tox said. 'He's made me and he's heading west towards Old South Head Road. I need a chopper and every available patrol car.'

'Forget it,' Nigel said. 'Whittacker has pulled a fucking miracle and tracked down Jax Gotten in an apartment in Erskineville. Let the lawyer go. It's the bikies we want.'

'Let the lawyer –' Tox shook his head, trying to clear his ears. 'I – You – Just trust me, Spader, it's the lawyer who's behind all this. I have proof.'

'And it's the bikie who's got the violent background and the nationwide manhunt on his back. We've got shots fired and

330

Whitt's trapped inside the building. We're about to move on the ground floor entry. I'll call you back.'

'But Mallally's family is –' Tox heard the line disconnect and roared the words anyway '– *in the back of the car!*'

Chapter 104

WHITT WAS DEAD. Two .38 shots entered his chest, a perfect military-style double tap, bullets that smashed through his sternum, his diaphragm, tearing holes in his heart and lungs, crumbling his spine on their way through him to the wall behind. The bullets collected his soul on their way out of his body, tugging it from his being far too soon. By the time he crumpled to the floor he was just the warm shell of the man he had been only seconds earlier, crouched behind a couch, trying to talk down a pair of killers.

That's what would have happened, anyway.

He considered the scenario of his almost-demise as he lay gasping for breath on the carpet. As the men talked above him, on the other side of the couch, Whitt reached up gratefully and slid his hand under his shirt, pulled the still-hot bullets from the surface of his bulletproof vest. He silently gave past Whitt all the thanks and praise he could muster for purchasing the vest when Harry suggested he should.

'We shouldn't have stayed,' Jax was growling. 'This was so stupid. *So stupid!* You said we could hide in plain sight. You said this apartment was off the books! Look, the building's surrounded. We're fucked, Ed.'

'It's gonna be OK, brother,' Romtus said. 'We'll explain. We'll explain everything.'

Whitt rolled over and clutched his way up the couch in time to see Romtus and Gotten embrace hard in the middle of the living room, both men gripping the other's shirt, their faces twisted in turmoil and their weapons sitting on a side table by the hall. He watched the hug in amazement and confusion for a few seconds. Then he raised his gun, his whole arm shaking and numb from the impact of the bullets to the vest.

When he spoke, both men turned to him.

'You can explain later,' Whitt said. 'Right now, put your hands up.'

Chapter 105

IT SEEMED MALLALLY had decided to head for the city, but when a busy intersection confronted him at Old South Head Road he turned left and headed south. Tox kept on his tail as much as possible, bursting through intersections and rolling up onto the footpath to get around parked and queueing cars. The Monaro crashed and bumped off guardrails, smacked over a stop sign without slowing, sent pedestrians diving into bushes.

Through the back window of the Chrysler, he could see Mallally's two little girls turned in their seats and watching him, their mouths open in silent, howling sobs. Shania Mallally was in the front seat beside her husband, which was a good thing, because now and then she tugged at the wheel when the car slowed, trying to get the panicked lawyer to pull over. But her position in the car was also a bad thing, because she was so far away from the kids in the rear seat. If she managed to get the car stopped, giving herself an opportunity to flee, Tox knew she wouldn't do it without her girls.

As the Chrysler roared down Arden Street, Tox wondered if he would find himself pursuing Mallally along the crowded promenade at Coogee Beach. The traffic was always terrible at the bottom of the huge hill before the sprawling ocean. His spirits lifted. And they lifted again when Mallally swung the wheel wildly and careered the car down Burnie Street.

'Yes,' Tox smiled. 'Good choice.'

Mallally didn't attempt the hairpin turn back onto Clovelly Road towards the city. He picked up speed past the back of the Clovelly Hotel. A pair of women in bikinis fell on their surfboards on the narrow shoulder of the road as the cars soared down the street towards the big car park that perched on the cliff edge before the sea below. There were plenty of cars there. Tox knew Mallally was trapped. He followed the car to the edge of the parking lot, south from the entrance, and parked behind it, trapping it into a wide space.

He pulled his gun and shooed away an old couple taking photos of the royal-blue sea beyond Mallally's car. Nearby, surfers making their way towards the stairs leading down from the cliffs stopped in their tracks. Tox pointed the gun at the driver's door and walked until he could see Mallally's profile, his hands gripping the wheel, staring at the rocky cliffs of Gordon's Bay. Mallally's window was half open. Tox was three metres away, but he could hear the lawyer's breathing.

'Turn the engine off!' Tox yelled. He couldn't get a clear shot at Mallally, not with his wife in the front seat and his kids in the back. He hazarded a couple of steps closer. 'Turn the engine off now!'

'She was extorting me,' Mallally said. 'She wanted hush money. I . . . I was defending myself. My business . . . my livelihood was threatened, and with it my family.'

'You killed Tonya,' Tox said.

'I tried to get someone else to do it.' Mallally shook his head. He slammed the steering wheel with his palm. 'I asked a hitman. I asked the bikies. They were all so squeamish. I tried to tell them I didn't care if the kid was killed or not. But I fell into the same trap they were trying to avoid.' He drew a ragged breath, gave a sad, hard laugh. 'The baby was just sitting there staring up at me after I'd finished with Tonya. I couldn't just leave her there.'

'Did you kill Rebel?' Tox took another step closer. 'Where is she?'

'Now I have nothing.' Mallally wrung the steering wheel. 'I have nothing left!'

'Listen to me,' Tox said. 'Use your right hand to shut the car off.'

'Louis!' Shania grabbed at her husband's arm. 'Do it, for God's sake! The girls are in the back!'

Tox glanced around the parking lot. Some beachgoers were hiding behind their cars, others filming on their phones, or using them to call the emergency services. He thought about shooting the car's tyres out. About firing into the front of the driver's door and trying to get Mallally in the legs, to show him he was serious. All he really wanted to do was yank the man out of the driver's seat and stomp his head into the asphalt. The girls in the back seat were beating their sweaty palms on the windows. Tox took another step closer to the vehicle.

It was a mistake. A shard of broken beer-bottle glass popped under his boot, startling Mallally at the wheel. The lawyer turned and looked at him, and Tox saw what was going to happen before it played out in front of him.

He raised the gun, shot out the front driver's tyre with a blast that made people scream around him. But it was no use. Mallally stomped on the accelerator, and the big car bumped and smashed over the concrete gutter running the length of the car park, careering over the clifftop.

Chapter 106

THE TUNNEL WAS empty up ahead. My mind was racing, trying to discern Anna's plan. The smell of smoke from the crash behind me still permeated the air through the rain of the sprinkler system soaking my clothes and hair. Above me, a message was blaring through the tunnel's safety announcement system in a calm, soothing loop.

Switch off your engine. Do not exit your vehicle. Safety personnel will arrive shortly to escort you to the emergency exits. Switch off your engine.

One thing was clear. Anna had to have had assistance in her escape plan. I knew this because she had been assisted before. She had been given a kitchen knife by a person with the ability to take the knife back to the kitchen and return it to its place before the search for Doctor Goldman's murder weapon took place. Anna must have had the knowledge – been given the knowledge – that the mace canisters in the prison riot gear were the exact size and shape of the prison-issue deodorant cans. She must have been snuck a can of paint from the workshops, because Anna Regent was too violent an inmate to ever be cleared to work in a room full of tools and sharp objects. Anna must have been allowed to leave her confines in solitary and walk to the third floor of C Block, unescorted and taking a route fast enough to get her there and back while the entire prison was distracted with the level-one alert. Someone would have searched Anna's personal items as she left for Long Bay and overlooked the black canister of mace in place of a canister of deodorant. It had to be someone who was willing to assist Anna enough to allow her to maim and kill on her way to freedom, but not someone strong enough to be the killer themselves, not someone who had ever killed before.

It had to be someone who controlled what Anna did and where she went. Someone with the power to allow her to visit me on the night of Doctor Goldman's murder in my solitary cell with a Cherry Ripe in her pocket. A little perk given to her by someone who loved her, someone who wanted to see the vicious child-killer set free.

Only a Johnsonborough guard could have helped Anna do all the things she had done. And only one guard had been hanging around the night Anna was let into my cell. Only one guard had warned me that I shouldn't try to help Dolly Quaddich get free of the accusation of killing Doctor Goldman, because that guard was in control. That guard was pulling the strings.

You're out there, and we're in here. There's nothing you can do to us.

I cursed myself for not seeing the guard named Steeler for what she was the moment she smashed my knuckles with her baton in solitary. She was a coward. Someone drawn to cruelty and pain. She was one of those terrible people lured towards a role in the police, military or corrections because it meant she could enjoy power over other human beings and get paid for it.

The tall, white-haired woman with the tattoo of barbed wire around her wrist would be just like the other terrible men and women who went into those jobs for the wrong reasons – without her gun and her baton and her uniform, she was just a loathsome coward. She would be cunning enough to sneak Anna a can of paint to disguise her deodorant can with, but not daring enough to swap the canisters out herself and risk being caught in the armoury, losing her job. She would be daring enough to give Anna the knife, but not daring enough to accompany her on the mission, to actually kill Doctor Goldman when she arrived unexpectedly around the corner of the C Block hallway. Steeler was the snivelling accomplice, not brave enough to hunt the wolf but bold enough to wear its fur. I was guessing, as I ran, that Anna would be heading towards Steeler and the getaway car. Steeler had facilitated Anna's escape with as few risks as possible. She was reckless enough to give Anna the truck's chosen route on that morning, to have spent her weekend calculating the seconds Anna needed to count from entering the Harbour Tunnel to an approximate crash point so that she would be able to meet Anna not too far away.

But she would not be there for the fire, the smoke, the screams. Just like she wasn't there when Goldman drew her last breath.

It was just my gut telling me these things. But I trusted my gut. I felt that I was heading towards one mastermind prisoner escapee and her hopelessly devoted, underhanded sidekick. Anna was smarter than she appeared. The hopeless, idiot sadist act had sucked me in, and Doctor Goldman, too. It had made Steeler give up everything that she was.

I knew that Steeler would wait for Anna to run ahead from the truck crash and get in her car, their getaway completely clear until emergency vehicles started responding to the disturbance in the tunnel from the city side. I knew there was little chance Anna hadn't made it to the getaway car yet, my feeling almost confirmed as a pair of fire engines and a police car roared past me in the dark, heading in the opposite direction. But just as I began to lose all hope, a car appeared in my vision, blinking yellow hazard lights, its nose turned in to a small emergency space cut into the side of the tunnel.

Chapter 107

I DID A lap of the car, my gun drawn, and saw no one. Behind me, the tunnel disappeared into the heavy rain falling from the sprinkler system. There was a concrete barrier on either side of the tunnel and a walkway leading to two bright-green emergency doors. I chose the door closest to the car, shoved my way in and checked both ways.

Empty. But beyond where I stood, fifty metres ahead in the direction of the city, the lights above had been smashed out, leaving a stretch of tunnel shrouded in pure blackness before a curve in the structure. I crept forward, my gun aimed into the dark, watching for the slightest movement.

'Anna,' I called. 'I know you're there. You were given a chance to do this the right way. You were on your way to Long Bay to get help, to get free one day without hurting anyone. I'm giving you one more chance now to stop the violence.'

There was no movement in the darkness. Another pair of emergency vehicles rushed past on the other side of the wall.

Beneath their noise, I thought I heard the shuffling of feet. I flicked the safety off on my gun.

'Anna,' I said. 'I'm warning you. I'm going to shoot if you don't come out with your hands up.'

Another siren and rush of cars, and now I was sure that someone was making their way towards me under the cover of the emergency vehicles. I lowered my weapon and fired low into the dark, hoping to wound whoever might be standing there, Anna or her accomplice, Steeler. But the flash of my gunfire lit the dark space, and all at once I saw the broken glass on the concrete floor, the emptiness there. I didn't have more than a second to feel shockingly, achingly alone. Another emergency door, one I'd paid no attention to in the dark, burst open at my side. I was shoved hard into the wall of the narrow tunnel, Anna's big arms wrapping me up while Steeler knocked the gun from my hands.

Chapter 108

THE BODY PANICS when the airway is cut off. It's impossible to think clearly. There are options available to the victim in a headlock, but for precious seconds all they want to do is grip wildly at the arm around their throat and pull. This is useless, because the attacker's strength locking their arm across their chest is far more mechanically efficient than the victim's strength pulling down and out with the forearms. For a second or two I fell into the trap, trying to work my fingers under Anna's arm, realising with horror my situation as Steeler retrieved my gun from the ground.

But Steeler's mistake came soon after mine. She straightened and pointed the gun at me, standing far too close. She wasn't going to shoot me. She was a weakling. Someone who had allowed herself to come under Anna's spell, who could hand over a knife but not do the stabbing. I used her proximity, pushing both of my legs swiftly off the ground and planting them in her chest, shoving downwards while I arched my back. I kicked Steeler away and sent Anna falling backwards, her impact on the concrete ground loosening her arm. I righted quickly, stomped on Anna's face as I turned to go for Steeler. What was important was the gun. Steeler had dropped it. We scrambled for it at the same time, nails scratching and fingers fumbling, and in the fray I butted her sideways with my shoulder, snatched the gun and wheeled sideways just as Anna was getting to her feet and rushing at us.

I put two bullets in the big woman, then backed up and blasted two more because the first shots seemed to have no impact at all. I watched in horror as she kept coming at me. She seemed like something inhuman, the monster that everyone had always told her she was. And I knew the fear of the little boy she had killed, a deep and primal and hopeless fear. She went down on her knees and Steeler pushed past me to catch her before she fell. I watched the two of them holding each other as Anna died.

Chapter 109

IN TIME STEELER stood up slowly. I held the gun on her, but she seemed almost to forget it was there. She was standing looking at me, and her face was red and tear-stained, her hands hanging by her sides. The rushing of a vehicle with a siren through the tunnel beside us seemed to bring her to her senses.

'She wasn't an evil person,' Steeler said.

'I'm sure that's what Doctor Goldman thought seconds before Anna plunged that knife into her neck,' I said. 'She was wrong, and you're wrong. I just saved you from whatever the hell she'd have done to you once the two of you were out of the woods.'

'You don't understand,' Steeler sneered. 'How could you possibly understand?'

'Because I've run across my fair share of cowards in this job,' I said. 'You weren't willing to do Anna's dirty work, but you would give her the tools she needed to do it herself. You're pathetic.'

Steeler shook her head at me. She looked exhausted, sad.

'I fell for Anna's bullshit the first time I met her, too,' I said. 'She was a master manipulator, there's no doubt about it. I do the same job you do, you know,' I said. 'I deal with criminals. Some of them are good people who do bad things, like Dolly Quaddich. Some of them are bad people who can be redeemed. And some of them are monsters.'

Steeler put her palms to the sides of her head like she was trying to block out what I was saying.

'It doesn't matter how hard you dreamed about being her saviour,' I said. 'Anna Regent was unsaveable.'

'Then so am I,' Steeler said.

I heard the wail of another siren coming up the tunnel, and so did Steeler. She turned, and though I'm sure my scream reached her, my fingers only brushed against her jacket as she fled through the door to the tunnel. I was just a metre behind her as she sprinted into the path of the speeding fire engine.

I was so close as she was hit that I felt specks of her blood hit my face as the vehicle passed me, dragging her body underneath it.

Chapter 110

TOX RAN TO the edge of the cliff, saw the Chrysler on its roof and sinking fast in the water fifty feet below. Then he ran back to the parking lot. The crowd was thick now.

'Don't do it, man!' A young surfer with blond dreadlocks held Tox's eyes. Tox ignored him, turned, and ran for the sheer drop.

He hit the water feet-first beside the car, his head full of silent screaming prayers that he wasn't about to be shattered on rocks beneath the waves. But he sank unscathed into white, swirling foam and pulled his way towards the surface, glimpsing people on the cliffs above looking down. Their cries were drowned out by the surf smashing on the rocks. He swam to where the car's right rear wheel was just disappearing beneath the waves and filled his lungs with air, ducked down and dived deep.

Four passengers. He was one man trying to rescue them all. Tox knew that if anyone was doomed, it was Louis and Shania Mallally, because he wasn't going to go home that night without having got the children out of the car. If he had time, he'd try for the adults.

Tox swam hard for the back of the car and grabbed at the hatchback door, trying to haul it open. An air bubble trapped at the roof of the car made it impossible to open the door, so he watched until the air was sucked away, leaving the two little girls wide-eyed and wide-mouthed, staring at him, panicking. When he pulled them out they latched onto him immediately, hard fingers and nails gripping his neck and shirt and hair, and he knew he was in trouble even before he turned for the surface and kicked off from the back of the car.

Their panic was like electricity. Winding and turning around him like a hot wire. One was gripped around his head, the other latched to his side, making it impossible to swim. The movement of the car seemed to be taking them downwards, away from the light. Tox struggled with the girls, his heart smashing against his chest, water finally slipping in with frightening ease, filling his throat.

Chapter 111

THEY BROKE THE surface together, gasping and coughing, but the children didn't calm, kicking and dragging him down. Tox pried one child from his head and pushed her away, burning with horror at having to let her go. He grabbed the other by the arms and ripped her from his side.

'I've got you!' He wound an arm around her tiny chest, dragging her backwards. 'I've got you!'

He swam, dragging one, and grabbed downwards for the other, who was sinking like a stone. A wave lifted them all, and he scooped up the other one.

'My mummy!' one of them cried. 'My mummy! My mummy!'

'I'm sorry, baby,' Tox said. 'I can't help her.' He would have to leave her behind, just as it seemed he would be unable to save Rebel Woods. His heart ached as he headed for the base of the cliffs, trying to find the spot where the waves were calmest and the rocks flattest. He knew that as he took the children further from the car, down there in the depths Louis Mallally was drowning, and with him any hope of knowing what had happened to Tonya's child. He reached the rocks, exhausted, and shoved the kids up before him.

Hard splashes behind him in the waves made him turn. He glimpsed two surfers, one of them the dreadlocked man who had told him not to jump, breathing hard and preparing to dive for the car. A little hope prickled in his chest as he dragged himself and the children to safety.

Chapter 112

THE MALLALLY HOUSE was surrounded by a ring of cops and journalists, local residents and people who had heard what had happened in the news and come to stare.

Whitt saw a group of men in suits, probably lawyers, arguing with police at the edge of the cordon, trying to get information on what had happened to their friend. He worked his way into the house, and the worried glances of his colleagues seemed to direct him up the stairs to Mallally's office, where someone was smashing and crashing through the items there.

Tox Barnes was still dripping wet, his jeans and boots sloshing as he moved about the trashed room. Whitt watched him for a moment, until he flipped the desk with an enormous crash, running his hands over the base and drawers, searching.

'Tox, you need to stop.' Whitt put his hands up. 'This is a crime sc–'

'Don't tell me it's a crime scene,' Tox snapped. 'It'll be a crime scene when I'm done with it. There must be something here that tells us where he's put the kid. If she's still alive we don't have much time.'

Whitt knew there was no chance Rebel Woods was still alive. From what he had learned from his fellow officers at the scene at Ed Romtus's apartment, and from radio chatter on his way to the Mallally house, he believed wholeheartedly that the little girl was dead.

Nigel Spader had told him that Tox Barnes and a group of his less-than-law-abiding friends had entered the Mallally home, conducted an illegal search and obtained a phone that held messages between Mallally and Tonya Woods. Their relationship, as well as their arrangement, had become clear. Mallally had begun his affair with Tonya Woods, and quickly turned her out to work for him, using her to listen in on the private conversations of clients in bars and restaurants, or to strike up conversations and flirt with prosecution lawyers to gain the upper hand on his cases.

Then he had come to her with a major proposition. A very dangerous, but potentially lucrative mission. Mallally had asked Tonya to seduce and sleep with Drew Bortfield, CEO of Sydney Airport. He wanted her to report to the police after the liaison that she had been raped by Bortfield. The scandal would delay the corruption lawsuit against Mallally's client, Antonio Santarelli, and throw doubt over the legitimacy of Bortfield's claim that Santarelli had bribed him. Mallally was offering ten thousand dollars for Tonya's services. She was a prostitute and a drug addict. She was a practised liar. It was a mission that wouldn't stretch her skills or her moral boundaries. All she had to do was have sex with a man and lie to police – a piece of cake for a girl like her.

But Tonya Woods didn't want ten thousand dollars. She wanted $1.2 million. She asked for the money as she sat before Mallally in his home office, after playing him a recording of a conversation between the two of them in which Mallally asked Tonya to commit acts that would not only have Mallally disbarred but thrown in jail.

Mallally had been backed into a corner. He needed Tonya to go away. He'd tried to hire a hitman, then put the bikies onto the job. When Jax Gotten and his crew in the Silver Aces Motorcycle Club refused his call, Mallally had gone to Tonya's motel room himself, killed her, and torn the place apart looking for the tape she had made of their negotiations.

There had been little Rebel, sitting, watching him through terrified tears. The man who had strangled her mother right before her eyes. Rebel knew Mallally. The tiny child had seen him a number of times. Was she too young to finger him when the police asked who had killed Mummy? Mallally had found himself looking down at Rebel and asking himself if he could kill her, something men far nastier than him had refused to do.

It only made sense to Whitt that a man so determined to save his own skin would have completed the job to its fullest. He'd killed Tonya. He'd hired Blenk to start violently steering Harry and her team away from the investigation. He'd have surely killed little Rebel Woods. Whitt watched Tox searching Mallally's office, swearing and throwing things, and felt hopeless.

Harry came up the stairs beside him, wet, like Tox was, parts of her streaked with blood. Whitt frowned at his exhausted friend.

'You went into the sea as well?' he asked.

'What?' Harry said.

'Tox just pulled the Mallally kids out of the ocean,' Whitt said. 'Some surfers got the mother out of a sinking car. They're fine. The lawyer didn't make it.'

'There has to be something here.' Tox leaned against the windowsill, breathless, watching the street. 'This can't be it.'

Whitt and Harry followed him through the mess to the window. A tow truck was trying to ease its way through the crowd. Whitt looked down and saw that the Mallally's yellow Maserati was outside one of the double garage doors. It would be taken away to be forensically examined for traces of Tonya and Rebel Woods.

Whitt felt Tox snap to attention beside him. The big man put a damp hand on the glass before him, his eyes fixed on the yellow Maserati in the driveway.

'Three cars,' Tox said.

'Huh?' Whitt said.

'The Mallallys have three cars,' Tox said quickly. 'A yellow Maserati, a red Chrysler and the silver BMW.'

'So what?' Whitt asked. He saw Harry's eyes widening as she caught on.

'So they only have a double garage.' She grabbed Tox's shoulder.

'Where do they keep the third car when two of them are at home?' Tox asked.

No one answered. Tox grabbed his car keys from the desk.

'Someone get on to the team down at the water,' he said. 'I want to talk to the wife.'

Chapter 113

NIGEL SPADER'S TEAM was the first to arrive at the storage facility Shania Mallally had told us about. I gripped the frame of Tox's filthy, smoke-choked Monaro as he bumped into the car park at a crazy speed, pulling up just centimetres behind Nigel's squad car. Seven people, my team and Nigel's, burst into the front office of the facility and barked at the frightened young woman behind the counter for the keys to Mallally's lock-up.

The primary name on the account was Shania Parker. The traumatised, near-hysterical woman had assured us that she'd wanted to tell Nigel's detectives about the lock-up, but her husband had forbidden it. Tox had hung up on her. It took some minutes for the office attendant to find the right keys. In the room, which was boiling with tension, Whitt and Nigel turned towards each other, the pair standing right in front of me.

'So do I get your badge now or later?' Whitt said. He wasn't smiling.

'Fuck off, arsehole,' Nigel sneered.

The two teams marched to the garage marked with Mallally's number. Tox snatched the keys off Nigel and fitted them shakily into the lock. The big man thrust open the door, revealing the silver BMW parked, cold and silent, in the space.

There was only one other thing in the garage. A pedestal fan plugged into the wall, turning slowly. Tox stormed in and did a lap of the car, tore open the passenger side door and grabbed the keys from the ignition. He opened the boot and slammed it, growling with frustration.

'What's that smell?' Whitt asked. The men and women around me all looked at Whitt, sniffed. There was an odour in the air. Whitt pointed to the fan. 'Turn that off.'

The smell thickened. Then I heard a shuffling sound. I put a hand on the wall beside me. Cold concrete. I ran my hand across the wall at the back of the garage.

Painted gyprock.

Chapter 114

TOX AND ONE of Nigel's guys kicked a hole in the false wall at the back of the garage. I tore at the gyprock as it splintered and crumbled away, slapping big sheets of it on the concrete. The space was no wider than Rebel's shoulders. The tiny child had no choice but to sit in the corner of the space, dripping with sweat, peering out at us. The ground was soaked in faeces and urine, scattered with the wrappers of sandwiches or snack bars.

Tox reached into the space and grabbed the filthy girl by her arm, pulled her carefully out. When he finally squeezed her to his chest, I felt a sob escape me.

'I knew he couldn't do it,' Tox laughed, clutching the child hard, his eyes wet and cheeks bright with relief or rage, I didn't know. 'The fucking bastard couldn't do it.'

Chapter 115

TOX BARNES PUSHED through the doors of the emergency room at St Vincent's Hospital for what seemed like the thousandth time. Only this time he was doing it with one hand, the other wrapped around a tiny, pale form held to his chest. It seemed like fate that Doctor Chloe Bozer was there, standing over the nearest bed with a patient chart in her hands, though he hadn't come there looking for her. The hospital was simply the closest to the storage facility he had just come from.

Chloe was so startled by Tox crashing into the room with Whitt and Harry at his side that she backed into a drip stand and knocked it over.

'This child has been living in captivity for two weeks,' Tox said loudly as nurses gathered around them. 'She's breathing but her heartbeat is weak. She fell asleep in the car and hasn't responded in about twenty minutes. I don't know how long it's been since she had water.'

'Give her to me.' Chloe took the child from him. For a moment he caught her familiar smell, the feel of her hands on his, and the heavy ache he'd felt since they'd parted broke through his panic for the child's survival. She looked back at him as she disappeared with the child down the ward, a crowd of nurses following her.

The three detectives stood, trying to recover mentally from the past few frantic hours, while the emergency room swirled and shifted around them with activity. The urgency and horror that had hit them all as they pulled away the false wall and spied Rebel Woods's small body at the rear of the concrete room had been palpable. It had not been easy in the car on the way to the hospital, and it hung like a shroud over them now.

Tox put a hand on Harry's shoulder and said, 'I'll stay with her. You two go before the press get here.'

Chapter 116

WHITT AND I sat in a booth at Jangling Jack's, a couple of streets away from St Vincent's hospital. The walk to the bar had been numb, silent. I ordered two tequilas and the waitress brought them swiftly. The sun was setting outside, casting the streets red. Before Whitt could remind me that he was a recovering alcoholic, I downed the two tequilas.

We sat for a long time in silence. Seeing a child that has survived in a crawl space, living in its own filth for two weeks, will do that to you. Watching a woman throw herself under a fire truck after the failed escape of her murderous lover will do that to you.

My joints ached and my mind could only grasp at fragments of thoughts. Whitt had slid down into his chair, the ice in his Coke melting slowly before him. A bunch of kids came and sat in the next booth and watched the footage of Tox jumping off the cliff at Clovelly together, huddled over one phone screen.

'What do you think he was going to do to her? To Rebel? What was the plan in keeping her?' I asked Whitt. He lolled his head towards me.

'I don't think there was a plan,' Whitt said. 'He was probably just working up the courage to end it.'

'He might have been thinking the problem would take care of itself,' I said. 'He gave her food but no water. Walled the crawl space off completely.'

We sat thinking about that. I ordered a wine and sat sipping it.

'The hero of the hour is here,' Whitt said. I turned and saw Tox at the street end of the bar, looking at his phone. 'I'll go get him.'

As soon as Whitt left me, my phone rang. I didn't even get a moment to say hello.

'Blue, I'm sorry,' Woods said. He sounded out of breath. 'I'm just sorry. OK? All of this has . . . I just can't . . .'

'Take a breath, big man.' I felt a small smile creeping to the corners of my lips. 'Is the baby OK or what?'

'She's fine.' He gasped a breath. 'She's doing great. I got here about twenty minutes ago. They let me see her. Oh. I just can't believe she's alive, Detective Blue. I'm . . . I'm so sorry for the way I've acted, and I . . .'

'Save it, boss,' I said. 'I don't need it. It was Tox Barnes who found your kid. Anything I did was just part of my job.'

'Yes, well, you'll be doing your job in an official capacity again from this moment on,' he said. 'I'm reinstating you. Whittaker and Barnes, too. I'm making the call. I'll speak to the prosecutor in your case right away.'

'Don't make any calls,' I said. 'Don't speak to anyone. Just go and be with your grandchild.'

I hung up on the Deputy Commissioner, and watched Tox and Whitt slide into the booth with me.

•

It was an hour before she appeared. Darkness had fallen outside the bar, and the light above us was making gold flecks in our drinks. Tox saw her and straightened in his chair, his eyes locked on her as she stepped over the threshold. Whitt and I looked. Doctor Chloe Bozer was looking uncertainly back at us.

Tox left us. I shifted to the seat beside Whitt so I could watch. It was clear Tox and the doctor had experienced some hard, heavy shift in their relationship, a devastating fight perhaps. There was fear and apprehension on both of their faces. As we watched, Tox and Chloe took stools at the counter, talking quietly, their heads together.

'What the *hell* is going on?' I asked.

'I don't know,' Whitt said. 'But it's dead serious.'

He felt me looking at him and glanced at me, blushed.

I turned my wineglass on the tabletop before us.

'You don't want me, Whitt,' I said.

Chapter 117

HE WAS QUIET. I drew a deep breath and let it out slowly. I had no plan. The words simply came, spilling out dangerously one after the other. Whitt took his drink coaster and held it like a life preserver as I spoke.

'You see that doctor with Tox?' I asked. Whitt looked over at Chloe Bozer.

'Yeah,' he said.

'That's the kind of woman for you,' I told him. I nodded at the doctor. 'She's brilliant. Measured. Normal. She probably grew up in a great family. Has a mother and father who love her to bits and think her being a surgeon is just the best thing in the world. She was probably popular in high school, and she fell into being a doctor because she cares about people and she works hard. She has a nice apartment with a balcony in the city. Every winter she goes down to the snowfields with a group of friends.'

'She's predictable,' Whitt surmised.

'She's safe,' I said. 'Why do you think Tox Barnes likes her so much? The guy's a boat without a sail crashing around in the waves. She's a secure harbour.'

'You can't tell me how I feel about you, Harry,' Whitt pushed his drink away. 'I care about you. I don't want to go skiing every winter.'

'You don't want to wake up to the sound of a bump in the night and wonder if it's the bikies coming for me,' I said. 'You don't want to answer the door of our house and find some serial killer standing there. This is my life, Whitt. This has always been my life. I'm chaos. I'm misery. I'm a storm that crashes and rages and never blows itself out. If I don't go looking for trouble, it's because trouble has already found me. That is not the life for you. You're not that kind of guy.'

'I don't care how chaotic you are, Harry,' Whitt said. He took my hand. 'I want to be with you.'

'Well, I don't want to be with you,' I said.

I slid my hand out from under his and walked out of the bar. Tox and Chloe didn't even glance up. He was whispering in her ear, and she was smiling.

Chapter 118

I WALKED DOWN Victoria Street towards the harbour. A wind was picking up, shifting the fig trees above me, carrying voices from busy Darlinghurst Road. I put my hands in my pockets, trying to shake off the feel of Whitt's fingers on mine, trying not to retrace my words.

I don't like lying, and it had all been lies. Of course I wanted to be with Whitt. From the beginning, the thought had risen now and then like a siren. Whitt was my safe harbour. But I knew, just as plainly as I knew it about Tox and Chloe – that there would be trouble on the horizon. The pain and darkness in my past never stayed away for long, and Whitt didn't deserve to get swept up in the kind of life I lived. I was destined for badness. Sometimes it came from inside me. Sometimes it was drawn towards me. Tox was the same. And I had known many others over the years like me, too. In the foster system. In group homes. In the prison where I'd spent the last four months. Even on the police force, carrying badges and guns. Some people are just walking disasters waiting to happen.

It didn't matter what I wanted. What mattered was protecting the people I loved from the curse that I was.

Chapter 119

SYDNEY DOGS AND Cats Home was on a quiet suburban street lined with pretty little houses with neat yards. I followed Pops and his trio of small, fluffy dogs up the stairs and into the foyer, which was crowded with people. Three families were standing in the little space between the high counter and the wall covered in posters and photographs, huddled together, faces lit with anticipation as my friend and his brood of hounds arrived. I stood in the corner and watched as an Asian family with two excited little boys, a young couple, and an older couple with their adult daughter took their dog from Pops, signed their paperwork, and carried their hairy bundle off, cooing and laughing with joy.

When it was all done Pops went to the counter and a group of three women stood chatting with him as he signed the paperwork reporting on the foster experience with the dogs he'd just seen adopted.

'Is this your daughter?' one of the ladies asked, spying me standing by with my hands in my pockets. Pops didn't lift his eyes from the paper.

'She's not far off,' he said.

'Can we tempt you into becoming one of our kitten foster mums?' one of them asked me. She took a small black kitten from the floor beneath the counter. 'We're overrun at the moment.'

'I would,' I said. 'But I'm technically homeless.'

The women didn't know whether to laugh at that or not. Pops finished up his forms and spread his big, hard hands on the counter.

'Alright, ladies,' he said with a resigned sigh. 'What have you got for me this time? Let me guess. A toy poodle in a little pink tutu.'

'Actually, we've got something a little different for you today,' one of them said. They were trying to keep straight faces, but I spied the lady at the back cracking a big grin as she walked off towards an office at the rear of the room. Someone handed Pops a key. 'She's in row three, enclosure twenty-one.'

There was furious barking as we entered the yard. Dogs of all shapes and colours and sizes were housed in separate enclosures, watching us as we entered, pawing at the gates and turning excited laps. Volunteers were hosing out empty enclosures and filling buckets with dog food. On every cage a laminated card gave the dog's name and a little slogan about their temperament. *Boston – I'm a rambunctious boy! Miffy – I'm a little nervous but full of love! Damon – I like naps on the couch!* Pops directed me to the third aisle and I followed, watching the dogs as I went.

'They think they're funny, those girls,' Pops said as we turned down the aisle. 'You watch. It'll be a pack of Chihuahua puppies wearing onesies.'

Pops looked into enclosure twenty-one before I did. He stiffened, and smacked a hand against his heart.

I looked in and saw a glossy Doberman staring at us, sitting at attention with her paws perfectly aligned on the damp concrete and her eyes big and attentive. The dog examined us with an almost human air of dignity, like a princess looking over the crowd huddled in the rain outside her palace, aloof yet curious. The laminated card zip-tied to her cage said *Antoinette – I'm pretty and I know it!*

'Oh,' Pops said, his hand still on his chest. He looked over Antoinette the way some men look at sports cars. 'Oh wow. Wow. *Wow*. She's so . . . She's so . . .'

'Beautiful?' I chipped in.

'Glamorous!' he corrected.

Pops led Antoinette from her cage with a proud, straight-backed gait. I followed behind. The dog was playing it cool up front.

But in the back, her little stumpy tail was wagging.

CHAPTER ONE

SOMETHING VERY BAD was about to go down.

There are things you know as a cop in Boston. You know how the city feels, because its streets are your veins and the voices of its people come through your lips when you talk. You know the smell of the salt in the harbor like the scent of the back of your wife's neck, and it's just as precious, reassuring. The hammering of footsteps out of Back Bay Station for the morning rat race wakes you up, and the wail of sirens in the old Combat Zone at night puts you to sleep. Every Christmas, you gather up some young wide-eyed uniforms to take poor kids from East Boston and Hyde Park into the toy stores, try to show the new cops and the kids that they can get along. You know that in a few years, some of those cops and some of those kids will end up killing each other. But that's how the city works. It's like a living thing. It sheds, and it hurts, and it bleeds.

I could feel what was about to happen in the air. It was an unexpected and dizzying heat, surreal against the snow on the ground outside the car.

When my partner Malone and I got a call to go to the commissioner's office downtown, I knew we were in for it. A Boston cop knows that being called to the commissioner's office is a bad, bad thing.

Malone always made fun of me for thinking I had Boston's pulse, a sense about approaching trouble in the city. On the morning of the marathon bombing, we'd been a mile up Boylston Street doing crowd control and I told Malone I felt hot and weird, like I had a fever. We felt the thump of the first blast under our feet a second or two later.

We were in the back of the cruiser, Malone looking out the window, joggling his knee and picking his teeth.

"Wait. I know what this is," he said suddenly. "This is about that baby. We're getting a medal for the baby last week."

The week before, Malone and I had been walking out at the end of a shift when a woman outside a café two doors from the station started screaming like she was on fire. She was standing in the street pointing at a balcony five floors above, where a toddler was sitting on the concrete ledge, having the time of his life. A crowd gathered, and it was quickly established that the mother was inside but wasn't answering the door or her phone. While some guys went in to try to break down her apartment door, Malone and I watched, pulling out our own hair, while the toddler crawled along the ledge and then, wobbling, stood up.

There was no time to decide who would catch the kid.

2

Malone and I both went in and snared him in a tangle of arms about two feet off the ground while the people around us hollered and screamed. Turned out the mother had been so damned tired from working two jobs that she fell asleep with the baby on the couch, the balcony doors open and a pot of peas cooking dry on the stove.

It was a good get, the kind of thing that wins you cheers when you walk into the station the next day. Ribbing about how tubby you look in the YouTube footage. Calls from the *Globe*. A medal, maybe. The toddler catch had gotten my wife, Siobhan, on the phone for a week, bragging to all her friends, telling them to watch the news, patting my head and saying she was proud of me like I was some kind of heroic dog.

But today wasn't about the kid. I could feel it in my bones.

"This is bad," I told Malone. "They only send a car for you when they know you'll be too fucked up to drive home afterward. We're in big trouble here. You better start thinking what we've done to piss off the top brass."

Malone, still twitching and joggling his knee, settled back and watched our driver. I gripped the seat belt and let Boston roll by, trying to guess what they were about to tell us.

The car dropped us at the building on Tremont Street. We went in, and as the elevator doors closed on us, I noticed that all Malone's twitching had suddenly stopped.

"I'm sorry," he said. His eyes were fixed on the floor. "I'm real sorry for this, Bill."

"You're sorry for what?"

He didn't answer. I had to hear it from the commissioner.

3

CHAPTER TWO

BOSTON PD LEGEND says that the visitor's chair in the commissioner's office is an old electric chair. I'd heard whispers around the department that some sadistic jerk occupying the top job had acquired the chair from a prison auction in Ohio and simply cut the straps and headgear off to make it acceptable for the office. Malone and I entered and took two identical chairs, either of which might indeed have been an Old Sparky sourced from the depths of the Midwest. The wood was eerily warm, and there were gouges in the arms that perfectly fit my fingernails.

I wouldn't have liked to be sitting in front of Commissioner Rachel McGinniskin even if the news were congratulatory. The red-haired, narrow-faced woman was a descendant of Barney McGinniskin, the first Irishman ever handed a police baton in Boston. From the moment Barney pulled on his blue coat, his appointment spurred hysterical newspaper reports, violent riots, and Irish bashings nationwide. The anti-immigration, anti-Catholic parties dumped him out of his job after only three years, and years later, Rachel McGinniskin had fought her way up the ladder in the force out of pure spite.

The commissioner opened a laptop and swiveled it on the desk so that the screen was facing us. She pushed a button and a black-and-white video began to play.

Only minutes into the video, I could feel sweat sliding down my ribs beneath my shirt. I looked at Malone, but he wouldn't meet my eyes.

McGinniskin pointed to a guy in the video. "Detective Jeremiah Malone," she said. "Is that you there on the screen?"

Her tone was strangely heavy, like she was the one getting the bad news. Malone didn't say anything. Just nodded, defeated. She let the video play a while longer.

"Detective William Robinson." She pointed at the screen again and looked at me, her eyes blazing. "Is that you?"

"It is," I said. Malone still wouldn't meet my gaze. *Look at me, you prick,* I thought. But the bastard put his face in his hands. McGinniskin turned the laptop back around and slammed it shut.

"You're both out," she said. The muscles in her jaw and temples were so tight, they bulged from beneath the skin. "And I've got to admit, gentlemen, after seeing that tape, it gives me great pleasure to say it. There's no place in my police force for people like you. Your discharge will take effect immediately. If I hear that either of you have inquired about pensions, I'll make sure you can't get a job in this city as a fucking *mall* cop." McGinniskin swept her hair back from her temples, chasing composure. "Give me your badges and your weapons," she said.

It was hard for me to get out of the chair. Gravity seemed to have tripled. I took my gun off, walked what seemed like a hundred miles to her desk, and put my weapon down at the same time Malone did. He finally looked at me as we took our badges off. Then we left. Neither of us spoke until we were outside her office.

"Bill," Malone said. "Buddy, listen. I—"

"I can't believe you did this." I was shaking all over. "I can't believe you did this to us. We're out. That's it. It's over. You lying, backstabbing piece of shit."

My job. My city. The walls of the old stone building were pulsing around me, closing in. Malone had killed us. We were being expelled from the living thing. Shed like dead skin, like waste. I couldn't breathe.

"I'm so sorry, Bill." Malone sounded panicky. "I was trying to—"

I grabbed my partner by the shirt and slammed him into the wall beside McGinniskin's door. It was all I could do not to knock his teeth out right there. I put a finger in his face and eased the words out from between my locked jaw.

"You and me?" I said. "We're *done*."

CHAPTER THREE

Two Years and Five Months Later

THE DEATH TOLL was eight, according to Cline's count.

He knew it was narcissistic, but every day he sat under the big bay windows on the second floor of his house where he could see the ocean beyond the cypress trees and checked the papers for signs of his work. Some days he told himself he was being too proud, and other days he knew it was just good business. Since he had moved to the tiny seaside town of Gloucester, there had been eight overdose deaths. Two a month. The papers were blaring out words that excited him. *Epidemic. Crisis. Downfall.* Whenever things started to slide, Cline felt happy. Being a criminal meant his concept of the world was upside down. Reversed. A downward slide for others meant an upward rise for him.

That didn't mean it was time to take it easy on anyone. As he sat reading the paper spread flat on the table before him, the way he used to in the can so that he could keep an eye on the movement of other prisoners, his lieutenants started assembling before him. Cline had made sure from the outset that his standards were known and respected. Tailored shirts. Cuff links. Ties for meetings. No speed-stripe buzz cuts, no neck tattoos, none of this gold-chain, bling-bling shit. They were a business, not a gang. The men who entered the room looked like a bunch of lawyers attending a daily meeting, but they came in punching each other and giggling and talking trash, and he silenced them with a glance. They were street thugs and prison bitches and violence-intervention-program dropouts he had recruited from rock bottom, but he'd make them true soldiers before long.

"Where's Newgate?" Cline asked when everyone was settled. "You fuckers know to be on time." There were uncomfortable looks around the crew, and then Newgate appeared with a baby in his arms. No, not a baby, a little girl, though she seemed like a baby in this setting, surrounded by hard men who made their living dealing in death. Cline stood and watched as big, muscle-bound, scar-faced Newgate put the barefoot child on the floor.

"I'm real sorry, boss." Newgate gave a dramatic sigh. "I had a fight with my girl and she dropped the baby on me this morning and ran off. I didn't know what to do."

Cline watched the girl toddling around the room, pulling books off his shelves, slapping her greasy palms on the huge bay windows. He felt a muscle twitching in his neck as he went to the desk and got his gun.

"No problem, Newby. These things happen," Cline said.

"I'm sure she won't cause us any trouble. Let's give her something to play with while we talk. Come here, little princess. Come on."

The lieutenants watched in horror as Cline loaded a full clip into his pistol and flicked the safety off. Newgate's daughter gave a coo of intrigue, tottered over to Cline, and took the gun. Squid, perched on the edge of the couch, didn't dare retreat but he hid beneath his gangly arms like they could protect from the child's aim. The little girl swung the heavy gun around wildly, then lifted the barrel to her eye and looked down into the blackness. Cline's eyes seared into Newgate's, daring him to protest. The little girl walked up to her father and pointed the gun at him.

"Bang-bang!" The girl laughed. Newgate reached for the weapon as his daughter fumbled with the trigger, unable to get her pudgy finger around the steel. Before Newgate could take the gun, Cline reached forward and grabbed it. He pointed it at Newgate, whose face contorted as he realized what was happening.

"Like this, princess," Cline said, smiling.

CHAPTER FOUR

PLANE CRASH, I thought. *That's the only thing that can save me now.*

I'd done everything I could to dissuade the residents of the Inn from holding a memorial service for my wife, Siobhan, on the second anniversary of her death. And yet here I sat at the end of a plastic foldout table in the forest of pines that surrounded the large house, tearing a yellow napkin into tiny pieces, waiting for it to begin, fantasizing about something that could interrupt it. Gas-leak explosion in the kitchen. Ferocious black bear suddenly appearing at the edge of the woods. Airbus A380 plunging into the slate-gray sea just visible through the trees. The truth was, nothing was coming. The people around me were going to talk about Siobhan, and I was going to have to listen.

They'd made a good effort, which was unusual for them,

because it was difficult to get the permanent residents of the Inn to collaborate on anything. They had nothing in common save Siobhan's recruitment of them in the months after I was fired. Siobhan had done everything to set up our new life in the north. She'd found the guesthouse for sale, sourced the furniture, got the licenses and approvals we needed to run a bed-and-breakfast by the sea—her retirement dream realized years earlier than she'd imagined it would be. She'd collected a motley crew of weirdos, down-and-outs, and deeply troubled characters, and she accommodated them all. I'd moped in my sweatpants about my lost job, having no idea that I was about to lose her too.

At the end of the table, Marni stood up. She was the resident wayward teenager, Siobhan's second cousin who'd been sentenced to the house for having constant screaming matches with her mother and running away multiple times. As I sat in my chair watching her prepare to speak, I felt a twinge of guilt. Since I'd lost my wife, Marni had been my responsibility, and like I'd done with everything else, I let her slip. She'd gotten a couple of piercings on her face recently, and there was a little pink heart on her left cheekbone that I wasn't convinced she drew on every day with lip liner despite what she'd told me. She was fifteen. Tattoos, piercings, and the attitude to go with them. She smoothed out a crumpled piece of paper extracted with some difficulty from the pocket of her jeans. A little speech. I rubbed my temples.

"Now, listen," Marni said, wagging a finger with chipped black nail polish at me. "We know you said you didn't want anything like this, Bill. But we've all got something to say about Siobhan, and we think you should hear it. The first year, nobody did anything, you know? It's kind of like we ignored it. And that just makes me totally sad."

"So get on with it, then." I gave a dismissive wave. My best friend in the house, Nick Jones, elbowed me in the ribs. Nick and I pull each other into line whenever we can, but it's not always easy. I like the muscle-bound black man because he's ex-army and has hundreds of horror stories from his time in the Middle East that are so hideous, they pulverize my own trauma like a sledgehammer smashes a walnut.

"Give it a rest, man," Nick said.

"You give it a rest." I took a croissant from the plate in front of me and tossed it at him. He caught it against his chest and started eating it.

"The thing I miss most about Siobhan," Marni told the gathering, "is her terrible taste in music."

Everybody nodded in agreement; some people laughed. I clasped my hands so tight, my knuckles cracked, and I searched the sky for planes.

"Siobhan was a great cook, and she used to play music in the kitchen," Marni said, looking at her paper for guidance. "You couldn't get from the back of the house to the stairs without her grabbing you and making you dance around the kitchen with her. It was so embarrassing. She filled the house with these lame love ballads. Whitney. Bonnie. Celine. Really ancient, weird stuff."

"Ancient?" I scoffed. I leaned in toward Nick. "The prime of Celine Dion's career was the mid-nineties."

"Shut it," he whispered.

"I liked the way Siobhan sang Bonnie Tyler with her arm

out and her face all crumpled up, using her wooden spoon like a microphone," Marni said. "I know all the words to those songs because of Siobhan, and even though they suck, I'll never forget them. I miss her so bad. I've already got a mom, but Siobhan was, like, my better mom."

Everybody looked to me to see what I thought of Marni's tribute. I folded my arms and sighed.

The second person to stand was Sheriff Clayton Spears. He too had a piece of paper with a prepared speech. For a moment, I appreciated the amount of planning that had gone into this breakfast memorial for my wife that I'd been railroaded into attending. The table was cluttered with yellow paper plates and yellow napkins, and someone had filled several glasses with yellow flowers. Her favorite color.

Clay was in uniform, likely because he'd just worked an overnight shift. His enormous belly sagged so low in front, it hid his gun belt.

"You all know, uh, that I came to the house because my marriage broke down." Clay's chin wobbled with emotion. "It's not easy to be a proud man when your wife runs off with someone else. Because of my position as the head of law enforcement in Gloucester, the whole town knows my story."

Sheriff Spears's wife hadn't run off with just anyone. She'd left him for a young male model who had been staying with some friends in the apartment next door to theirs for a single weekend. It had taken him all of two days to convince Mrs. Spears to dump her life with the sheriff, pack a bag, and jump in the car with him and a crew of beautiful nineteen-year-old men. She hadn't been seen since.

"Siobhan stayed up with me many nights, listening to me talk through my breakup," Clay said. "She was the best listener. She was endlessly encouraging. We would sit out here in the garden eating slices of pepperoni pizza and looking at the stars and . . . and she just made me feel like . . . you all know I'm no George Clooney. But Siobhan told me that I deserved love and that I was a great man, and I believed her."

Clay sat down quickly, perhaps attempting to get his butt planted before he burst into tears, and the plastic lawn chair beneath him creaked in a concerning way.

I noticed a car drive up to the house and stop with a spray of gravel.

"My name is Angelica Grace Thomas-Lowell." The third speaker had risen from her chair. Angelica had lived in the house for more than two years, but for some reason she always introduced herself with her full name. "I'm a vegan. Activist. Provocateur. Bestselling author."

The car at the front of the house was a welcome distraction. I leaned to the side in my chair to see around Angelica, but her thin, veiny arms were in the way. The paper she held looked like a full page of typed notes.

"'I'd like to announce firstly my sincere appreciation for Siobhan's constant willingness to act as a confidential sounding board for my ideas,'" Angelica read. "'The creative process isn't always straightforward. It's fluid, magnetic, sometimes chaotic. Though Siobhan's reading history was firmly located in trash novels, I found her somewhat naive critiques of my works in progress—those few I entrusted to her—refreshing.'"

Nick suddenly stood up beside me. I looked over and

saw a woman running from the house toward the gathering. Not a plane crash, gas-leak explosion, or ferocious bear, but *something*. I stood with him.

I recognized the woman from town. Ellie Minnow. She grabbed Nick by his scar-covered arm.

"Nick, Bill, you've gotta help me. It's Winley."

"What is it?" Nick asked. "What's happened?"

"We'll help." I grabbed my phone from the table. "Whatever it is, we'll help."

Marni was already pouting. I brushed her shoulder in consolation as I passed. "Sorry, everyone, duty calls. Feel free to continue on without us."

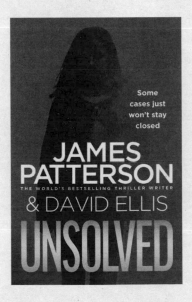

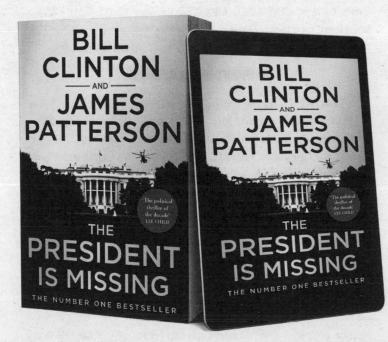

Also by James Patterson

ALEX CROSS NOVELS

Along Came a Spider • Kiss the Girls • Jack and Jill • Cat and Mouse • Pop Goes the Weasel • Roses are Red • Violets are Blue • Four Blind Mice • The Big Bad Wolf • London Bridges • Mary, Mary • Cross • Double Cross • Cross Country • Alex Cross's Trial (*with Richard DiLallo*) • I, Alex Cross • Cross Fire • Kill Alex Cross • Merry Christmas, Alex Cross • Alex Cross, Run • Cross My Heart • Hope to Die • Cross Justice • Cross the Line • The People vs. Alex Cross • Target: Alex Cross • Criss Cross

THE WOMEN'S MURDER CLUB SERIES

1st to Die • 2nd Chance (*with Andrew Gross*) • 3rd Degree (*with Andrew Gross*) • 4th of July (*with Maxine Paetro*) • The 5th Horseman (*with Maxine Paetro*) • The 6th Target (*with Maxine Paetro*) • 7th Heaven (*with Maxine Paetro*) • 8th Confession (*with Maxine Paetro*) • 9th Judgement (*with Maxine Paetro*) • 10th Anniversary (*with Maxine Paetro*) • 11th Hour (*with Maxine Paetro*) • 12th of Never (*with Maxine Paetro*) • Unlucky 13 (*with Maxine Paetro*) • 14th Deadly Sin (*with Maxine Paetro*) • 15th Affair (*with Maxine Paetro*) • 16th Seduction (*with Maxine Paetro*) • 17th Suspect (*with Maxine Paetro*) • 18th Abduction (*with Maxine Paetro*) • 19th Christmas (*with Maxine Paetro*)

DETECTIVE MICHAEL BENNETT SERIES

Step on a Crack (*with Michael Ledwidge*) • Run for Your Life (*with Michael Ledwidge*) • Worst Case (*with Michael Ledwidge*) • Tick Tock (*with Michael Ledwidge*) • I, Michael Bennett (*with Michael Ledwidge*) • Gone (*with Michael Ledwidge*) • Burn (*with Michael Ledwidge*) • Alert (*with Michael Ledwidge*) • Bullseye (*with Michael Ledwidge*) • Haunted (*with James O. Born*) • Ambush (*with James O. Born*) • Blindside (*with James O. Born*)

PRIVATE NOVELS

Private (*with Maxine Paetro*) • Private London (*with Mark Pearson*) • Private Games (*with Mark Sullivan*) • Private: No. 1 Suspect (*with Maxine Paetro*) • Private Berlin (*with Mark Sullivan*) • Private Down Under (*with Michael White*) • Private L.A. (*with Mark Sullivan*) • Private India (*with Ashwin Sanghi*) • Private Vegas (*with Maxine Paetro*) • Private Sydney (*with Kathryn Fox*) • Private Paris (*with Mark Sullivan*) • The Games (*with Mark Sullivan*) • Private Delhi (*with Ashwin Sanghi*) • Private Princess (*with Rees Jones*)

NYPD RED SERIES

NYPD Red (*with Marshall Karp*) • NYPD Red 2 (*with Marshall Karp*) • NYPD Red 3 (*with Marshall Karp*) • NYPD Red 4 (*with Marshall Karp*) • NYPD Red 5 (*with Marshall Karp*)

INSTINCT SERIES

Instinct (*with Howard Roughan, previously published as* Murder Games) • Killer Instinct (*with Howard Roughan*)

STAND-ALONE THRILLERS

The Thomas Berryman Number • Hide and Seek • Black Market • The Midnight Club • Sail (*with Howard Roughan*) • Swimsuit (*with Maxine Paetro*) • Don't Blink (*with Howard Roughan*) • Postcard Killers (*with Liza Marklund*) • Toys (*with Neil McMahon*) • Now You See Her (*with Michael Ledwidge*) • Kill Me If You Can (*with Marshall Karp*) • Guilty Wives (*with David Ellis*) • Zoo (*with Michael Ledwidge*) • Second Honeymoon (*with Howard Roughan*) • Mistress (*with David Ellis*) • Invisible (*with David Ellis*) • Truth or Die (*with Howard Roughan*) • Murder House (*with David Ellis*) • The Black Book (*with David Ellis*) • The Store (*with Richard DiLallo*) • Texas Ranger (*with Andrew Bourelle*) • The President is Missing (*with Bill Clinton*) • Revenge (*with Andrew Holmes*) • Juror No. 3 (*with Nancy Allen*) • The First Lady (*with Brendan DuBois*) • The Chef (*with*

Max DiLallo) • Out of Sight (*with Brendan DuBois*) • Unsolved (*with David Ellis*) • The Inn (*with Candice Fox*) • Lost (*with James O. Born*)

NON-FICTION

Torn Apart (*with Hal and Cory Friedman*) • The Murder of King Tut (*with Martin Dugard*) • All-American Murder (*with Alex Abramovich and Mike Harvkey*)

MURDER IS FOREVER TRUE CRIME

Murder, Interrupted (*with Alex Abramovich and Christopher Charles*) • Home Sweet Murder (*with Andrew Bourelle and Scott Slaven*) • Murder Beyond the Grave (*with Andrew Bourelle and Christopher Charles*)

COLLECTIONS

Triple Threat (*with Max DiLallo and Andrew Bourelle*) • Kill or Be Killed (*with Maxine Paetro, Rees Jones, Shan Serafin and Emily Raymond*) • The Moores are Missing (*with Loren D. Estleman, Sam Hawken and Ed Chatterton*) • The Family Lawyer (*with Robert Rotstein, Christopher Charles and Rachel Howzell Hall*) • Murder in Paradise (*with Doug Allyn, Connor Hyde and Duane Swierczynski*) • The House Next Door (*with Susan DiLallo, Max DiLallo and Brendan DuBois*) • 13-Minute Murder (*with Shan Serafin, Christopher Farnsworth and Scott Slaven*)

For more information about James Patterson's
novels, visit www.jamespatterson.co.uk